MADISON MICHAEL

Besotted

A BEGUILING BACHELORS ROMANCE

BOOK FOUR

Besotted by Madison Michael

Copyright 2018, 2022 Madison Michael

All rights reserved. No part of the book may be used or reproduced in any manner whatsoever without prior permission of the author/publisher, except in the case of brief quotations embodied in reviews.

All characters in this book have no existence outside the imagination of the author and have no relation to anyone bearing the same name or names. Any resemblance to individuals known or unknown to the author is purely coincidental.

Cover: Amanda Walker Designs

Contents

"The course of true love never did run smooth"

William Shakespeare

A Midsummer Night's Dream

Prologue

How the hell did I end up here? Me, the boy handed everything on a heaping platter—looks, brains, the best schools, the right friends, the perfect pedigree.

How is it that almost twenty years later, despite my privileged life, I am still paying the price for one little indiscretion? Sure, I got an ivy league education, and I can still practice law—which was a lucky break after everything that happened. My friends are still my friends too, but would they be if they knew I had kept such an enormous secret from them all these years?

What a fool I have been, taking all this for granted instead of facing it head-on. The pressure now is enough to make my head explode. I can't sleep, I can't eat, I can't pursue Regan. Shit, what a mess I have made of my life.

It was a big nothing back then. I was a kid who didn't know better. If only I'd been honest, this would all be over by now. But I was young and stupid. I took my cue from my parents. Not quite 18 years of age, who wouldn't?

I went along with the cover-up that my family devised, the complicated litany of emails describing Geneva, Paris, Barcelona, and London, the Photo-shopped selfies of me with tons of friends, tons of women. Hell, we were so thorough, even I started to believe my bull-shit.

Then it's no surprise Regan fell for the whole charade. All I ever wanted was a cozy life with my buddies, my girl, meaningful work, and a house along the lakefront. A family life similar to the one my parents had when I was growing up. Big suburban home, a wife I adored, a few brilliant kids to be proud of. I wanted all that, and I wanted it with Regan. Dammit, I still did.

Instead, here I was, mid-thirties, still blessed with my buddies, brains, and brawn, but without the girl. Instead of having a life with Regan, I was sitting at her desk, doing her job. Being the CEO of the Lyons Howe Real Estate empire was the pinnacle of success and I knew it. No complaints about that.

But there were these nagging problems with my current situation. First, a dangerous group of Russian thugs was blackmailing me, and their demands were getting harder to meet. I was running out of options and the stress was getting to me. Looking over my shoulder wherever I went was not conducive to reviving a romance.

Second, I was filling in for Regan at the helm of her family business so that she could marry a god-damned cabinet secretary who could rival a young Jack Kennedy. How's a guy supposed to compete with that?

Third, and worst of all, I didn't know if I could win Regan back before she walked down that aisle and shut the door on us forever. Could she even love me again?

I had promised myself the waiting was over. No more dragging my heels where Regan was concerned. I loved her. I'd always loved her. Instead, I was running for my life, scared to let these assholes know someone was important to me for fear of what they might do to her. And that meant keeping my distance, allowing a smooth-talking politician to steal Regan from me.

I wish I could turn back time. I was desperate to get these thugs off my back. I needed to win the girl.

Chapter One

"How could you do this to your mother and me?" Emmett Winthrop's face was red and apoplectic. "I am so ashamed of you. I can hardly look at you."

Tyler was not apologizing again. He had said he was sorry in every way possible for the last thirty minutes, to no avail. He sat sullen and exhausted in the corner of the barren room, waiting for the expensive lawyer to arrive, avoiding eye contact with his furious father.

"I heard you the first time, Dad."

"Don't you dare speak to me like that, young man. I get a call from the police at one in the morning telling me they have arrested my son, and you give me lip?"

"Don't think I am going to take this crap from you. First, it was the motorcycle, then the late nights, then the marijuana—oh yes, I smelled it on you—and now this. Tonight is the last straw. Do you think your brother would humiliate us this way? Not a chance."

His father knew exactly how to provoke Tyler's worst insecurities, but the entrance of the lawyer saved Tyler from another opportunity to be found wanting compared to his older brother. Tyler watched silently as his father shook hands with the family lawyer and the father of a school friend.

"Oh shit, this will be all over school now," Tyler complained, unaware he spoke out loud.

"You have attorney-client privilege, fortunately, so we should be able to keep this quiet," his father tossed over his shoulder, pulling the lawyer to a far corner of the small room and lowering his voice. Tyler strained to hear what they were saying but caught only a word now and then. The lawyer said something in a low voice that resulted in his father turning a disapproving stare on Tyler while he pointed an accusatory finger at his son and shouted. "This is not the first time?"

"You did this before? You got caught doing this before and did it again? What kind of idiot child did I raise? That's it, Tyler. I am done with you." Tyler feared his father would have a heart attack right on the spot. Although he was healthy and active, his face was mottled red and spit was flying from his mouth. Tyler had never seen his father this angry about anything.

The lawyer placed a calming hand on Emmett's arm and spoke soothingly to him. "Not a chance," his father's voice erupted. "He needs to learn his lesson."

The lawyer spoke some more. "What about the press? Our reputation?" his father asked as Tyler finally gave up waiting and moved closer so that he could hear their conversation. "You sit right down, young man. Don't you move," his father ordered. Tyler did as he was told, dropping into the battered metal chair, lowering his head and picking at his nails.

The two men continued quietly for another three minutes, frustrating the hell out of Tyler despite his apparently docile behavior.

"That would work," his father finally told the lawyer, his head nodding enthusiastically. "Marjorie and I will have to work at the subterfuge, but we'll find a way." Emmett turned to glare at him. Tyler didn't like that look on his face. His father looked calculating. He looked mean.

The lawyer approached as Mr. Winthrop left the small interrogation room. "Well, young man, it appears your father is not in a forgiving mood. Let me tell you about your future."

"That doesn't sound good to me." Tyler knew whatever they'd discussed, his father would protect their name, which meant buying off some judge most likely, like last time. Tyler just wanted to go home and crawl into bed.

"It could be worse." The lawyer was less than reassuring. "Be grateful you haven't turned eighteen yet. If they'd caught you next month, this would have been a lot worse. Here's what's going to happen."

The lawyer outlined the charges against Tyler—stealing a car, drug possession, and evading arrest. They sounded formal and ugly as the man recited them without emotion. For the first time, the joy rides Tyler and his buddies took in stolen cars sounded horrible.

"I'm sorry, Mr. Diamond. I didn't know the car was stolen."

"Nice try, Tyler, but I think even you knew your friends didn't own a Ferrari."

Tyler had the grace to look ashamed.

"No more lying. I am your lawyer now, and you and I need to be straight with each other. Your father has washed his hands of you. I am the only one standing between you and jail."

Tyler felt the words like a punch in the gut. "Jail?" The word barely came out on a choked breath. "No way I am going to jail. Don't I have a say here?" Tyler found the last bit of bravado from deep within, but the withering look from the lawyer sent it scurrying back into hiding.

"Well, your father is adamant. He won't pay your bail."

"Great," Tyler spat the word. "That's just fucking great. I'll use my college money."

"That won't wash, Tyler. The judge won't release you on your own recognizance. Your parents want you to suffer the consequences. They want you to straighten up. Frankly, I am not sure I agree with the methods, but as a parent, I can't help but agree with the sentiment."

"Great, so no one is on my side." Tyler was feeling abandoned, and angry. "I thought you were my lawyer, but it seems you and my dad are judge and jury."

"You should have thought about that before you lied to your parents, the first time you got pulled over with a warning. That warning was your lucky break, and you threw it away. You have dug yourself a deep hole here, Tyler. Fortunately for you, juvenile hall awaits instead of jail, since you are underage. You need to understand what's happening. You need to be contrite before the judge. Juvie is a godsend, my boy. Jail would have been the lesson your father preferred."

"My father wants me to go to jail?" Tyler never felt more alone. What had he done to make the man hate him so much?

"He wants you to learn your lesson," Mr. Diamond said, exasperated. "Sixty days, then your record will be expunged. You will head to Cornell, and life will go on with you, hopefully, a wiser young man."

"You gotta be kidding me?" Tyler was finding it hard to soak this all in. His father, who had catered to his every wish, who had millions of dollars in the bank, was letting him rot in juvie? "What the hell!"

"As I told you, Emmett believes you need to learn a lesson. You're lucky it's not worse, Tyler."

"Lucky, my ass," Tyler countered, getting up and pushing the chair halfway across the room in anger. "Lucky would be if my old man paid bail, and we all went home and got some sleep."

"Well, son. You are going home for four more days until school is out. Then you'll spend sixty days in juvie. Consider yourself lucky. Your cohorts in crime will serve prison time for sure.""

Tyler felt his legs give out and sank to the floor as the truth of his circumstances sank in. This man was laying out his only option. His father was turning his back on him, making him pay for his behavior by forfeiting his summer.

"Doesn't my father care I am a straight-A student, that this was one small indiscretion?" Tyler begged.

"Not one indiscretion. You had a warning less than two weeks ago when you got caught at the beach with a stolen car and drugs. If it had been an isolated incident, if there wasn't a serious warning that you ignored, then maybe your dad would have helped. But he has washed his hands of you, Tyler. It's time to pay for your unacceptable behavior and then put it behind you. Now come over here and let me walk you through the details."

"I'm not sure I want to know the details."

"That's your choice, Tyler. Either way, you're going to do time."

Chapter Two

He's breaking up with me. I know it. Why else would he be so nervous? It made sense. Tyler was heading off to Cornell in two months, while she had two more years of high school. Regan knew her brother, who had never liked the idea of the two of them together, had been harassing Tyler to end this relationship. She overheard them talking in the hall and had been struggling to hold it together ever since.

Regan had been barely two steps into the hallway when she spotted Tyler accosted by his three closest friends, Randall, Alex, and Wyatt. Wyatt wrapped a friendly arm around the shoulder of his oldest friend, slowing him down and looking him hard in the eye.

"Where you headed in such a hurry?" Wyatt pried. "It better not be to sniff around my baby sister."

"Oh, leave the poor guy alone." Alex bumped into Wyatt just enough to make his point and shake his arm loose from Tyler's shoulder. "He's crazy about her, and you know it. So cut it out. Besides, Ivy, your threats are falling on deaf ears."

"What are you going to do for the next four years, T, pine for the girl? You need to break it off and move on," Wyatt recommended. "College girls await us, my man. You need to be free to partake."

"Spoken like a true player, Wyatt," Tyler accused.

Regan's friends approached at that moment, but Regan shushed them and shamelessly continued to eavesdrop.

"And what's wrong with being a player?" Randall asked, rushing to his friend's defense. "Especially when you're as good at it as Ivy?" Randall tipped his head toward Wyatt. "He's stolen every girl I've ever wanted. Just be grateful Regan is his sister, or he'd steal her, too."

"Ew." Wyatt cringed at the idea. So did Regan. What a disgusting image. Just remembering it revolted her.

"Seriously, what're you going to do, Tyler?" Wyatt prodded. "You can't string her along for the next four years."

"I know," Tyler admitted reluctantly. "I'm having 'the talk' with her after school, so get off my back." Those words, combined with the air quotes Tyler put around "the talk," sent despair stabbing into Regan. She put a fist to her mouth to stifle a sob.

Regan's friends tried to drag her away. She knew she shouldn't be listening. Her reward for eavesdropping had been a sharp ache in the region of her heart. She'd anticipated this breakup. It was logical for Tyler to start college and leave her behind, but she hadn't expected it to hurt so much.

Not wanting to hear any more. Regan stepped away. Her friends moved to follow, but Regan stopped again, listening to her brother and his friends while the girls' whispers swirled around her. Would she never learn her lesson?

Wyatt was talking so loud that it was easy to hear. "Good. I'll feel much better when you break up with her. Regan's a smart girl; she has to know it's coming."

"She may know it's coming, but it will still break her heart," Alex added.

"Who cares, Alex?" Wyatt tossed out. "I just want him away from her instead of in her pants." Regan would make him pay for that callous remark when they got home.

Randall gave Wyatt a stern, disappointed look. "Wyatt, that's your sister you're talking about."

"Yeah, but you guys know Tyler. Would you trust him with your sister?"

"Oh shit, good point," Randall conceded as his eye caught sight of Regan and her friends. Regan quickly joined the clique of girls, pretending she had just arrived. "Speak of the devil."

Regan flashed the boys a brave smile, knowing she looked good. She wore a bright blue sweater that clung to her body, a straight black skirt that stopped well above the knees and boots with a high heel too sexy for a girl her age. Regan had borrowed the boots from her friend Suzie to impress Tyler. Now she wondered why she bothered.

"No way my mother let her out of the house dressed like that," Wyatt muttered under his breath. He quickly closed the small gap between them, and Regan felt her heart sink even lower. Getting right up in her face, Wyatt checked her out from head to toe and bragged, "Caught you! You're in so much trouble now."

"Please Wyatt." Regan's pouty lips turned down further as she fought back tears. She didn't need this problem on top of everything else. "Think of all the secrets I've kept for you. Don't tell."

"Leave her be, big brother," Alex suggested as the fellows caught up with their friend. Regan flashed Alex a grateful smile. She could always count on Alex to calm Wyatt down.

"I'll think about it," he teased. "But you better not come home looking like that, Ree. And you better wash off the makeup too, or Dad will ground you for sure."

Regan sighed in relief, unclenched the fists she had made instinctively, and promised Wyatt that she would do as he asked. She had intended to change, anyway.

Tyler just stared, catching her eye briefly. She gave him no indication that she'd overheard him, that she knew what he wanted, that her heart was breaking smack in the middle of the Lake Forest High School hallway as people moved around them, oblivious. She was trying to throw her brother off the scent, rather than toying with Tyler, but she could see she was adding to her boyfriend's anxiety.

Regan turned on her heel, moving away with her girlfriends, at least two of whom turned to glance at the handsome quartet over their shoulders. Not Regan. She kept on walking, wiggling her butt and swishing her long blond hair as her stride ate up the distance to the library. She avoided him from then on, but school was ending now. The period would end, and so would her world.

The note in Tyler's hastily scribbled handwriting was barely legible. Regan studied it again and checked the clock. She looked at Tyler, fidgeting at the library table, his knee going a mile a minute. He was nervous. He looked up at her, and Regan quickly averted her gaze. She was afraid she would cry if she made eye contact.

"Mr. Winthrop, although you only have two more days of high school, I would appreciate good demeanor." Mr. Finley skewered Tyler with his most threatening glare. Tyler gave a polite nod and stopped his knee from rattling the table above it. Mr. Finley was barely around the corner before the table shook again.

When the bell sounded, Regan dragged her feet, noticing that Tyler shot out of the room like a man on a mission. Her heart pounded in her chest as she made the three-minute walk to their meeting place.

"What took you so long?" Tyler grabbed her arm as soon as she came into view. "I've been waiting for hours." Tamping down tears,

Regan gave him a quick peck on the lips. Tyler slid his hand down her arm until they were holding hands. He tugged at her hand, leading her deeper into the cool shadows until she leaned against the heavy metal exit doors, hidden from prying eyes in a dark alcove.

Caging her in place with a hand braced on either side of her head, Tyler leaned in until only their lips touched, kissing her softly. Regan struggled against her desire, barely returning his touch. Tyler stepped back, putting space between them, but saying nothing about her lack of response.

"We need to talk, Ree." Regan swallowed hard and watched as Tyler wiped his hands on the sides of his pants. He must be as nervous as she was. She felt sorry for him.

"I know, Ty, I've been expecting this. Only two days until you graduate. I get it. I understand that a college man, especially one as handsome as you..." Regan ran her finger down Tyler's cheek, causing him to shudder slightly. "A college man isn't gonna stick with lil' ole me," Regan's voice was breathy, her fake accent heavy as she leaned into Tyler seductively.

So much for feeling sorry for him. She would not make it simple when he was breaking her heart.

"Cut that out, Ree. I'm serious. You aren't helping."

Pushing him away as if he'd slapped her in the face, Regan dropped her flirtatious stance and stood tall. "Well, excuse me, but since when am I supposed to make breaking up with me easier?"

"Damn it, Ree, I'm not breaking up with you."

Regan stood still, forming a small 'O' with her mouth, bright blue eyes huge on her face. "You're not? But you said it was serious." She was stunned.

"It is. Just let me talk for a minute, would ya?"

"Sorry," she apologized, taking his hand in hers again and pulling him closer. If he inhaled, his chest would touch hers. She was so close and so happy. She wanted to get nearer, but she could see that he was trying to concentrate. "I'm listening, Tyler."

Stepping back, Tyler looked her in the face, took a deep breath, and sputtered. "We both knew this day would come, Regan, when I had to leave for college, and you would stay here. But I think we both assumed this thing between us would burn out before that and it would be no big deal. For me, at least, it's a huge deal."

"Me too, Tyler. I'm going to miss you so much."

Tyler nodded and continued. "I know that long-distance relationships rarely work, so I don't want to leave things uncertain between us or leave anything left unspoken. You're a beautiful girl, Regan, and popular. I suspect you will make homecoming court next year..."

"You are so sweet to say that," she interrupted, flattered by his compliment.

"Anyway, the minute I am out of the picture, guys are a gonna flock to you, and I'll understand if you want to be free to date them, to play the field. You've only been with me, and you're young to make the kind of commitment I'm asking."

"You are asking for a commitment?" Regan felt her breath leave her body. Tyler had her complete attention.

"Wyatt wants me to break up with you. In fact, he thinks that's what I am doing right now. He thinks you should be free to date other guys. He loves to remind me you're only a sophomore."

"And he wants you to be free to hang around with him. He needs a—what do you guys call it again?"

"A wingman," Tyler supplied.

"Yeah, a wingman." Regan despised the idea of Tyler being her brother's sidekick. Wyatt was always picking up girls everywhere he went. She figured it was only a matter of time before Tyler succumbed to the wiles of one of them.

"Maybe, if we're honest, he does want that, but mostly he wants us separated. He worries about you, and he thinks I'm stupid to tie myself to a high-school girl. He doesn't understand that you are not just some girl to me."

"Yeah. He's always on my case too, about you being too old for me, but he really hates that his friend is dating his sister and he doesn't get all the juicy details." Regan loved keeping what she and Tyler did together a secret, then rubbing Wyatt's nose in it, but she didn't share that with Tyler.

Tyler had told Regan how much the secrecy bothered Wyatt, along with his cohorts, Alex Gaines, and Randall Parker. The four were inseparable and shared stories of their conquests every Monday. Not Tyler. "After all, Ree, what can I say in front of three protective boys, all of whom feel like they are your brother?"

Regan laughed when Tyler told her that, but she never failed to use it against Wyatt, teasing him with her secrets, making him think she and Tyler were doing more than they were.

"Wyatt has been on my case all year about you. He hounds me with remarks about 'making an ass of myself' or 'sniffing around you.' Just this morning, he started in on me again."

"I heard some of it," Regan confessed.

"You did?"

"'Fraid I was eavesdropping. Sorry about that. He didn't mind when we were younger," Regan reminded him, trying to get him to move past Wyatt's objections. She knew he was swayed by his friend's opinions too much. "When you were pulling my pigtails, and I was sticking my tongue out at you, no one paid attention. But once I entered high school, things were different. Suddenly, Wyatt was my overprotective big brother. And this year, my dad..."

"They're no dummies, Ree. You're not a kid anymore, and they're afraid we'll get into trouble. Have you looked at yourself lately?"

Regan knew she was more grown-up, but what was the big deal? "So I'm not skinny with pigtails anymore."

"You are clueless, Regan. You've blossomed into a stunner. All the boys have noticed. I sure have," Tyler finished, reaching for her and giving her a soft kiss on the lips.

Regan lingered against him, savoring the sensation of his lips pressing hers, of his tongue exploring her mouth as the kiss became more demanding. Regan wrapped her arms low around Tyler's back and pulled him close, feeling the bulge growing between them with wonder.

Finally, he pulled back. Regan hid her disappointment by fidgeting, adjusting her sweater with a twitch. "Wyatt is just afraid you'll hurt his reputation, Ty. It was never about me. You guys are the big deal seniors. He's embarrassed you're hanging around his kid sister."

"You may be right about that, but he is concerned about you, too."

"I know, but he should trust you. Although," Regan continued, "my parents don't seem to trust you as they used to, either. That doesn't help."

They both knew why. Tyler had changed during the last year, changed enough that he stood out around conservative Lake Forest. Not in a good way. While his friends wore oxford shirts and Dockers, he had swapped them for a supple, buttery leather jacket and skin-tight jeans. His hair was longer than his friends, and now that school was about to end, he was growing a goatee. He looked like the consummate bad boy, despite his wholesome upbringing and salutatorian status. Wyatt was valedictorian, of course.

The look was bad enough, but a scant two months ago, over the objections of his parents, Tyler had purchased a Harley Dyna Super Glide, adding to his new image. It had changed him. Regan knew that late at night he was hanging around with a different crowd. He was edgy, but she found his bad boy persona sexy and appealing.

Wyatt and his friends were unfazed by his new look. He still played sports and got high grades and was—well—Tyler. Only Regan knew that Tyler liked to sneak out to the beach to smoke a little weed with a group of bikers. He invited her to join him, but she always said no. It might have been her imagination, but she thought he was relieved, not wanting her to be part of this aspect of his life. It hurt a little, but when she was honest, she admitted that she was afraid of her own emotions, and her hormones, as well as worried about getting caught.

She was too young for sex, although many of her friends were losing their virginity. She knew that Tyler longed to sink his body into hers. They could barely keep their hands off each other. No wonder her parents were worried about her innocence. They realized what he was thinking, and could read him like a book.

"They like me, but they like me better when I am far from you," he acknowledged. "Far away. That's why I wanted to talk to you, Ree."

Tyler was uncertain in a way she had never seen before. A confident young man raised with all he desired—wealth, family support, brains, and charm, it was uncharacteristic for him to be so reticent and nervous. "I'm going away," Tyler finally blurted out. "For the summer."

"What do you mean, Ty? Are you taking a vacation?" She was confused. So what if he took a week or two and went away? It wasn't surprising, even if it was unplanned.

"No, Ree. I mean that I am going away for the whole summer. I am leaving this weekend. Right after graduation."

"Where? For how long?" Regan was confused. Tyler was usually forthcoming, but he was offering her nothing.

"My folks decided I should go with my brother Denny for the summer. We're going to backpack all over Europe." Tyler didn't sound at all excited, and he was kicking at the ground with his Nikes. Usually, this behavior meant Tyler was hiding something, but Europe with his brother was nothing to hide. Regan couldn't help being excited for him.

"That's fantastic," she gushed, giving him a huge hug. "You will have the best time. Why don't you seem happy about it?"

"It's just I'll be away from you all summer, and then I leave for college."

Regan's face fell. She hadn't realized he would be gone that long. "All summer? Can you get out of some of it?" She felt like Tyler was breaking up with her, after all. They wouldn't see each other for months. Tears were building behind Regan's eyes, threatening to spill over. She struggled to hide them from Tyler.

"That's why I needed to talk to you today."

Regan chewed on her bottom lip, a nervous habit. Tyler was staring at her mouth like he wanted to kiss her, but she just wanted to sob. "Tyler, I don't like the feel of this."

"We're fine, Ree," he reassured her, taking her in his arms and holding her tightly. "We are better than fine. You know how I feel about you, right?" Regan felt his breath in her hair, his arms around her. Here was her Tyler. If he said they were fine, they were fine. "You have always been the only girl for me."

Regan was reassured by his words, smiling broadly despite their impending separation. Her smile faded with his next words.

"Chicago and even Lake Forest have a lot to offer you. You have that summer internship to keep you busy. And Ree," he hesitated and released her. She looked up into his serious face. Feeling her lip start to tremble, she bit down hard on it. She was going to lose it any second. "I get that you might find somebody new, somebody you like better than me."

Was he pushing her away and waiting for her to break up with him? "I won't, Tyler. I know I won't," she rushed the words in a breath as the sobs started.

Tyler took her in his arms until she quieted, then held her at arm's length. "I won't find someone else either, Regan. You are the girl for me. I need you to know that I will still want you, even when I am away at college. Will you wait for me too, Ree? Will you be my girl?"

Regan couldn't remember when Tyler had said so many words together in his life. He stopped, holding his breath, eyes staring hard at her bottom lip.

Regan beamed pleasure at his words, pink rising in her cheeks, her wide eyes sparkling, tears gone. "I feel just the same, Tyler."

"I hate the idea of you being with some other guy, and I have absolutely no interest in being with any other girl. Promise you'll wait?"

"I don't know," she said, suddenly feeling light and playful. Tyler wanted her. He had proclaimed it out loud. "What will you be doing all those years, while I am being good and waiting for you?"

"Me? I will be loving you, Regan. No matter where I am. No other girl is going to be special to me, Regan. It will always be you. Someday I am going to marry you."

"Marry me?" Regan stood dumbfounded. He loved her. He was talking about marriage. This discussion was miles from where she thought they would be when she started this conversation. She was bursting with happiness, even though he was leaving for the summer.

"Yep. I promise you, right here, right now. Someday you will be Mrs. Tyler Winthrop." Tyler finally swooped in, gently taking her pouty lip between his teeth before swirling his tongue in her mouth, exploring the warmth there. She could feel him relax after his speech. He leaned into her, their bodies touching from lips to thighs as he plundered her mouth, his short breaths mingling with hers until he came up for air.

"Jeez, Ree, what you do to me?" Tyler exploded in a shaky breath. "I have loved you since you were six years old and you brought me that frog from the pond. I will love you when I am 96 years old too. I swear. Say you will wait."

Regan's heart was pounding in her chest. She was floating, feeling an odd urge to dance. She threw her arms around his neck and breathed into his ear. "I will wait, Tyler. I love you too and always have." She spoke the words with total conviction, the sincerity and promise of a grown woman, not a 16-year-old girl. The tears returned, lingering on her eyelashes before falling to her cheeks.

"You understand, this is our promise?" Tyler asked, sighing a huge sigh of relief. Regan nodded an enthusiastic yes, then kissed him again, but reverently. She stepped back to gaze at him, to reassure herself that he had meant the words she had heard.

"This is forever." His voice came out just above a whisper, giving her the reassurance she needed.

Regan looked deep into Tyler's dark eyes and vowed, "Forever."

She watched as Tyler preened with pride. He took her head in his hands and kissed her again and again. She returned his passion until she felt him about to pull back. Regan grabbed his hips and spun Tyler around, pressing him back against the cold steel doors, and taking his mouth, stroking her tongue in a bruising embrace. A small moan of pleasure left her lips as her body ruled her mind. She pressed her groin into his hips, her breasts tight against his chest, and pushed him harder into the door, deepening the kiss.

His teenage hands wandered under her blouse, then hesitated. She knew he was waiting to see if she would stop him. When she didn't, he continued, slipping his hands along her skin, fingers rough against her as he cupped her small breasts. He caressed her as she returned his kisses with fervor. Regan felt a jolt low in her belly as her nipples pebbled.

Regan encouraged him, and Tyler grew bolder, rubbing the hard nubs and gently squeezing. Regan's blood was heating, the skin where he touched her was ablaze. Tyler always had this effect on her. She wanted more. Grinding her hips into his groin, Regan pinned him hard against the door, her heart pounding like a freight train.

Regan knew Tyler was losing control, and she savored the moment until he finally pushed her away.

"Stop, Ree. Remember where we are. Wyatt will kick my ass if he sees us."

Always the practical one, Tyler would never make it past second base. Regan heaved a sigh of frustration as Tyler adjusted his leather jacket, then the front of his pants.

"This isn't private, Ree. We need some privacy, which we never seem to find anymore."

"I am sure no one can see," Regan insisted, teasing him with her fingers on his belt buckle. He shoved them away. She knew she wouldn't get him to continue. Logic had overtaken his longing. It was written all over his face.

"That's not the only reason I stopped. You push me too far, Regan. I'm only human."

He kissed her again, but was more circumspect. Regan felt her body cooling, coming down from that all-consuming desire. When they heard voices in the near distance, Tyler pushed her further away from him. She was forced to comply.

"God, I want you," she rasped in a harsh voice, shocking even herself. So much for calming down. Her body was curious, and desire was coursing through her veins. "Why the hell are we still waiting?"

"You know why." The air crackled with the question.

"Because you love me," Regan replied simply. Tyler was calm finally, touching Regan's hand with just the tip of his fingers.

"Yep, I do. And we have forever."

Chapter Three

D read and shame filled Tyler's every waking thought, even as he longed to see Regan again. It had been months of lies, elaborate fabrications and missing her until he ached with want.

College was challenging, and Cornell was exciting, but he couldn't get the taste of juvie out of his mouth. From what he had heard, the place he had been in was heaven compared to a real jail, but for a spoiled rich kid from Lake Forest, it was hell. The rooms were bare and the place was noisy and overcrowded. There was never enough to stimulate his active, inquisitive mind except planning for more trouble. Tyler had sworn to avoid that at all costs.

It wasn't easy. If college hadn't been waiting, there were plenty of kids ready to recruit him into their gangs. They pressed hard, threatening, cajoling, cornering him at all hours of the day and night. He still had nightmares, sometimes waking with a shout, drenched in sweat.

The subterfuge meant telling lies to Wyatt, who believed Tyler spent an idyllic summer in Europe. Everyone did. His parents had negotiated his college tuition for his silence.

"You will not destroy your mother or the reputation of this family," his father commanded on his last day of high school. His friends were preparing to celebrate as he packed a minimal wardrobe to the sounds of his mother's tears. She had begged his father to pay the bail, but his father was an unforgiving asshole.

His older brother had been no more sympathetic. It would be his job to send postcards from his travels, signing them as Tyler, making it appear as if Tyler was by his side. Denny didn't appreciate 'baby bro' encroaching on his summer. "You owe me, jack off, and I will collect someday," Denny told him. "What a screw-up you turned out to be."

Tyler would never forgive his father. He would never again be close with Denny. Never. Yeah, he hated his father for sending him to juvie, but he hated him more for the intricate network of lies and deceit that would always be between Tyler and his friends, and between Tyler and Regan. Each lie added a brick in a wall, rapidly erected and continuously growing between him and those he had been close to his whole life.

Tyler had trouble remembering which lie he had told when and to whom, causing him to withdraw more and more. Despite all his efforts, though, Tyler's problems were magnifying. Worst of all, when they began, he had no one to advise him.

At just 18 years of age, Tyler would typically have turned to his father for help, but his pride would not let him. He hated his father and Tyler no longer trusted that Emmett would have his back. He might have turned to his older brother, but they were barely on speaking terms by the end of that awful summer.

The old Tyler wouldn't have hesitated to ask his friends for help, and they would have rushed to his aid, but there was no way to do so without breaking his promise to his parents and losing his tuition. He had learned a hard lesson about life. It could be hard and ugly. He had seen those kids in juvie with no futures. College was his ticket out. He was desperate to succeed now that he could only rely on himself.

Then there was Regan. He missed her until it was physical pain, but each day apart, each lie, drove a wedge between them. He was struggling to hold on to what they had together when the calls and threats began. While he was unable to solve the problem, at least he could contain it. If he did that well enough, he could salvage his present life. He could have Regan.

But containing was challenging. It was clear—painfully clear—that Tyler would have to let Regan go until he found a better solution, a way out. She was his angel, but he had fucked up. His hands were too dirty to touch her. Until he dug himself out of this mess, he would have to say goodbye.

He had been away from her for four months, and already he was going crazy. He had stayed loyal, despite all the college girls making their interest in him more than evident. Girls were throwing themselves at him in class, in the library, in the dorm.

When did girls get so damn aggressive?

"Come on, Tyler," Wyatt had prodded just days ago when they were sitting in the Cornell library. "You can't expect to stay a monk for four years. Regan is history, man. A high school crush. Or maybe you got so much action in Europe this summer that you still need a rest?"

"I promise you that I do not need a rest. Quite the opposite, in fact."

"Then get in the damn game. These girls are ripe and ready, and they want us," Wyatt pointed out unnecessarily. "Just pick one and let's get the hell out of here."

"And if I do that, which of us gets the room tonight, huh?"

"Oh yeah, I hadn't thought about that. OK, you've stayed down the hall more than your fair share. You take the room, and I'll throw out Stu and Alan and take theirs. They can sleep in the lounge or something."

"Nice, Wyatt. You are such a thoughtful friend, but until I officially break up with Regan, you can have the room. All women are off limits."

"You've basically broken up already, Ty. It's just a phone call away. She'll never even know, you dolt."

"I'll know, and if I know, one look at me, and she'll know, too. I know you want me to leave her alone, but I have to do this my way. Just go, damn it. Just go." Tyler turned his back, not waiting for Wyatt to leave, his frustration surfacing uncontrollably. He needed to hit something, and Wyatt was no punching bag.

Wyatt didn't have to be told again, finally singling out a cute co-ed from his math class and making his move. He had been tutoring her in calculus for about a month, although no one believed she needed the assistance. All the men on the dorm floor knew she wanted Wyatt. She was anything but subtle.

Poor girl. Tyler considered warning her. She would be tossed over for the next one within a week. They all were.

So it had gone almost every Thursday, Friday and Saturday since the friends had arrived at Cornell. Tyler studied late and lamented his situation while Wyatt went through women like candy. Soon Wyatt would run out of the freshman, but that was no problem. The senior women were equally interested in Wyatt's handsome face, his jock status, and his millions.

Not Tyler. Instead, here he was, leaving Regan's family home, driving away while adjusting the crotch of his trousers, driving too fast on the quiet, late-night streets, wondering if a cold shower would even do the trick. She had looked stunning tonight, but Tyler should never have run his hands over her body. Not when he knew he had to break things off with her.

Tyler wriggled again in the small seat of his MGA, struggling with four months of pent-up sexual frustration. He loved the vintage car, but right now, he wished he had a nice big bench seat to move around in—not that he would find any comfort.

Was it only two hours ago that he had picked Regan up, thinking that he could break this off graciously? "Regan, you need to understand," He had whispered the words over Lou Malnati's famous deep-dish pizza. "I thought this would work, this long distance thing, but I was wrong. You need to date other guys and me…"

"You need to get laid. I get it, Tyler." Regan threw down her pizza slice, her clipped words wounding Tyler just as she intended.

"That is not it," he insisted. "It's not about the sex. I swear, it is not about sex. I am out there in the wider world, and it's helped me realize we need to be with other people."

"So you're breaking up with me after asking me to wait? Forever sure is short to you," Regan sat shredding the napkin in her lap and allowing her tears to fall unchecked.

Tyler glanced around the restaurant furtively, wondering if everyone was watching him make this pretty girl cry. Thank God, no one was paying any attention.

"I just want to go home," she begged quietly. "Please, just take me home."

"Ree, I think we should talk about this. We have been friends for a long time."

"Friends? Friends?" Her voice was rising as she leaned in and placed her balled fists on the table. "Is that what we have been, Tyler? We've been friends all these years? I get it. I misunderstood before, but now we're on the same page."

"Ree, that is not what I meant." Tyler signaled for the check, desperate to leave the small restaurant as Regan became louder and more accusatory.

"No? What did you mean, Tyler? Did you mean you would love me forever, or did you mean we were friends?"

"Regan…" he pleaded with the one word, throwing some crumpled bills on the table and steering her from the restaurant. He was messing up. "Things change. I'm doing a poor job explaining it, obviously, but they have just changed."

"They have changed for you, you mean?"

"Yes, things have certainly changed for me," he whispered.

Regan dropped her fighting stance and leaned closer. "What did you say?"

Tyler inhaled the fragrance of her shampoo as she flipped her mane of hair over her shoulder. He recognized the defiant move. He longed to hold her and soothe her anger.

Moving closer, he placed a whisper of a kiss on her cheek. He intended to stop there, but Regan turned to face him, her tears shimmering under the streetlights, looking more beautiful than he could remember.

"What?" she asked, trying to understand the sudden change in Tyler's expression.

"I can't remember when you have been more beautiful," he whispered in awe.

"Cut it out, Ty. You can't have things both ways. Either we are through, or we aren't."

Tyler knew if he touched her, he was a dead man, but his mouth descended on hers, claiming her pouty lips with his own and kissing her thoroughly. He coaxed her lips to open with a sigh and slid his tongue in to explore her warmth. She tasted of oregano and honeyed sweetness. It was a heady combination.

She was his. She had always been his and nothing could change that. His hands slipped under the edge of her short jean jacket, sliding up to pull her closer. Her skin was warm and smooth like velvet. One hand slid down the waistband of her pants to cup her small behind. Hers followed suit, her fingers slipping under the front of his belt and pulling him closer. Tyler gasped as her fingers moved lower.

A car coming toward them on the dark street caught them in its headlights, and Regan quickly withdrew her hand, using it to push Tyler away. He pulled her out of the road and against the car, trying to resume where they had left off.

"Ty," her voice quivered, "I don't know what you want from me. Are we breaking up or not? Do you love me or don't you?"

"I love... It is not about whether I love you, Ree. You are jus better off without me. You are perfect, Ree, but you are young. You need to learn more about life, about people." His excuses sounded feeble, even to him, but he tried again to explain the unexplainable, repeating the same phrases as he pulled her back into his embrace.

"Then we should stop," she said, even as her mouth lifted to his, brushing his lips lightly with her own. He took the invitation she offered, kissing her again, hands sliding under her clothes to return to her silky skin. He leaned against her, pressing her against the car, rubbing his growing erection against her, painfully aroused.

She allowed him to grind against her only until his hands began moving from her back to her front, and then she pushed him back. "We need to stop, Tyler. You need to stop."

Taking deep breaths to calm down, Tyler pulled back immediately, knowing she was right. He opened her car door, still trying to get his breathing, and his erection, under control. She slid into the small car without looking at him and remained quiet during the fifteen-minute drive home. When he moved to get out of the car, she stilled him with a hand to his knee.

"So this is goodbye," she said, a quiver in her voice.

"Not goodbye, Regan. I will see you around." His voice cracked on the last word. He reached over the gear shift and pulled her close. She moved reluctantly into his arms and returned the friendly hug that was all he offered. She stepped from the car, closing the door behind her with a final click.

Regan moved two steps toward her front door but halted only feet from the car. She stood like a statue for ten seconds, turned, yanked the car door open and poked her head back into the dark interior.

Her voice was strong and sure when she spoke. "You won't see me around, Tyler. Not if I can help it. Someday I will be a big shot executive, Tyler, a Harvard graduate. I have big plans, and from this moment forward, they do not include you. Go fuck your college girls and have a good time. I don't need you anymore. I won't miss you, and I won't think about you, but I promise you this. You are going to remember every kiss and every touch, and you are going to miss me."

Regan slammed the door, shaking the small car. Her words galvanized him. Tyler threw the car in reverse, spewing gravel and screeching tires in his need to be gone, and gone fast.

Throwing the car into drive, speeding down the long drive, Tyler went only a short distance before taking a deep breath, slowing and pulling over in front of the neighbor's house. Tyler killed the engine and rested his head on the steering wheel. He had never heard Regan lose her temper like that and certainly never with it aimed at him. He had never, ever heard her swear.

Squirming again to get comfortable around the slowly diminishing bulge in his pants, Tyler was swamped with regrets. Why couldn't he spill his guts and tell her what was swirling in his head, in his life? She might have understood. She might have loved him, anyway.

Memories of his father and his brother and their treatment of him these last few months swamped his emotions. They had turned their backs on him, so why wouldn't she? Why take the risk? He was better off letting her go. They were kids. They would forget each other by the end of the month.

Chapter Four

"You did what?" Tyler's voice rose above the noise in Hugo's Frog Bar. Tyler turned to Wyatt in horror, feeling his heart thudding as his blood chilled. "What the hell could you have been thinking?"

Tyler's stomach dropped at Wyatt's pronouncement. After all, his best friend wasn't asking a question, he was presenting a fait accompli. How could he wriggle out of this? Raking his fingers through his hair with nervous energy, he caused it to stand up straight. Impossibly, his messy hair only made him even more attractive. Two passing beauties caught his eye and flashed him come-hither smiles.

"It's a brilliant idea," Alex Gaines praised, slapping Wyatt on the back with enthusiasm and recapturing Tyler's attention. "Did you come up with it on your own, or was it Regan's idea?"

"No way Regan came up with this plan," Randall Parker asserted. "She might be his plus one for every event in town, but that friendship is strained to the breaking point." Randall put air quotes around 'friendship,' watching Tyler cringe as he did so. "Haven't you noticed?"

"Guys, I really don't need this shit right now. I have too much going on." He loosened his already loose tie and struggled not to down his expensive whiskey in a single gulp. These men knew him too well; they would see too much.

"Like what exactly?" Wyatt pinned him with a stare. Tyler knew making eye contact with his oldest friend would be a serious mistake. He would know something was going on. Tyler fidgeted with his cellphone and ignored Wyatt's prying for more details.

It was a busy Friday night, and the men were tucked in a corner of the trendy North Side bar where they went unmolested and they could usually hear each other over the din. Although women tried to catch their attention repeatedly, none approached. Had they tried, they would have been swiftly rebuffed. It was boys' night out.

At least once a month, the four gathered in the bar above Gibson's Steak House. They claimed it was to catch up, although they spoke almost daily in the earliest hours of the morning while working out at the East Bank Club. These Fridays were a ritual the men had carried over from their graduate school days and now, after more than ten years, they considered the time sacrosanct.

"I offered you to head up Lyons Howe," Wyatt repeated with a smug grin. He was clearly enjoying Tyler's discomfort.

"What's the problem?" Randall egged Tyler on, rolling up the sleeves of his custom-made shirt and leaning into the conversation with his characteristic gusto. "You don't care about the girl, you have the skills. Wyatt is willing to facilitate the time away from Tech Solutions, and it will be another notch on your resume."

"Notch on your belt," Alex corrected calmly. "He's right, Ty. If you ever abandon Wyatt, it would look fantastic on your resume."

"Thanks, man," Randall smiled at Alex and slapped him on the back. "Appreciate the backup. It's not like you care about her, right, Ty? You're not in love with her or anything?" Randall's tone and his broad grin told Tyler his friend was fully aware that he was irritating a sore spot.

Tyler considered throwing a punch into Randall's smug face. He had never discussed Regan with any of them, not for twenty years, and he didn't intend to start now. Wyatt had approached the subject earlier in the year, and Tyler regretted the brief conversation. He had shared too much of his feelings then, but he didn't intend to do it again. What could he say to make them all understand without saying too much?

"Get off my back, Parker," Tyler hissed. "That train has left the station."

"Yeah, and Tyler is not abandoning me, guys, so do not give him any resume ideas." Wyatt got the conversation back on track.

"Well, it's not a bad idea to jump ship if you are so willing to banish me," Tyler challenged. "I thought we were partners. I don't understand why the hell you would agree to this. You should have at least consulted me first."

A constant buzzing of text messages to Tyler's phone caught his attention, giving the three men time to discuss the situation without him. They were obviously in favor of the arrangement.

"He really would do a fantastic job and it would give him a chance to spread his wings a bit," Randall said.

"I love the idea, too. It will be a real growth opportunity for Tyler, but Ivy, you know better than to play matchmaker," Alex warned his friend.

"Matchmaker?" Tyler rejoined the conversation. "Is that what this is about? Me and Regan?"

"No, of course not," the three answered in unison.

"It is a real step up for you, Tyler, and you know it. You went from the law firm to my company. This is a chance to be in charge of something. You have worked your whole career for this moment."

"I like being your legal counsel, Ivy. Are you trying to get rid of me?"

"Not a chance," Wyatt reassured him. "Truth is, my father was hollering at Regan about being away too much…"

"Well, damn it, she is away too much," Tyler interjected, earning him a knowing look from his friends.

"From the office, away from the office, I meant." Tyler moved to finish off his drink, but found the glass empty. Shit. He needed to do something about these nerves. He twirled the glass slowly between his palms. *Damn these guys, they never let up.*

Wyatt laughed at Tyler's hangdog expression. "My father made a compelling argument. He said the Board was complaining."

"Ethan? Couldn't he fill in?"

"Even I know Ethan isn't ready," Randall interrupted. "He is still too immature to guide the giant deals. The competition would eat him alive."

"He's coming along, but Randall is right. He's not ready yet," Wyatt agreed.

"He isn't even 30 guys. Give the fellow a break," Alex reminded them.

"Yeah, AJ, and how many companies were you heading by thirty?" Wyatt pressed his friend.

Tyler appreciated having the spotlight off him for a moment and tried to keep the topic alive. "Yeah, see, AJ agrees with me about Ethan. He might turn out to be a child prodigy. After all, Alex was."

"I was not a child prodigy and my situation was different," Alex countered. Alex was whip-smart and born responsible, so his ability to take the helm of two major corporations at a young age was no surprise to any of them.

"Ethan isn't you, Alex." Wyatt stated the obvious.

"Hey, why didn't anyone ask Charlotte? She could do it for sure." Alex bragged about his wife, who was Director of Finance for LHRE.

"Well, Regan is obviously more considerate about your wife's current condition than you are," Wyatt sneered at his friend. "Come on, that was not an option and you know it."

"I am not inconsiderate, but I know Charlotte plans to return to work six weeks to the day after the baby is born." The other men, unaware of the happy news, offered hearty congratulations.

"Another round of drinks," Randall hollered to the server. "We're celebrating over here. You know, Alex, Sloane said that too, and she didn't go back to work for twelve weeks, and then not without buckets of tears."

"It's easier for Sloane, too," Wyatt reminded his friends. "Keeli provides her with daycare on the premises. Charlotte will have to leave the baby home. Anyway, AJ, it's just bad timing or she would have been Regan's first choice. I am sure of it." Tyler listened with a sinking heart as Wyatt shot down his other options.

"Yeah, I guess you're right," Alex conceded, mollified by the explanation. "Frankly, I am surprised Regan agreed to Tyler at all. Not that you aren't exceedingly qualified, Tyler," Alex continued when Tyler was about to argue with him, "but your relationship is..."

"Friendly. Totally and absolutely friendly. Regan knows I would walk across hot coals for her, for all of you."

"Great. So you'll do it," Wyatt concluded.

"Hey, wait a sec! I never said that," Tyler argued, realizing that he had just walked himself right through the door and allowed it to shut behind him.

"Yeah, Ty, I think maybe you just did," Randall confirmed with a smile.

"I've been had. You planned this. Not fair," Tyler complained, but the friends swore they had not arranged or even known anything until Wyatt had brought up the subject.

"You'll be great though, and if, as you say, Regan is just a friend, you will have no problem working closely with her. Very closely. Wyatt, this is a great plan." Alex slapped Tyler on the back. "Buck up my friend. You just got a big promo, Mr. CEO."

"Ty, remember what you said to me a few months ago, that it was time? I think you were right, man. Whatever has been holding you back, it's crunch time." Wyatt stared hard at his friend, communicating without a sound.

Tyler groaned, laying his head on his arms that rested crossed on the high top until the server arrived with their drinks.

"I don't know what I was thinking when I said that, Wyatt, but things are different now. Don't think I don't know what you are up to."

"Hey, don't complain," Randall defended his friend. "If you are very lucky, Ivy will succeed."

"And we all know you want him to," Alex seconded.

Instead of agreeing or disagreeing, Tyler looked again at his phone buzzing on the table.

"Who keeps texting you?" Wyatt asked. "Is it work?"

"No, it's nothing," Tyler responded, distracted. "Let me just deal with it. I'll be right back." Taking his phone, Tyler headed toward the doorway. He looked over at his friends and moved out of their line of sight to prevent them from seeing his increasing agitation with the caller. He hung up quickly, overhearing his friend's conversation as he approached.

"What do you think that's all about?" Alex asked.

"No clue, but he's been getting a ton of texts at work for the last two weeks. He is playing it very close to the vest."

"Maybe it's legal and he can't talk about it."

"Nice try, Randall, but he works for me. He could tell me."

Tyler returned to the table, gratefully sipped his replenished drink, and offered no excuses or explanations. "So, where were we?"

"We were wondering who you were talking to?" Alex answered bluntly.

"No one, AJ, it was nothing." Tyler sat silent for a moment, wanting to unburden himself to his friends. But how to explain now what he was unwilling to share twenty years ago? Tyler further messed up his already messed up hair, took a deep drink and opted to keep silent a bit longer. That's why he'd paid all that money, after all, to prevent anyone from knowing.

"Oh yeah, we were talking about my great new job. So, when do I start?"

"As soon as you and Regan can arrange it. You'll have to work out the details with her. You'll need Board approval. I am releasing you from Lyons Tech, but she actually has to hire you into Lyons Howe."

"Jeez, it sounds like you guys own the world," Randall joked.

"Not all of it, Randall, just most of it," Alex teased.

"Yeah, AJ. You own the rest, right?" Randall shot back, causing the four men to laugh. Any remaining tension dissolved, and the conversation turned to hockey and their winter vacation plans.

"AJ, if Charlotte wants to skip a Blackhawks game or two, you know who to call," Randall offered. "I could be very comfy in that box of yours."

"Randall, you know I can make room for you anytime Sloane will let you out of her sight, or both of you could join us. You'd have to leave Amelia with a sitter, though."

The men teased each other fondly, but they were right about Randall. He was a changed man in the last few years. He had been hard-drinking and wild until Sloane Huyler finally looked his way. Since their marriage, he had been just as much fun as ever, but seriously committed to his family. With the recent birth of his first daughter, he was never far from home. At the mention of her, he pulled out recent pictures like the doting papa he was.

"Look at you," Tyler observed his lifelong friends. "All three of you married, one of you with a baby, another with one on the way. Three years ago, who would have believed we'd be sitting here like this now? Wyatt, you were engaged to Sloane back then."

"Hey, that's my wife you're talking about, so be careful," Randall threatened gently.

"Alex, you were dating a different model every night," Tyler continued, as if Randall had never spoken. "Randall, you were partying all the time. And look at you now."

"No complaints from me," Alex admitted freely. "But you, Tyler, have failed to progress, haven't you? Fifteen years ago you were in love with Regan but unwilling to do anything about it and here we are today and you are still in love with Regan and unwilling to do anything about it."

"Yeah, what the hell is up with that?" Randall queried.

"Why do you think I suggested him for the job, assholes?" Wyatt pressed his friends. "I'm not stupid. Until now, I never saw a threat to Tyler ending up with my sister."

"Except you," Alex interjected.

"Yeah, except me," Wyatt agreed with a proud, big-brother grin. "But I have mellowed over time. When we were kids, it was different. I had to protect Regan's reputation and maidenly virtue. I knew this guy." He jerked his thumb in Tyler's direction. "I couldn't let him be alone with my little sister. It's different now. He can have her if he can catch her. That would be better than her marrying Brandon and moving away."

Marry Brandon? Where had that come from? Tyler grabbed his drink and gulped his whiskey, choking down the fiery liquid. She couldn't marry Brandon. Regan belonged with him and only him. Tyler's head swam. He couldn't think of a solution.

"What's wrong with Brandon?" Alex pierced Wyatt with a hard stare. "Remember you are talking about Charlotte's good friend."

"Nothing, as far as I can tell. Not a god damn thing." Tyler grumbled.

"Well, he's not you, for starters," Wyatt answered, looking over at Tyler.

"Since Regan was old enough to take care of herself, I haven't seen her date anyone that was a threat to our boy Tyler here," Randall patted Tyler on the back. "He'll prevail when he's ready."

"She's barely dated anyone but our boy Tyler," Alex corrected.

"Until now. I think this is different. Brandon Hockney could give you a serious run for your money, Ty." The men sat stunned by Wyatt's words, letting them sink in.

"You need to step up to the plate, man. It's long overdue," Alex said finally.

"Thanks for the concern, AJ, but he can have her. If they love each other, then I am just happy for Regan." Tyler said the words, but he didn't mean them.

"That's total bullshit, and you know it," Randall hissed. "You are completely in love with Regan Howe and you have been since you were eighteen years old."

"Oh, way before that. I think Ty has loved her since we were seven or eight."

"On the nose, as always, AJ. He has loved her since she brought him a frog from the pond. She won his heart forever with a frog," Wyatt shared.

"Enough. First of all, I am sitting right here, so stop talking about me like I'm not. Second, I am not the man for Regan." Tyler felt the words burn his lips. He may not be the man for her under the circumstances, but she was still—always—the woman for him.

"And why not?"

"She's in love with the senator, that's why not." *Tell them.*

"She's in love with you, dimwit, but you won't do anything about it. Is the poor woman supposed to wait forever?" Tyler's composure slipped as Alex hit an already raw nerve.

"It's not going to happen, so just drop it," Tyler shouted, exasperated. When heads turned, he took a deep breath, lowered his voice and said, "Look, I missed my chance with Regan and now we both understand it's too late for us. She has moved on."

"If you believe that, then great. You and Ree won't have any problem working together." Wyatt came full circle. "I'll let her know that you said yes."

"You do that," Tyler responded, a combination of belligerence and resignation mingling in his voice.

"Just one more thing, though. Personally, I think Regan needs help to fend off her senator. She is looking for an excuse to stay in Chicago and LHRE. You should have heard t talking at dinner Sunday. I never saw a woman feeling more pressure to marry a man she didn't love."

"Marriage? You didn't tell me she was marrying him." Tyler's shock was palpable.

"Ah, I see I finally have your attention," Wyatt responded. "Not yet, but he is hinting broadly and leaning hard on her to move in with him. Hence the need for someone to manage the business here. You can still stop her, Ty. I believe she would welcome the assistance, especially coming from you."

Tyler's phone buzzed again, just as he was about to respond to Wyatt. He clutched the phone, swigged the last of his expensive scotch without relish, and said a brusque good night to his friends. It would do no good to share. They might be temporary help, but he could not drag his friends into his problems. Not with these thugs leaning on h im.

"Something is going on," Tyler heard Randall say as he moved out of earshot. He hesitated as he answered the phone. "Hang on."

He stood like a statue listening to his friends' replies.

"And I think it is time we got to the bottom of it. We have been patient long enough."

"Too long," Wyatt agreed. "I have done my part to throw them together. Now, what are you two going to do? Let's make this happen before my sister does something we'll all regret."

If only they could do something, Tyler dreamed. Then he returned to the waiting phone call, his voice impatient. "I'm here. Now what?"

Chapter Five

"**I**s this awkward for you?" Regan asked politely, gesturing toward an armchair in the enormous conference room. "I want you to be comfortable."

"No, it's fine Ree. I am completely fine with this. I think it's a great idea." Tyler stood politely until Regan took her seat at the head of the large table. Was he being serious or sarcastic? Regan couldn't tell. He took a seat to her left, his back to the wall of windows facing the corridor, where curious employees kept strolling by and peeking into the room.

"It's just that the last time we talked on the phone..." she hoped she could get him to open up.

"That was nothing, Regan. I felt bad catching you so late, and while you were on a date, too. I didn't enjoy interrupting anything."

"We went through this already, Tyler. I was not on a date and you didn't interrupt. You were so chilly on the phone that night; I didn't know what to think. You were all, 'are we going or aren't we?'. It was so brusque. I wasn't sure you would be comfortable with this entire p lan."

She wasn't being completely honest. Tyler had offered to talk that night, his usual supportive self. She had refused. Why couldn't she admit that and come right out and ask if he was jealous?

"I am good with it. I am pleased with it. I am looking forward to working with you and your team, to mentoring Ethan and getting out from under Wyatt for a while."

"You are just trading one brother for another," Regan pointed out.

"Yes, but I get a sister in the bargain, too." Regan blushed and Tyler looked out at the Chicago skyline, breaking the brief connection that flared between them. "It seems a great deal has changed since that conversation, Regan. Let's just put the past behind us. I called because we made plans for the Rita Hayworth Alzheimer's fundraiser. Let's ignore the rest."

The rest. That would be the interrogation he conducted about who she was with, where they had gone, what they had talked about. She had played down everything, never mentioned Brandon's suggestion that she move East, but the fact that he was here now meant that he knew all the pertinent information.

Regan pivoted back to business, where she felt safe and in control. "Yes, well, in that case, I thought we could discuss timing, responsibilities, concerns from the Board of Directors, salary and the like, before you meet with the LHRE team this afternoon. And, of course, I want to answer any questions or concerns you might have about your role."

"That sounds perfect, Regan, and I want to be sure we discuss potential conflicts of interest. That will be important here and at Lyons Tech."

"Yes, that is on my list, too." Regan smiled at him and tapped the paper in front of her with an elegant Mont Blanc pen. "Coffee?"

"That would be great," Tyler thanked her, and she punched a number into the intercom, requesting a pot of coffee for the two of them. While they were waiting, she noticed him staring at the view. The offices at LHRE had the best view in the building, top floor looking over the river at the Wrigley Building to the North, all the way up Wacker Drive to the lake looking East.

"Get used to it," she gestured at the windows. "Your office is right next door." Feeling her mouth grow dry at the words, she added, "I will be down the hall, right next to you, in case you need me for anything."

"When you are in town, of course."

"Yes, of course."

It was torture. Regan questioned again how she would survive this. It would be different if she could read his mind, or if he would just reveal what he was thinking and feeling. Regan wondered if he was feeling anything. He acted like he didn't care, so she would learn not to care either. Regan reminded herself that she was going to Washington to fall in love with Brandon.

Brandon. He felt like a stranger since she'd been home. She had quickly been pushed him to the background where she didn't have to worry about the relationship or the future. Now that Tyler was coming on board, her last excuse for dragging her feet was disappearing.

The coffee arrived, cutting Regan off from her counterproductive thoughts. She leaned forward in her chair and poured for them both from the expensive porcelain set. She unconsciously added just a touch of cream to his cup, exactly the way he liked it. He noticed, raising an eyebrow and causing her to rattle his cup on its saucer.

Regan admonished herself. Get it together. Just stay focused on business. "Let's start with a division of responsibilities," Regan spoke in a cool, professional tone as she poured her own cup. "Knowing who is accountable for what will be critical to our successful working relationship."

Almost three hours later, she and Tyler had agreed on how they would divide their CEO role for the next twelve months, what he was authorized to determine on his own and when to seek her counsel.

They had arrived at a more than generous salary and benefits package and determined how interactions between Lyons Howe and Lyons Tech would be handled. Pending transactions for buildings and developments, the financial status of the company, outstanding loans and commitments, and even certain personnel issues were reviewed in detail.

"That was easier than I expected," she admitted with relief, sitting back in her chair and rolling her head to release the tension in her neck.

"Well, we approach problem solving the same way, Ree. We always have. It helps that we see eye to eye on so much."

"It doesn't hurt that you're quick to pick things up."

"Thank you for that," Tyler nodded, acknowledging the compliment.

"We also deal well together, don't we?" Regan continued. "We could always read each other's thoughts." Regan almost laughed out loud. She sure as hell couldn't read his thoughts these days.

Regan was proud of herself. She had been organized, effective and professional throughout the long meeting, and she was determined to stay that way now that they were finished. She had been careful not to be overly friendly or condescending, although Tyler called her boss and ma'am throughout the conversation. She suspected he was just baiting her. She was emotionally drained from the experience, but she conceded that she was leaving the company in very capable hands.

"I just need to keep things all business," Regan repeated to herself as she had all morning. Hell, she had been reiterating those words since the appointment had been scheduled.

Tyler didn't seem to be having any trouble with their roles, so she reminded herself to get over it. He would be terrific at the job. She would be out of town in DC two or three weeks each month. She could rely on him to run things capably and keep their interactions to a minimum. They would have no trouble working together.

The only issue, Regan admitted, was that she didn't want minimal contact. She wanted Tyler. No, she reminded herself, she wanted Brandon. Brandon would make her happy, and he loved her.

"Ms. Howe," Regan's assistant, Donna, knocked gently at the door, "your reservation is for 12:15 and it's noon now. Also, Ms. Roche called to say she can't join you."

"Would you ask Ethan instead, please?" Regan asked.

"Afraid to be alone with me?" Tyler taunted.

He should only know. "Don't be silly. We've been alone for the last three hours. No. Of course not," Regan babbled before shutting her mouth sharply, stopping herself from protesting further.

"Mr. Howe is at a client location, Ms. Howe," Donna stood in the conference room doorway, "Should I try to reach him there?"

"No, just let the restaurant know we will only be two for lunch," Regan thanked the assistant. "Can you just grab my coat?"

"I have it, Ms. Howe," Donna moved to pass it to Regan when Tyler reached to take it. Flashing him a slow, burning and highly flirtatious smile, Donna was reluctant to exit the conference room.

"Thank you, Donna," Regan repeated, pointedly. The assistant made a hasty retreat after one last glance in Tyler's direction.

Tyler showed no response to the obvious come on, helping Regan into her Burberry trench, his hands lingering briefly on her shoulders.

A chill shivered through Regan, where Tyler's hands had whispered along her skin. A sensuous warmth followed behind it.

"Where are you taking me, boss?" Tyler queried. Boss. Tyler was determined to keep their roles front and center. Tyler's words brought her back to the business at hand, and her body returned to room temperature. If she asked him to stop calling her boss, she knew he would just do it more.

"I made reservations at Catch 35 so we wouldn't have far to walk. Okay with you?"

"Sounds perfect."

They were being so careful with each other, friendly but not warm, cordial but aloof. Regan hated it, but it was safe, and frankly, she wasn't sure of the best way to move to anything more familiar, at least not comfortably. Then there was the 'boss' and 'ma'am' thing, keeping that wall between them.

Five minutes later, Tyler solved the problem for her in his usual forthright manner.

"Is this strictly business now, or can we just be friends for an hour?" he asked once they were seated in a cozy booth, quiet despite the full tables and soaring ceiling. "It would be nice to just be us for a while."

"We are us, Tyler, but I know what you mean. We will have to find a balance between our business personas and our friendship. I would like to just be us, too." Tyler leaned forward, elbows on the table, about to be very casual, so Regan added "at least during lunch." There, she thought with satisfaction as he sat upright again, that will keep him on his toes.

But Tyler lounged back in the chair after a moment, completely relaxed. "So first, give me the lowdown. How did your father take the idea of letting me fill this position? Did it give him a coronary?"

"Don't even joke about a coronary." Regan paled at the thought. "Actually, he was better about this than he was about letting me run LHRE."

"That's not saying much."

"He is so conservative. I think he is happy to have a man back in charge. It's hard to forgive his chauvinism, but I know I can't change him. Of course, this little move of mine just reinforces his antiquated thinking. If I run to DC for a man, it confirms his prejudice. I helped set the advancement of women back a generation."

"Are you moving for sure?"

"Oh no, nothing is for sure yet, but I am leaving the option open. It's tempting now that I have been approached about another job, a government appointment. It would certainly sweeten the deal." Regan saw Tyler lean forward, ready to ask a million questions, and headed him off. "It is way too premature to discuss that, though."

"Tease," Tyler responded, his voice dropping low. Regan fidgeted with the napkin in her lap. The situation was fraught with possibilities. Tyler's double entendres didn't help, and she didn't want to discuss DC with Tyler, of all people.

"So," she quickly returned to the earlier topic, "my father feels like you are family. He's confident that when the time comes, you will step aside for Ethan or return the reins to me without an argument." Return the reins to me? Why had she said that? She shouldn't have reminded him the option existed. "We know you will give it your all, despite the temporary status."

"And of course, I am a man."

"Yes, you are a man." The words were barely out of Regan's mouth before a blush stole into her cheeks. It was the understatement of the day to say that Tyler was a man. He was all man.

Tyler was walking temptation, with his beautiful brown eyes, deep set and penetrating. She loved the way his dark hair mostly behaved, but always stuck up after he ran his hands through it.

The man was a brilliant lawyer, a hard-driving hockey player with a sharp brain and a rock solid body. He wasn't overly tall, but he had several inches on Regan. He was broad-shouldered and narrow hipped. She loved his stride, the way his long arms and legs swung easily, reminding her more of a dancer than an athlete. He could sit still for long periods of time, giving nothing away, a real asset when he was in negotiations. He never fidgeted, always appearing in control—which he usually was.

He exuded confidence and was completely disarming when he revealed a true smile, not that self-deprecating smirk he automatically presented, or the slight tilt up of his lips. No, a real smile could bring Regan to her knees. When he tilted his head slightly to the left and let his sensuous lips expose his perfect teeth, his eyes would crinkle and one tooth would just nibble on a corner of his lips, she was a goner. His dimples, large but not deep, would be on full display, and that roguish twinkle would light up his eyes. Then she would remember every moment they shared over the years, every laugh, every touch, every kiss. When he really smiled, Regan could not resist him.

If their server or the women staring at them from nearby tables were any indication, it was obvious other women could not resist him, either. They only saw his good looks and his confidence, the width of his shoulders beneath his expensive custom suit. They could sense his allure while they guessed at his wealth, wondered about his personality, but she knew; he had the whole package.

He was inundated with women handing him their phone numbers. Even today, despite Regan's presence, a leggy beauty in a short dress stopped to hand him her card. Regan flashed her a dirty look, but what could she do or say when she was involved with Brandon? It was gratifying when Tyler ripped the card in half, tossed it on his plate and let the server carry it away.

"You will never change your father's mind about women, but I know he is fully aware of your ability. He knows you have increased revenues and fueled LHRE's expansion, even if he doesn't say so."

Tyler pulled Regan back to the conversation and away from the danger zone where her memories were headed.

"Yes, but it would be nice to hear it once in a while."

"Well, I am happy to tell you that you belong at the helm, and that I believe we are going to be a powerhouse couple—team, I mean. No one will be able to compete."

"I think you are right, Tyler," Regan agreed, ignoring his slip of the tongue. "It is going to be fantastic to look at things with your fresh perspective."

"There we go, talking business again. I am determined not to do that while we are sitting here. Tell me about Missy and the kids. I have not seen them in ages."

Regan bragged about her nieces, flashed pictures like the doting aunt she was, then shared the latest about her mother's charities. It felt like before Brandon, before Tyler's displays of jealousy, when she believed she had Tyler firmly in the friend column and was comfortable with him there.

She asked about his older brother. It was a sore subject and one he usually was reticent to discuss. Tyler struggled to feel worthy in his parents' eyes compared to Denton, who was four years his senior. They had been close as children, but the comparisons had been relentless and their summer together in Europe had finally driven them apart.

"Denny is good," he told her now, with no animosity evident. "Denny is always good. He's wintering in Florida with his family, but he is hard at work. His eldest will be looking at prep schools next year, then college. It doesn't seem possible."

"He married young, though, right out of graduate school."

"True, and he has sure put the pressure on me to marry and have kids. My mother never stops talking about it."

Regan nodded her head in agreement. "Mine either." They both fell silent. Regan always thought she would marry Tyler and have a family quickly as well, and he knew it.

Regan took a breath and plunged back in. Who knew that simple discussions about family could conceal so many conversational land-mines? "How is Denny's work going?"

"Great. He feels he is on the verge of a breakthrough."

"He always says that." They shared a laugh at the truth of her statement.

Denton Winthrop was a famous cancer research doctor and head of a small biotech company affiliated with the University of Chicago Medical School.

"If anyone can cure cancer, you know it will be Denny. At least my father thinks so."

"Most of the world thinks so, Tyler," Regan added softly. She wished she could take the words back immediately. She understood the rivalry between the brothers. She had observed it firsthand.

Throughout their childhoods, Tyler's father had lavished his attention and praise almost exclusively on Denny. While most children worried that their parents loved their siblings more, in Tyler's case, it appeared to be true. Emmett Winthrop had doted on his eldest son to the detriment of Tyler, and Regan believed the situation had pushed Tyler to pretend a bravado he didn't feel until his confidence caught up with him after law school. But she knew it had left scars, too.

"Let's change the subject," Tyler suggested with a small, self-deprecating laugh. "How did the Howe Museum fundraiser turn out?"

"You were there. You know it was a sell-out."

"I meant how did they do financially?" he clarified.

"Oh, sorry, of course. They beat all of their goals, which was fantastic. The family was very happy and the trustees ecstatic."

"That's great. I am so pleased for Stephen and Missy. They worked like dogs on this one. Speaking of benefits, you and I are still on for the Rita Hayworth ball next month, right? Would you rather I bow out so you can bring your senator?"

"Would you stop calling him mine, please?"

"But he is yours, Regan. Otherwise, why would I even be here right now?" Tyler looked away, fiddling with his silverware. "You're happy, right? This is what you want, isn't it?"

There it was, unavoidable, now that Tyler had asked a direct question. Regan found herself uncharacteristically tongue-tied and suddenly paid careful attention to her halibut and risotto. After taking a moment, perhaps expecting a response that she didn't offer, Tyler put his finger under her chin, tilting her gaze until it met his. "You know you can always talk to me, Ree. About anything. If you're not sure about all this..." he let the thought trail off.

"Of course we are still going together to the fundraiser," Regan prattled, avoiding the question of her happiness. "We made these plans ages ago, and being together makes more sense than ever." Tyler's eyebrow shot up in surprise at her statement. Regan blushed. "What I mean is that we will be at the LHRE table and now that you are heading LHRE, it only makes sense for us to attend together. I am sure Brandon will understand."

"Are you? I am not so sure," Tyler mumbled under his breath. "If he does, he's a fool. I know I wouldn't be happy if it were me."

Chapter Six

"You have to stop calling me here. I can't keep doing this," Tyler ground out through gritted teeth into his cellphone. Standing in the newly furnished office, listening to his voice reverberate off the hard surfaces, he prayed the space was soundproof. If Regan caught a whiff of his conversation, all deals would be off.

"Not a chance, lover boy. We aren't going anywhere." The heavily accented voice was menacing, even through the phone.

"I told you I am in a new profession, remember? I just got here and it would be nice to keep my position for more than a couple of weeks. You are asking me to risk everything." He paused to listen to the speaker.

"Like I give a shit."

"Maybe you don't care, but I do."

Surprisingly, Tyler was excited to be leading LHRE for the next year or two. After only two weeks, he was in charge and full of ideas for ways to move the business forward. Of course, working closely with Regan, even from a distance, was an enticing benefit. They had enjoyed a blissful week working side by side and then he suffered an agonizing week while she was in DC. At least when she was gone, he didn't have to worry about these damn phone calls.

"Right, like I told you, I have left Lyons Tech, so I can't help you." Not that I would have anyway, Tyler added under his breath.

"I don't remember asking you, asshole," the voice shouted so loud Tyler had to shift the phone away from his ear. "This is not a negotiation anymore. You want your precious job? You want your friends to stay safe, or your family? You will do as we asked and stop stalling."

Anyone standing twenty feet away would have heard the shouting coming through the phone. "I am not lying. Call over there, they will confirm it. Go find another patsy."

"You are the patsy, Tyler," the man threatened, savoring Tyler's word as he repeated it. "The boss made it perfectly clear from the beginning that if you wanted to roam free, live your life as you choose, there would be a price. This is the price. We don't want your money anymore. We have bigger fish to catch and your friend's databases are the source of those fish."

The caller spoke at length, while Tyler listened attentively. Eventually, there was a break in the diatribe and Tyler replied. "I can't do that and you know it. Your demands are ridiculous."

"Fine. I will tell the boss and he will decide how to exact punishment. I can promise, and you know I mean it. The price will be high and it will be messy. Your pretty blond friend, perhaps. You seem to have a soft spot for her. Or your mom? She's getting old and unable to defend herself. Your father would move heaven and earth to protect her. We can drag your friend Wyatt into this now, too. Of course, it could mean the end of his business."

Hearing the response, Tyler sank into his office chair, the color draining from his face.

"That's crazy. You know we'll get caught. Do you want to take that risk?"

"We can mitigate the risks. You should have joined us back in juvie and stopped trying to play Prince Charming. But now you have more to cover up than you did then, Tyler. All those payments to Russian gangs won't look good."

Tyler knew he was right. A small infraction at eighteen would have been easy to bear, although he hadn't thought so then. Now he was deep in the Russian underworld and had been for years.

"But that was blackmail," he stated, hoping the law was on his side.

"It doesn't change the facts, you entitled prick. You have been funding illegal operations for years. You don't think we've thought about this. We can destroy you and you know it and so this is exactly what you will do."

More shouting caused Tyler to hold the phone away again, but he continued listening, scribbling notes on the pad in front of him.

"Yes, I heard you. Yes, I understand. I don't think I can help you, I really don't. No matter what, this has to stop. Enough is enough, and this is way out of my league. Money was one thing, but this is criminal activity. I am out of options here and I've paid long enough. You are being unrealistic." Tyler tried to keep his voice level, but strong. He needed to get his point across without showing the fear gripping every molecule of his body.

"Enough? There is no enough. You are in this, man. You are in for life."

More shouting ensued. Tyler rose to his feet in response and began shouting in return. So much for not showing emotion.

"You tell the boss I am not in this forever, and I mean it. This is the last time. This is no idle threat. It was one thing when it was just me he was hurting, but this is out of the question."

More hollering came from the other person, mixed with a menacing tone that sent shivers up Tyler's spine. One wrong word when he was eighteen and he had been paying ever since. He refused to drag his family and friends into his problems.

"You sure as hell aren't going to get me to bring Wyatt into this. I cannot drag him into anything. I cannot jeopardize his business. Even if I still worked there, the answer would be no."

"I understand that you want to protect the people you love." The caller calmed down and Tyler retook his seat, lowering his voice as well. "Maybe we can do something with your new employer and leave your buddy alone. Where are you working now?"

"Where? Why do you care where? You just need to know it's not Lyons Tech Solutions."

"You think we won't find out?"

"You don't…"

"We have spies everywhere," the caller interrupted Tyler.

"You don't…" Tyler tried again. "You don't need to know. It's not relevant." He started to hang up the phone, but something the caller said stopped him, hand in midair and Tyler listened attentively.

"Our methods are ruthless Tyler. We can easily leave bodies in our wake."

"You wouldn't dare," he breathed, clearly shaken. "You wouldn't dare."

The caller said one last sentence, "I wouldn't test that," and hung up. Tyler was holding the phone to his ear, listening to silence, his heart racing, his blood chilled.

"Shit, shit, shit," Tyler finally mumbled, hurling his cell against the wall. It left a dent in the Sheetrock before falling to the Berber carpeting. He sank lower in the chair and dropped his head into his hands, defeated. "What the hell am I going to do?"

He sat for a solid minute before walking over to pick up the phone. He moved like an old man, or a humbled one. He checked the phone and seeing that it still worked, dialed a number.

"Mother," he said without preamble, "it's time to bring Father into this mess." He listened to his mother's response. "I wouldn't if I could avoid it. No, no, I am absolutely sure. I have no other choice."

His mother said something that caused Tyler to pause as he nervously paced the carpet from wall to window. In a small, insecure voice he asked, "Do you think he will help?"

Chapter Seven

"What the hell are you wearing?" Tyler barked at Regan.

"Marchesa," she replied calmly. "Do you like it?"

"Don't play this game with me, Regan. You look indecent."

"Tyler, you sound like my father. Or Ivy, which is worse."

"You would never have worn that if your father or your brother were attending tonight, and you know it."

"But they aren't, so come dance with me." She turned her back and strolled away on ridiculously high heels, a triumphant smile on her face, listening to Tyler trying to control his angry breathing.

She was determined to get an honest reading tonight. She knew Tyler. He would do everything possible to keep his emotions in check. Regan was determined to do everything possible to get under his skin.

They had done beautifully, driving the twenty minutes to the Rita Hayworth Gala. She had discussed current events and political tidbits that she had gleaned from her new congressional friends. Tyler had kept his side of the conversation solely about business.

But as she had known this would happen, Tyler couldn't control his reaction when he helped her remove her coat. The dress was barely there, a knee-length dress of nude, layered lace. The bottom looked like a Disney concoction, except it was sheer, displaying most of her thighs.

That was nothing compared to the top. The top was nothing more than a sheer corset covered in lace. The stays were visible, along with a lot of skin.

Selecting the dress had been tough. She loved knowing Tyler would see so much, but she worried that everyone else would, too. Her nipples were hidden, but barely.

Tyler's reaction was worth every agonizing moment. She had made the right decision. Regan watched as Tyler's mouth went dry. He lost his tongue, his manners, and control over his erection. He was worse than a randy teenage boy, and unable to hide it.

When Tyler caught up with the quickly disappearing Regan, all he could ask was, "Can you dance in those shoes?"

"Let's find out," came Regan's snappy retort.

Tyler seized two glasses of champagne off the tray of a passing server, passed one to Regan, gulped down the other, and moved into the vicinity of the dance floor. Business people, politicians and philanthropists slowed their progress several times, seeking their time, their connections, their advice or their money. Both Regan and Tyler were astute at handling requests and moving away quickly, having made no promises.

Then she was in his arms. He fit around her like a glove and smelled like Tyler. She buried her nose in his tux, imprinting the moment in her memory. He was holding her slightly too close. Regan let her slim body go soft in his arms, let Tyler run his hands over her warm skin.

"You feel like velvet," he whispered as he danced slowly around the room. His fingers played over her arms, back and shoulders in small, involuntary movements, leaving a trail of fire behind. When she rested her head against his chest, he placed a whisper of a kiss on the top of her head, so soft that she feared she imagined it. She savored the moment of perfect synchronization, in mood, and movement.

"We dance well together, don't we—even in these shoes?" she teased him as the song ended and they moved to mingle with the crowd. "Tell me again why we don't do it more?"

"Because of your senator." And just like that, the connection was severed. Regan wasn't sure if he was lobbing an accusation or a question, but she was instantly defensive.

"Really, Tyler? You want to have that conversation here and now?"

He looked unapologetic, and the look in his eye emboldened Regan. There was something between them, despite all his denials. He gave himself away in the dance—the way he held her, that soft brush of his lips. "How long did you really think I would wait for you?"

They were interrupted by their host, the Executive Director of the Alzheimer's Association. LHRE was a big supporter of the cause. Talk about bad timing. Regan wanted a serious talk with Tyler about their relationship, but she thought they would do it privately. Now that she had put it out there; would he take the bait? And would it end in an embarrassing shouting match, or another romantic spin about the room?

Time was passing them by. Regan needed Tyler to act now, commit to her once and for all. Otherwise, she needed to move on with Brandon. Tyler had been the boy for her, and she believed he could be the man for her, but for some reason, he refused to step up. Tonight was so promising. His movements, his touches, were definitely those of a man interested in more than friendship. If this dress didn't do it, nothing would. She had been driving the relationship from the beginning, she realized. He had always held himself in check.

"Hey jerk," she hollered to him across the playground the first time she had ever seen him. He was tongue-tied and clumsy around the young Regan, but she was brash and confident in pigtails with two skinned knees. She walked over, her hands cupped in front of her, and said, "I'm Regan. Here," and gently placed a frog in his hands. She flashed him a proud smile, "I caught it myself, in the pond."

Tyler smiled, took the frog, and gave her a tiny kiss on the cheek, spun on his heel and returned to his friends. He was gone, and she was a goner.

Since that day, their lives had come together and separated, always hovering on the edge of romance. Before she accepted a job in Washington and the advances of another man. Regan would need Tyler to step up or tell her unequivocally that it was over in words.

"Let's not discuss it now," Tyler ended the conversation, spoke quickly with the director and relinquished her only briefly to another donor. Taking Regan back in his arms, he swept her on to the dance floor. They moved in time to the music, eyes locked, in a world of their own.

"I could dance with you all night," he whispered, his breath warm on her ear, "and never let go."

Before she could reply, had she chosen to, the emcee announced dinner. Regan heard the huff of impatience leave Tyler's lips, feeling the same. Speeches and polite table talk took over the evening, and Tyler and Regan transitioned as they were required to do. The moment on the dance floor gave way to business.

They put their heads together throughout the evening, discussing how they would approach potential clients, who would take the lead, and who would say what.

"Okay, so we have a game plan," he announced, a determined air about him.

"You make this so much easier than working the crowd alone," Regan freely admitted. "I am glad you are here, Tyler. You are so good at putting our big clients at ease."

"I'm glad, too," he mumbled with a smoldering look, running his index finger up her bare arm, leaving no doubt of his meaning. Could he see the play of emotions on her face? She was so pleased and so confused. Did he want her? Was he just teasing? Would he rope her in only to push her away again? When they were younger, she had read him easily, but he was secretive now, confusing her. She was playing with fire and needed to stop unless he would commit to their future.

Regan turned her focus to the needs of LHRE instead of her own. She and Tyler were a strong sales team, playing good cop, bad cop once or twice, with outstanding results that gained LHRE a previously reluctant new client before dessert.

Later, when they again huddled close, this time over the list of items up for auction, Tyler was back in control, keeping things friendly, laughing and teasing Regan over her choices. She didn't care about the items. She was all about raising the needed dollars for the charity. She bid recklessly on theater and sports tickets, dinners and brunches and even high-performance driver training. She had no idea what she would do with any of it if she was the successful bidder.

Tyler's cellphone vibrated incessantly until Regan finally suggested he read the texts and deal with whomever was so demanding.

"Sounds like an emergency to me."

"It's fine," he responded without looking at his phone. He was curt with his response sheltering the screen, as if he feared that she might read over his shoulder, or that someone else might. Finally, he relented.

"Forgive me, Regan, I think I will take this," Tyler pardoned himself, and stepped away from her.

Regan feared she had lost her chance to get Tyler to communicate. He was preoccupied when he returned to the ballroom, barely able to give Regan the attention she deserved. Tyler failed to follow the conversation several times and refused to answer when Regan repeatedly asked if anything was wrong.

"I give up," she told him in a crisp, cold voice, crushed by her failure to make this night go as she hoped. "Maybe we should just go? Your attention is obviously elsewhere and you aren't great company."

"I was listening to the speeches."

"They ended ten minutes ago, Ty," Regan argued. "You are ignoring the music, ignoring me, and you're not working the crowd anymore either. It's been a long day. Just take me home."

"No, you're right," he finally turned his full attention to Regan. "Come dance with me again." He wiggled his eyebrows and pulled her close. "It would be a crime to waste that dress."

He swung her out to the dance floor in a move that sent her skirts flying about her. Brandon be damned. This was what she had wanted her whole life and maybe, finally, Tyler was willing to show his true feelings. Tyler's arm circled her waist, and he pulled her close. Regan leaned into it, the feel of the fine wool on her skin, the scent of his aftershave tickling her nose, the warmth of his breath as he nuzzled her neck.

She couldn't be happier if she had scripted this moment in her own fairy tale. Now, this was more like it.

Chapter Eight

Regan was just too damn alluring in that dress for him to ignore. He wanted her. Desperately.

He was an idiot. He should have told her years ago. He should have told everyone. Despite the tongue-lashing he was silently giving himself, Tyler was certainly no fool.

"The professor" to his friends, Tyler was generally serious and professional. He had the smarts necessary to obtain both an MBA and a law degree, and he was now acting CEO of LHRE, on hiatus from one of the fastest growing tech companies in the country. He kept his cool in general, but again and again he behaved like an imbecile around Regan.

Since that damn frog almost thirty years ago, he had loved no one but Regan. Sometimes they made it work together, like in high school, but most times not. His feelings were unchanged, but something always stopped him from declaring his feelings and asking her to do the same. This time, it was something insurmountable.

Yet Tyler couldn't stay away. He was the proverbial moth to the flame, flirting with disaster every time he flirted with her. He had vowed to stay away, to keep her safe, but the attraction was undeniable. Yep, prize idiot.

Returning to the ballroom after the latest threats, Tyler briefly considered sharing the conversation, coming clean with Regan and perhaps moving their relationship forward. He was at a fork in the road, knowingly choosing the wrong path, unable to summon the will to fix it. Not only were his problems unsolvable, but Regan was involved with Brandon. Even Tyler could see that Brandon could offer her the world. He felt hopeless.

He was preoccupied, just as Regan accused, despite feeble efforts to give Regan the attention she deserved. He failed miserably at each attempt until Regan suggested they just leave. That got his attention. Who knew when he would have the chance to hold her in his arms again?

"Come dance with me again. It would be a crime to waste that dress."

Encircling Regan in his arms, his body responded to her nearness even as his mind worried over the earlier texts. He was unaware of his hand stroking her back, and fingers lightly skimming over her bare skin. He wasn't thinking clearly when he pulled her close or when he dropped kisses on her hair. He wasn't paying attention, just acting on instinct. Regan was responding, her breath growing uneven, her hands clinging to his shoulders.

Tyler reflexively pulled her closer, allowing his hand to slip lower on her waist, pulling her tight against him. She tilted her head up, a quizzical look in her eye. Tyler left her in no doubt of his feelings, lowering his mouth to hers. He wasn't a complete idiot. He remembered that they were on a public dance floor, that she was in the spotlight these days, but he didn't slow down and she didn't stop him.

Tyler sampled a small taste of her sweet lips, coaxing her to respond, to open and allow him to explore her honeyed mouth. His left hand joined his right, low around her body, closing what small gap was still between them, the bulge growing between them proclaiming his desire.

Tyler, nearly thirty-six years old, had been keeping his distance from Regan for two decades. In this moment of weakness and preoccupation, he stopped fighting and just tasted her, felt her, breathed in the essence of the woman he loved. He allowed the promise of her to tease his senses and kissed her again. It might be the last chance he ever had, he told himself, as if that justified his actions.

Less circumspect once she responded, Tyler gripped Regan's neck lightly in his large hand, holding her head still as he plundered her mouth. His hard body, all muscle, engulfed her small one as he felt lust pulsing between them.

A small moan from Regan brought him back to his senses with a jolt. The dance ended, Tyler released Regan, and after dropping a quick kiss on her rosy mouth, he placed one hand on the small of her back protectively and guided her off the floor.

"Let's get out of here before we're splashed all over tomorrow's news," Regan suggested before he could communicate a similar desire. She picked up her miniature jeweled handbag, looped her arm through his, and rested her head on his shoulder. "Besides, my feet are killing me." They shared a laugh at the poor excuse for their rapid exit.

Still in a fog of external problems and internal desire, Tyler followed her suggestion with alacrity and soon they were seated in his Tesla, moving through the inky darkness of the cloud-covered night.

"So now what? You want to come to my place or go to yours?" Regan asked, straightforward as always. Her hand reached across the console to slide over his muscular thigh, massaging higher with each stroke.

Tyler's erection was painful, but his conscience kicked back in. What was he thinking? Had she had too much to drink? His pulse raced with the possibility of the situation, but so did his mind. "Maybe we need to slow down, Regan. You've been drinking, remember, and we are working together." A scowl formed between Tyler's brows. "Then there's Brandon to consider."

"I had a couple glasses of champagne. I am fully aware we work together. Brandon isn't here but you are. If you want out, say so, but I know what I am doing. My relationship with Brandon is my issue."

"You made it my issue when you hired me so you could marry him."

"I hired you so I could explore a relationship with him, Tyler. We have no commitments to each other, certainly not marriage."

"So the press has it all wrong?"

"I appreciate your concern, but let it go. I don't want to discuss Brandon. I don't want to think about Brandon. I don't want to talk about another man, about giving up my home and everything I've worked for. I want to see where this takes us. Do you?" Regan caught her breath and waited for Tyler to reply. He remained silent. "Stop fighting me, Tyler Winthrop. Stop fighting yourself. Just this once, turn off that brain of yours and allow yourself to feel."

Tyler remained silent, battling his desire with his conscience exactly as Regan imagined. He was desperate for her and desperate to do the right thing, but unsure at the moment exactly what the right thing was.

Regan sighed. "At least come back and have a drink with me. It doesn't need to be anything more."

"Ummm," Tyler stalled, his brain clamoring for answers, for something reasonable to say. "I don't know how to read you anymore, Ree. This could be a very bad idea. You could get hurt."

Tyler thought she would take him at face value since he was making it about her, not him. He needed to do something before he started something she would demand they finish.

"What are you talking about, Tyler? What are we talking about? You have known me my whole life. I have never hid my feelings for you, or my ambitions. Brandon clashes with everything I worked to achieve, but he is offering me a future. You are offering me nothing, or at least that was the case until thirty minutes ago."

Regan turned in her seat to face Tyler in the shadowed interior. "Tyler, I am sick to death of this game of cat and mouse. You are worried that I could get hurt? Don't you know how many times you have broken my heart?"

Regan's voice rose unsteadily, choked with emotion that hurt Tyler to hear. He wanted to reassure her, apologize, make everything right, but how could he?

Regan took two deep breaths, then continued in a soft, resigned voice. "Either you are interested or you aren't. I believe you are. I thought tonight you were finally putting your cards on the table. Was I wrong? Am I wrong?"

"Yes, well no." Tyler fumbled. "Jeez, I sound like an imbecile." Tyler pulled to the side of the road and threw the car into park. "Everything I do, I do to protect you, Regan. Your welfare is paramount to me. But tonight—" Tyler ran his hand through his hair in exasperation. "Tonight I was distracted, Ree. I let my guard down."

"You let your guard down?" Regan's voice rose three octaves. "Do you feel like you have to ward me off? I am completely confused, Ty. Let me make this simple for you. Ever since I have known you, and certainly since that promise we made to each other in high school, I believed we would end up together. I wanted to end up together, despite your there today, gone tomorrow behavior. Now, after almost two decades of you running hot, then cold, then hot, then cold, I am asking for a definitive answer. Once and for all, what do you want from me, Tyler Winthrop?"

Tyler hesitated too long. What could he tell her when he wanted her and always had? He recognized the moment that Regan gave up on him and turned to look out the window.

"Find, whatever, I don't care anymore." Her anger and disappointment wrapped around every syllable. He felt it bubble up inside until he wanted to explode. "Come up for a drink or don't. I'm done with all this."

"It's complicated Regan," he said, the words inadequate to his own ears. Why had she offered him another chance when he treated her like this? He wanted to deserve her, but how? "You know how much I care about you, but you are CEO of Lyons Howe, responsible for the fates of hundreds of people, not to mention the support of your family. You testify before congress, you are seen about town with a potential vice president. Shit, Ree, I work for you now. You are an important woman."

"You bet I am," she said, whipping her head around to face him. "And you are a hot-shot lawyer and now a CEO. What does any of this have to do with us? Either you love me or you don't. Do you? Do you love me?"

"Of course I love you, Regan."

"Not like that! Not like a sister, or the sister of your best friend. Do you want to spend your life with me? Do you hunger for me? Because if you don't, or if you are not sure, let me out right here and I will get an Uber." Regan reached for the door handle, and Tyler instinctively pulled her close. No way he could let her go.

What did he want? Tyler knew the answer, had always known the answer. He wanted her by his side always, but he wanted her safe, too. He hadn't yet figured out how to accomplish both.

"Don't go, please." He pulled into traffic before she could try to slip away again. "I just need some time to work a few things out, Regan. I know I have said that before—"

"Like a million times," she muttered under her breath.

"And I know it sounds like an excuse, but I swear it's not."

"My life is complicated too, as you so charmingly pointed out. But I am telling you what I want. It's time for you to decide what you want, Tyler, and let me in. Let me help you."

They pulled up in front of her high-rise, the doorman approaching to open her door. In that split second, Tyler risked everything. "You, Regan. I want you."

"Park it," Tyler commanded the fellow, getting out and taking Regan's hand in his steely fingers. "Let's go inside. I think I might need that drink."

Tyler followed her down the corridor to the elevator, breathing freely now that he had admitted his desire. He admired her long legs in the tall heels, enjoyed the view of a vast amount of slender thigh through her sheer dress. He watched her short hair swing softly and remembered watching her walk the halls in high school. He couldn't say no anymore. He didn't want to try.

They each stood looking forward on the long ride up. Tyler didn't dare touch her or he knew he would combust.

"So, they haven't finished the hotel yet?" he asked, cooling his blood as best he could, already knowing the answer. "You moved in anyway?"

"I couldn't resist. I know I have to sell it eventually, but while they complete the building, the penthouse is mine."

"You've done a beautiful job with this project, Ree. Everything is beyond luxurious, and the condos are rumored to be over the top."

"They are. Wait until you see my place." He didn't care about her place, but stalling was vital at the moment. He feared ripping her clothes off and taking her against the door as soon as they were alone. "Breathe."

"Did you say something?" Regan asked. Tyler shook his head, remembering to breathe.

They reached the top floor of the 60-story building in what felt like a flash. The quiet doors whooshed open on an enormous foyer with no furniture in it, the inlaid marble floor set off to perfection in the empty space. Regan's heels echoed and reverberated.

"It's too big to bother furnishing, since it's temporary," Regan said as she led the way to the living room, dropping her coat on one of the two oversized chairs dwarfed by the open space. "Scotch?"

"Please," Tyler responded, stalking around the enormous room. "Just how big is this again?"

"You should know, Ty. LHRE is developing the property."

"I know the half floor condos, not this one."

"Just over 70,000 square feet," Regan announced, watching his face for reaction. His jaw dropped and a sharp whistle escaped his lips. "See why I had to move in? I'll never live like this again."

Laughing with her at the absurdity of it, Tyler allowed her to give him a quick tour. They wandered the outdoor space—11,000 square feet—and the bedrooms, all seven, not including the guest suite that held three more. He hesitated at the door of the only room with a bed in it and took a gulp of his drink. The liquid was golden fire in his system.

"Who will buy something like this, Regan? I know you did your research, but seriously—"

"Someone foreign with too much money and possibly a large number of wives. They will run their business out of it. After all, there is a full office, secure internet, and a car and driver. Someone will have everything they need."

"You could put my condo in one tiny corner of this place and it's nothing to sneeze at. I am impressed, madame."

"Don't be, Ty," she said. "The company owns it, not me. I am still just me." She turned toward the hallway, and Tyler took her hand, tugging until she faced him, their mouths only inches apart.

"Are you, Regan? Are you still just you? You jet between here and Washington, you run a multi-billion dollar company, you're plastered on the covers of magazines. You date a cabinet secretary. A rich, handsome cabinet secretary."

"You are rich and handsome, Tyler. You run a multi-billion dollar company, not me. And your face was on the cover of 'Inc.' just last week. Don't think you're not good enough."

"I know I'm not, but no one—no one—will ever love you more than I do."

"And you know all my secrets, a whole lifetime's worth."

Tyler started to say "and you know mine" but checked himself. She didn't. But she would soon. He would tell her everything, they would be partners, share everything. He would never make the same mistake again. He could never let her go.

"Do you think Wyatt will get over having me in the family?"

Regan laughed, blushing a pretty pink. He hadn't meant to say anything about family, it had simply slipped out. But she had to know he was in this for keeps.

"It may take him a while, and he may exact payment."

"You're worth whatever he demands, Regan, and more. I have been a fool not to make that clear sooner."

"You know you didn't hide your feelings, even if you didn't express them. You were very confusing."

"Well, I plan to be crystal clear going forward," Tyler said, pulling her into his arms and kissing her soundly. "I want to shout it from the rooftops, Regan."

"Go right ahead, crazy man. I've waited a lifetime to hear it."

Tyler hesitated, leaning his shoulders against the doorjamb, looking past the bed to the dark windows. He sipped his drink, quiet and pensive. He leaned closer, so his lips brushed hers as he spoke.

"If we start something, Regan Howe, there is no going back. I am in this for the long haul or I am out of here. No more Brandon. You break that off. You understand? You will be all mine, or not mine at all."

"I understand," Regan nodded, reaching over and taking the scotch from his hand to place it safely out of the way under the only other furniture in the room, a folding chair. "Ty," she said in a whisper of breath, "I have always been yours."

It was the invitation Tyler required, had been waiting for but refusing to hear. He pulled Regan against his body, wrapped his arms tightly around her waist and plundered her mouth like a starving man finally offered his favorite dish.

Regan led the way deeper into the master bedroom, a huge space of floor to ceiling windows, the bed standing insignificant in the center. She bent to turn on a table lamp sitting on the floor beside the bed. The sight of her firmly curved backside, framed by the corseted dress, furthered the lust raging through Tyler's veins. He took Regan in his arms, fell back upon the bedding, and pulled her down on top of him.

Fine strands of hair fell forward to cover Regan's face. Tyler slid them back gently, his hands skimming her face. Regan rested one cheek in his large palm, turning to place a kiss on it. Her mouth was moist, hot and inviting. Tyler rolled them into the engulfing bedding and kissed her with twenty years of pent-up desire, trying to compensate in one kiss for years of want, frustration, and denial.

"I need to savor this, Ree. Take it slow. We have waited too long not to." His voice was gravelly. "I want to try to take it slow."

Regan nodded her agreement, untying the bow tie from around Tyler's neck and gently undoing the top studs of his shirt. She planted small gentle kisses on the smattering of dark hair she revealed, kissed his neck and jaw as her fingers opened his shirt wider. He loved the feeling, but craved so much more. Finally, she lifted her head, and he claimed her mouth.

Tyler took control enthusiastically, his lips seeking the warm heat of her mouth with his tongue. His hands worshipped her body from thigh to shoulder, exploring every delectable inch. Her skin was soft as velvet over her long arms and legs. Tyler stroked the muscles beneath, felt the strength of her under the incredible softness. The ability to touch her was indescribable. Tyler had waited a lifetime to allow his fingers to linger over her shoulder, her hip, her breast. He felt her nipple pebble under his touch, heard her small moans of pleasure, and wondered how he could hold on. He was as hungry for her as air.

Gasping for breath, he pulled away, watching as the dark crescents of her lashes lifted to reveal languid desire in her turquoise eyes.

"I'll never go slow at this rate."

"Maybe we should get this first round over with," Regan whispered, "then we can go slow the next round."

"Rounds? Are we in a prize fight, Regan?"

"That remains to be seen, champ," she teased.

"I forgot my boxing gloves, and—how embarrassing—a condom. Do we need a condom?" he asked, pink tingeing his high cheekbones as a dimple made a brief appearance with his awkward smile.

"Not embarrassing." She actually seemed pleased. "Good to know I wasn't a sure thing, and that you didn't have other plans."

"I never have other plans Regan, not for ages. How could I want anyone but you?"

"Well, I am on the pill, so if you are safe, I am, too."

"Well, thank God for that," Tyler told her, dropping his weight down upon her again and kissing her eyes, her cheeks, her jaw and sliding his tongue down her neck to nestle in her cleavage, just above the edge of that temptation she called a dress.

"How do I get you out of this thing?" he asked, even as his hands slid up under the full skirt, tugging gently at her panties beneath it.

Regan moved her legs to help him divest her of the scrap of lingerie, then pushed at him until he lifted off her. Silently, she rolled until she was facing away from him, kicking off her shoes as she moved.

Tyler went to work immediately on the back of the dress, unlacing the skin tight corset with deft fingers and pulling Regan back to face him as it fell away from her breasts, exposing her to him for the first time.

"You're beautiful," he said in a hushed whisper. Lowering his head to her breast, he sucked hard on the nipple, feeling it harden under his tongue and mouth. Tyler wrapped his hand around the other perfect orb, feeling Regan arch under his ministration. He pulled back to blow a tantalizing breath on the wet nipple, watching it tighten even more before he covered it with his hand to squeeze gently. She felt amazing, better than his teenage or adult brain had imagined. She was the perfect fit for his hand, responsive as hell under his lips. A small moan escaped her as he nipped Regan's other nipple between his teeth. The pressure in his groin grew urgent. He willed himself to slow down.

Tyler tugged the dress down Regan's body and followed the confection with kisses, stopping to pay homage between her thighs. She shuddered and clawed at his back in demand.

So much for going slow. Tyler yanked the dress over her toes and allowed it to fall to the floor, followed by his shirt, the last of the studs flying about the bed in his haste to remove it.

Regan, naked in the soft lamplight, caused Tyler to stop breathing briefly before the iron spike in his pants demanded release. Tugging clumsily at his zipper, he finally wrenched down his pants and briefs and fell upon her body.

"Am I crushing you?"

Regan shook her head no, and Tyler, holding what weight he could on his forearms, dropped his mouth to hers again. Nibbling at her lips, he pressed forward, sliding his leg between her thighs and pushing them apart. She moved willingly, her hands massaging the long muscles in his back, clasping him to her tightly as her body writhed beneath his, begging for possession.

Tyler gave in to the sheer bliss, pushing at her slick entrance and sliding in with excruciating slowness, holding his breath, savoring the tight, wet heat clenching around him. A sigh of pure pleasure escaped her as he began to move within her in slow, controlled movements. He thrust into Regan's welcoming body with measured strokes, listening as her breathing sped up, feeling her body arching and shaking under him.

"God, you feel incredible," he muttered over and over again like a mantra, kissing her deeply, his tongue thrusting in time with his hips. When he felt her body pulling harder at him, her heels digging into his butt, her hands clawing at his shoulders and back, he sped up, giving her what she needed.

Regan wrapped her legs tighter around his hips, withholding nothing, her body all but begging Tyler to move faster and harder. He thrust deeper and quicker until he felt her body grow taut and her breathing halt. Kissing her hard enough to bruise her lovely pouty mouth with his teeth, he pushed himself to the brink, until he felt her body shiver and pulse around him, her orgasm rippling through her, her core clenching, impossibly tight around him.

Tyler tried to catch his breath, tried to hold on, moving more slowly, waiting for the spasms to subside, but he was hanging on by a thread and within moments, it snapped. Tyler throbbed and exploded into Regan's warmth, hoarsely shouting her name.

They lay in the afterglow, laboring until their breathing slowed and evened, obsessively stroking each other's skin, feathering each other's faces with tiny kisses.

"Oh my god," Regan finally laughed.

"Worth waiting twenty years for?"

"Yeah, but I don't plan to wait more than twenty minutes for the next round, champ."

Tyler happily obliged.

Chapter Nine

Regan awoke to find the sun in her eyes, a tenderness between her legs and a warm, muscular body wrapped around her naked body. Smiling at the decadent combination, she lazed briefly, basking in the pleasure before she sidled sideways out from under Tyler, working hard not to wake him.

Padding to the bathroom on quiet feet, she washed her face, doing her best to remove stray signs of last night's mascara. Regan brushed her hair and teeth, grabbed a light robe, then headed to make a big pot of badly needed coffee. They had been up most of the night, and she was tired. Tired, but elated.

It was already close to 10 am. Regan couldn't remember the last time she'd slept that late. She poured her first cup of java, inhaled the rich aroma, and went looking for her purse. Digging out her phone, she texted Missy as she found a plug to recharge it.

"Good morning," she wrote. "All is right with the world at last. You'll never guess who stayed over here last night."

"WHOA!" came the almost instant response. "Talk?"

"Calling," Regan returned. Rapidly dialing her sister, Regan barely got out a hello before Missy peppered her with questions she did her best to answer.

"How? What did you have to do to get him to step up at last? Was it worth the wait? Please tell me it was worth the wait? Are you in love? Never mind, that's a stupid question. What about Brandon? Did Tyler say anything about the future? Were you surprised?"

Regan's answers were vague. She was bursting to share, but didn't want to give away too much. "First, you better breathe before you burst, Miss. Surprised? Most definitely, I was surprised. It just happened. One minute he was pushing me away, the next he was pulling me forward."

"Who made the first move?"

"Me. I made the first move," Regan confessed, "well, after he kissed me on the dance floor."

"He kissed you on the dance floor? He kissed you in public?" Missy's voice was unnaturally high and squeaky.

"I am not even sure he was aware of what he was doing. He seemed preoccupied after a phone call."

"Did he say anything about the call? Perhaps it would explain his change in demeanor?"

Regan listened as Missy speculated on Tyler's behavior before responding. "Who knows, but before the call, he was aloof; not after." Regan couldn't wipe the satisfied smile off her face.

"How not aloof?"

Honestly, Missy? I am not answering that."

"Was it hot? Worth the wait?"

"That either," a blush rose in Regan's cheeks. She was grateful her sister wasn't there to see it. "Yes, it was definitely worth the wait," she said, keeping her voice low so as not to wake Tyler.

"I am delighted to hear that," a deep voice rumbled in Regan's ear, as a pair of powerful arms wrapped around her from behind. "But I don't think we should wait anymore, do you?"

"Missy. I love you. We'll talk later. Gotta go." Regan disconnected abruptly, turning into Tyler's arms in a fluid movement. He lowered his head to kiss her thoroughly, holding her low around the waist, his hands cupping her butt to keep her close to his gloriously naked body. His erection rose hard between them. Regan could feel the heat of it through her robe, which Tyler was fumbling to untie.

"Coffee?" Regan queried, breathless from Tyler's kisses.

"Mm," came his positive response, "then you. A lot of you."

Regan moved reluctantly from Tyler's embrace, pouring a steaming cup of fragrant coffee with added cream, then topping off her own. He swallowed almost half the liquid quickly, while she barely had time to take a sip before Tyler lifted her onto the cold granite countertop and undid the belt holding her robe closed.

Stepping between her legs, Tyler slid his hands around her, warm skin caressing warm skin. He kissed a trail from her eyes down to the tip of her nose. He settled on her lips again, gently sucking her pouty lower lip between his and sliding his tongue into her mouth. His kisses grew rougher, more demanding, as Regan met his tongue thrust for thrust in a simulation of the lovemaking soon to follow.

She was breathing quick, shallow breaths when he lowered his head to slide his tongue down the long column of her neck, causing her to shiver in response. Man, he knew how to turn her on. She felt a craving for him rise in her body, hot and demanding. Tyler feathered a row of soft kisses from collarbone to collarbone, then captured one hardened nipple between his teeth, feeling it harden. Regan gasped as a jolt electrified her every nerve ending.

"Like that?" Tyler asked, his teeth lightly scraping her breast. "I want to learn everything that excites you, Ree. Everything."

Regan threw her head back and allowed the luxurious warmth to spread throughout her body. She felt the wetness pooling between her legs, but Tyler was in no rush to fulfill her growing need. Her hands scrabbled to bring him tighter against her, begging him to satisfy her desire. Rather than comply, he continued sucking and nibbling her breast until it was deep pink, the nipple rigid, tight with the sensation of needles and pins.

When he moved to her other breast at long last, Regan released a sigh of pleasure, bringing her hands up to hold Tyler's head hard against her body.

Tyler swiveled Regan on the corner of the oversized counter to accommodate her entire body. He gently coaxed her until she was resting flat on her robe, with her legs dangling over the counter's edge. Then he dipped his head lower, moving down her body until she felt his hot breath on her throbbing center.

Regan experienced a gut-wrenching desire, her arousal pulsing like a living thing. Small moans and sighs escaped from her of their own volition. Tyler kissed the inside of one white thigh, then moved lower to her knee, then the arch of her foot. He shifted to the other foot, then knee and up the other thigh. He was taunting her, making her wait as her need escalated.

Finally, he granted her what she was craving, his sensual lips wrapping around the tiny nub of nerves at her core. His tongue stroked her with firm strokes, then light ones, doing an expert dance with his mouth until she shattered into a million pieces. She was moaning with pleasure, her body throbbing inside and out, as she held Tyler's head steady, waiting for the staggering sensations to subside.

If Regan thought Tyler would release her, let her come down from her incredible high, she was sadly—or not so sadly—mistaken. He pulled her buttocks closer to the edge of the counter, placed several more kisses between her legs, then nibbled on her again.

"Stop, Tyler, please," she begged. "It's too much. Too intense."

He stroked her with his tongue and then nibbled again.

"Seriously, it's too much. I need to rest."

"Do you?" he asked mischievously, barely lifting his head as she braced herself on her forearms to make eye contact. "Your lips tell me one thing, but your body is saying something completely different."

He was right. Regan slid her body closer to him with each nibble, seeking the pleasure she knew he could provide. Regan's legs held Tyler's head tight against her in a vise-like grip. Even as she asked for rest, she felt a second orgasm pulsing through her body, gaining power.

"Do you really want me to stop?" he asked, lifting his head from where he was doing an extraordinary job, bringing her to the brink of ecstasy. She noted his wicked smile and knew she had met her match.

"God no, don't stop now," she cried, dropping her head to the counter and allowing herself to succumb to the orgasm swamping her body. She shook with the force of it, feeling her body pulse and shiver around Tyler's talented tongue.

Tyler released her almost immediately and slid her closer to the counter's edge until only the top of her buttocks and Tyler's muscular hands kept her from tilting off. He positioned himself carefully, and in one powerful stroke, slid deep and hot into her still pulsating body. She was slick with her juices, wet and welcoming.

The last of her orgasm was still subsiding even as the next built. No way she could have three orgasms in such rapid succession. No way, she mused as she lost coherent thought. Her body slipped up and down the counter with his movements, her robe sliding smoothly on the hard surface.

Tyler held her shoulders, bending over her body, squeezing her so that her body created a contrasting push to his thrusts, creating a steady rhythm that increased in pace and intensity as his arousal intensified. He grew impossibly thicker inside her, filling her completely.

That tightness of desire was building again, her toes curling as the friction of his body against hers brought her trembling to a precipice, in need of release.

With several hard thrusts, Regan's body unleashed, shattering and throbbing around Tyler, who, thrusting even harder, immediately found his release pulsing deep into her body. They rode the storm of bliss together for a long moment before he rested his head on her breast and his body softened inside her.

Catching his breath, Tyler slid out of Regan. She felt the loss immediately, longing to maintain that close connection, although she was exhausted and sated. He planted tiny kisses on each nipple before helping her to sit up.

Tyler nonchalantly handed Regan her coffee mug before sipping his cold brew like he wasn't standing naked before her, like he hadn't just rocked her world. He gave her that Tyler smile. "So? What shall we do today?"

"I think we just did it, didn't we?"

Laughing, he pulled her close and planted a hard kiss on her lips. She tasted coffee and that salty, musky flavor of herself. "It was the start, Ree. That was only the start."

"Just the start? If that was just the start, I am not sure I can survive the ending."

"Well, that depends. How sore are you?"

"Sore?" she asked, although she understood the question. Did he want more? She would definitely need a rest first. The man was insatiable.

"Yes, sore. We have been a little frisky," Tyler smiled at his understatement. "Could you ride a bike? It's a glorious spring day, Ree. Let's get out of here and remind you why you need to stay in Chicago."

As if the best reason to stay wasn't standing right in front of her.

Chapter Ten

Tyler and Regan behaved like young lovers the entire day, appropriate since their pairing was young and fresh despite the length of their enduring love. Tyler suggested the Sofitel Hotel, and they walked the few blocks hand in hand, then kissed and cuddled like teens while they awaited a romantic outdoor table.

"I just can't decide," Regan spoke earnestly, surveying the French-influenced brunch menu. "Everything looks scrumptious."

"It's breakfast, Ree," Tyler said. "You were going to serve me a lowly carton of yogurt. No matter what you order, it will be better than that."

"Well, I could have a quiche or an omelet, but the waffles and French toast look good, too," she vacillated, staring longingly at the plates placed on nearby tables.

"What are you having?" she interrogated Tyler, spearing him with her bright blue gaze like his breakfast decision was a matter of state.

"Eggs Benedict."

"Oooh, that sounds good too," she whined, unusually indecisive.

"We could share, Regan, would that help? Then you only have to narrow it down to two things." He would have happily ordered her every item on the menu. Anything to make her smile. Anything to make her stay.

"Perfect." She quickly settled on the brioche French toast and Tyler's eggs Benedict, along with mimosas and fruit.

"See how good we are together?" Tyler reminded her with an impudent grin. "I can even fix your food decision issues when necessary."

"Well, I worked up quite an appetite," she flashed him a sassy smile.

"And I intend to help you burn a lot of calories today," Tyler announced with an accompanying leer.

"You already did."

"Oh, honey, I am just getting started."

They laughed together, as Regan reached across the glass table to squeeze Tyler's hand. When she went to remove it, he held on fast.

"We have a lot of time to make up for, Ree," he told her solemnly before placing a sensual kiss on the palm of her hand. She nodded her agreement, and they stayed touching until Tyler was forced to release her so they could eat.

It was a perfect April day, just warm enough for sitting on the terrace and luring Chicagoans out with the promise of Spring. Regan kept turning her face to the sun until Tyler insisted they rearrange her seat to be shaded by the large, bright red umbrella above them. "I intend to take great care of you, Ree, and helping you avoid a sunburn is part of that."

"You know I am a big girl, Tyler, right? You know I can take care of myself?"

"But you wouldn't deny me the pleasure of spoiling you, would you?"

"Well, when you put it that way..." Regan beamed with pleasure. It reminded Tyler of their high school days, before everything exploded, when he was able to get her to smile easily.

After overeating, they walked a few blocks along the Gold Coast streets, admiring the stately old mansions and enjoying the dappled shade of the budding trees. When they were tired of walking, they rented Divvys—the bright turquoise bicycles placed strategically about the city for commuters and tourists.

Tyler was concerned about Regan after the night and morning's sexual activities, but the ride was short, and she bragged to Tyler "she was tough." Still, they abandoned the bikes after a short fifteen-minute ride, leaving them in a Divvy rack near Lincoln Park and continuing on foot.

First, Tyler suggested the Conservatory, a stunning 1890s glass structure boasting the Spring Flower Show. It did not disappoint. Tyler and Regan wandered the palm and orchid houses—then entered the show house—weaving between couples and families, admiring colorful azaleas, elegant hydrangeas, exotic orchids and fragrant hyacinths. They swung clasped hands like teens when they had space and ducked behind a rather large display of ferns for stolen kisses until Tyler feared he wouldn't be able to walk. She had a high-voltage effect on his body.

Next, they found themselves strolling the park walkways, stopping to admire statues of Benjamin Franklin, Abraham Lincoln, and Hans Christian Andersen they had seen a thousand times. "It's as if I am seeing everything for the first time," Tyler confessed to Regan.

"I know," she agreed, dropping a quick kiss on the tip of his nose. "I feel like a tourist."

"I just feel incredible," Tyler admitted. "I'm sorry I stayed away so long, Ree..." he began, wondering if he was crazy to come clean here and now. Their relationship was changing. Regan would need to know the truth.

"Ooh, popcorn," Regan gushed as they approached the zoo entrance, saving Tyler from his confession. "That smells so good."

"Do you want some?" Tyler was already reaching for his wallet.

"Yes, please, although God only knows where I will put it." She patted her flat stomach as if it protruded. "French toast and popcorn. I will get fat."

"I'll help you work it off later." Tyler pulled her tight to his side as he made the promise and they kissed and laughed, delighted by the idea.

Wandering into Lincoln Park Zoo, Tyler stopped to purchase them each a drink before they meandered past the zebras, triggering a conversation about Regan's trip to Africa many years earlier for a safari.

"I have never been, but it's always been high on my bucket list," Tyler confessed.

"We could go together. I would love to go back again, spend more time in Cape Town and the surrounding wine country. You will love it. It is a lot like San Francisco, but different."

"Alike, but different," he laughed. "I like that. Do you have photos?"

"On my computer, not on my phone. Remind me to show you later."

"Do you realize how many things we missed doing together all these years? What a waste." Tyler grew wistful at the thought. He was about to say more when Regan interrupted.

"Don't go all melancholy on me, Ty. It's not like we are too old and too late."

"No, but I have been an ass to wait this long."

Tyler chose not to say more, wanting to preserve the mood and keep Regan smiling. Later he could worry about coming clean, worry about putting Regan in jeopardy. Even now Tyler could be exposing her to danger, but with the sun shining, the fragrance of spring flowers, popcorn, and animals filling his nostrils, crowds of children laughing and Regan's hand trustingly folded in his, threats and danger seemed a million miles away.

As they moved past the swan pond, speaking of nothing and everything, Tyler enjoyed the perfect day and the pleasure of Regan's company. They joined the crowd in front of the seals, admiring their sleek bodies and laughing at their antics. It was a gorgeous day, and throngs of Chicagoans were outdoors after a long winter hibernation.

Suddenly Regan was falling hard against Tyler, ultimately losing her balance. His strong arms reached out instinctively to catch her, holding her close against his chest, adrenaline sending his pulse racing as she regained her lost composure and her breath.

"What happened?" he asked in alarm, righting her on her sneaker'd feet.

"I got knocked over by those kids." Regan pointed to the retreating backs of two children, aged four or so, who were careening into people willy-nilly while being chased by a frazzled father.

"Kids," Tyler said, relief swamping his emotions, exasperation clear in his voice.

"Don't you want kids?" Regan turned to him in wide-eyed surprise. "I always assumed you wanted to be a father."

"You know, Ree, I never actually thought about kids much, but with you, yeah, I am sure I want kids with you."

Regan glowed at the words, a blush stealing over her fair skin and a broad smile lifting her small mouth. She took off the sunglasses hiding her bright blue eyes and gave Tyler a kiss better saved for a moment of privacy.

Not caring about who was watching, Tyler wrapped his arms around Regan and pulled her body close against his. He sank into the kiss, moving his lips across her softer ones repeatedly as his arms ranged over her back. She wrapped her arms around his neck, running her fingers through the dark hair curling at the nape of his neck. The kiss went on until a nearby child cried out to her companion, "Ew, gross."

Tyler raised his head, smiled at the small girl and chastely pecked Regan on the cheek, looking to the child for approval. He got a small, shy smile, before the girls walked away, headed to see the lions. Regan turned to follow in their wake when Tyler forestalled her, placing a restraining hand on her arm.

"Let's skip the lions," he suggested. "Let's skip the rest of the zoo." Regan looked disappointed until he added in a husky whisper, "Let's go make a baby now."

A vibrant smile lit Regan's face. She lifted herself onto her toes to place a short kiss on the wicked grin Tyler was sporting. "Or at least practice."

Chapter Eleven

It was late Sunday night when Tyler went home to his luxury condo. The 5000 plus square foot modern apartment seemed small and overly furnished after Regan's penthouse. Tyler laughed at the idea as he settled at his desk and went to sort through the mail. The lingering smell of sex emanated from his exhausted body.

He had been like a horny teenager, falling on Regan all afternoon. They emerged long enough to have Chinese food delivered for dinner, which they ate on the floor in front of the 60-inch flat panel television in her media room. The audio-visual system was state-of-the art, but no comfy armchairs were available to complete the space.

"How long have you lived here?" Tyler asked, gesturing toward yet another empty room. "Don't you think it's time to get some furniture?"

"The company will hire one of our designers to stage everything when we are ready to sell this unit, so what's the point?"

"Comfort?"

"I'm fine. I am never here anymore, anyway."

Tyler fell silent, looking down uncomfortably. Regan instantly realized that she had killed the mood. There it was, the one topic they had avoided all weekend—Brandon.

"I'm sorry, Tyler. I shouldn't have brought that up."

"You need to deal with it, Ree," Tyler commanded, albeit gently.

"I know, Tyler, and I will."

"Soon. Very soon."

"I agree, but I need to do it in person. I am sure you understand."

"I don't like it, but I understand. When are you planning to be in D.C. again? This week, right?"

"Yes, I will head out on Tuesday night. I have an interview Wednesday that Brandon arranged for me."

"An interview? Don't you want to cancel that now?"

"No. Don't get upset," Regan said quickly, watching Tyler bristle at the news. "I want to see it through, even if I have no intention of accepting. It's more professional than canceling, besides I am curious about the position."

"And what position is that?"

"I'd rather not say, even to you. We've kept things silent, and I want to respect the people who are considering me. You understand, right?"

"Well, no, not really." Tyler sat pensively for a moment, his appetite lost. "Well, when will you be home?" Tyler sounded like a petulant child. He knew it, but could not help himself.

"I was supposed to stay through the weekend, but I will talk to Brandon Wednesday night and fly home Thursday if I can get a flight."

"If you can't get a flight, use the jet."

"Don't be irresponsible, Tyler, that is the LHRE corporate jet."

"It's a Howe family personal jet, and we all know it. I will miss you, Regan. I want you here where you belong."

"When did you get to be so possessive, Ty?"

"When I knew how amazing you felt in my arms," he admitted, swooping Regan into an embrace and kissing her until she pushed the food out of the way and laid back on the floor. Tyler quickly divested Regan of her yoga pants and tee shirt and shucked off his jeans.

Tyler fell upon Regan, twisting as he did so to absorb any friction from the carpet. She straddled his legs, wasting no time in pressing her already willing body down on him until he was lodged deep within her.

Letting out a satisfied growl, Tyler began moving Regan up and down, his steely fingers digging into her hips. "I want you back here," he told her, his words coming in time with his thrusts. "Now that I have you in my life, I don't want to let you out of my sight."

Feeling the lust pulsing between them like a live wire, Regan agreed with alacrity, responding breathlessly, "Thursday, even if I have to get the jet."

Rolling on top of her, Tyler was careful not to pound her into the carpet, but he increased his speed until they could neither breathe nor speak. The couple rushed toward orgasm, clinging and kissing one another with a level of desperation they had not experienced previously. Almost savage in their need, they demanded everything from one another. Tyler's sweat-slicked skin slid over Regan's wet body, hands seeking to touch every inch of her. Bordering on exhaustion, and sensing she was too, Tyler reached his hand between their bodies, finding and lightly stroking the nub of nerves that would send Regan over the edge. She peaked quickly, and her spasms squeezed Tyler so that he rapidly followed suit. They lay wrapped in each other's embrace, panting from the exertion and exhilaration as their heartbeats gradually returned to normal.

Laying still with Regan in his arms, Tyler listened as her breathing slowed and evened out, as did his own. When her body had relaxed completely, he rolled her back over, pulling out reluctantly and took her weight upon his own. She rested her head on his chest as he stroked her back to finish calming her.

"I don't want to be possessive," Tyler admitted after several moments, just listening to her breath. "I trust you completely, Ree. I don't want to waste any more time."

They lay like that for quite a while, talking and planning, before he reluctantly acknowledged that he needed to go home.

"I need clothes for tomorrow, Regan. I can't rely on whatever is in my gym bag for another day. And we both know we will get no sleep if I stay."

"I am kind of tired, and you look so damn fine in those suits of yours. Okay, I guess I will let you go."

He pulled on his jeans and carried the cold, disregarded Lo Mein to the kitchen, then went in search of the remainder of his clothing. Regan, wrapped in a spa robe that dwarfed her, called down to the lobby and asked the valet to bring Tyler's car around.

They stood at the elevator, kissing and touching like they would be apart for months and not the nine hours until they would reunite at the office. Being at work would feel different, so Tyler cherished this private moment.

The car felt chilly, and the short ride put too much distance between them for Tyler's peace of mind. He considered grabbing a change of clothes and returning to Regan, but logic won out, and he remained at home. Then he debated showering. He loved the slight scent of her perfume and the stronger scent of her body that still clung to his skin.

Who knew you were a complete romantic?

Shaking off his desires as 'sappy,' Tyler stood under the hot water, reviving himself and changing focus. Pulling on a pair of sweats, dragging his briefcase from where it had remained unopened all weekend, he pulled out his laptop and a hefty pile of contracts and dove into LHRE work. When he rubbed his eyes with exhaustion, it was after one. Setting the alarm for 5:45, Tyler dragged himself to bed, cognizant that this exhaustion would haunt him when the alarm went off.

His prediction was mistaken. The exhaustion he anticipated was absent, and Tyler was quickly wide-awake and ready to go when his phone alarm blared CeeLo Green singing "Bright Lights, Bigger City." When Randall arrived at 6:30, Tyler was in the gym, full of energy and drive.

"You are unusually cheerful for a Monday," his friend quickly observed. "Good weekend? If I didn't know better, I'd think you got laid."

"Don't be crude, Randall," Tyler scolded before his expression morphed into a huge grin.

"Oh my God, you did get laid. You waited long enough. It's been ages. What's her name? Is it serious? Is she hot?"

"Aren't you a married man?"

"What does that have to do with anything? I'm a man, aren't I? I'm just asking. And if you are deflecting, it must be serious."

"Would you just drop it?" Tyler grunted as he lifted the heavily weighted metal over his head.

"Very serious," Randall pondered. "Hmm, who have you been with lately? You haven't been this close-mouthed since your..."

Randall stared at Tyler, awareness spreading across his features.

"... Are you back with Regan?"

"Shhh, idiot. I am sure Wyatt is around here somewhere."

Randall scanned the room and lowered his voice before continuing, "Are you back with Regan? How the hell did that happen? What about her move to Washington, and her senator?"

"Good morning." Wyatt snuck up behind them despite the wall-to-wall mirrors. "What about the senator? Did Regan say something at the Alzheimer's Gala Saturday night? You know she has spent a lot of time with his family, but we hardly know him. If she said something useful, you need to share."

"Don't bother getting to know him," Randall responded cryptically, a sly smile on his face. He ignored the scowl Tyler sent his way. "I have a strong feeling he's a short-timer."

"What are you talking about, Randall? Regan says they are just biding time until they announce their engagement." Tyler cringed at Wyatt's statement.

"Nah, I don't think so. Have you talked to your sister lately? I think she's going to change her mind."

"Do you have any idea what he's talking about?" Wyatt asked Tyler. Tyler dropped his head. If Wyatt got the chance, he would read Tyler's expression instantly – after all they had been best friends for 30 years. It didn't matter. Even without being able to see Tyler's face, Wyatt read him like a book. "What have you done, Tyler? What don't I know?"

Tyler remained silent, lifting the massive weight with a grunt, then lowering it smoothly and repeating. A sheen of sweat covered his face and dampened his tee, masking the added shine created by coming under Wyatt's scrutiny. "Are you back with Regan, Tyler? Answer me."

Wyatt's insistence reminded Tyler of his father at his worst, demanding and cold, but entitled to an answer. And as with his father, Tyler found himself unable to dodge his friend's inquiries. He dropped the weights with a clunk and faced his friend.

"Yes. We are together, I love Regan, and she loves me. We are staying together this time, Wyatt, so do your worst."

"Do my worst? It's about fucking time!"

Chapter Twelve

"Donuts? You brought donuts?" Donna squealed so loudly that half the office could hear her. "I could kiss you, Tyler. I mean…" she stammered, blushing scarlet, "I'll get some napkins."

She rushed past Regan, who had emerged from her office in an elegant Armani suit to witness her assistant's embarrassment. Was she harboring feelings for Tyler?

"I heard the squealing." Regan looked at the retreating Donna, but Tyler was ignoring the situation. Regan decided she was imagining things. "Did you bring donuts? Is it a special occasion, or are you just trying to give us all a sugar high?"

"I walked past the Donut Vault on my way here, and I couldn't resist." Checking to verify they were alone, Tyler dropped a quick kiss on her mouth, which formed a surprised 'O.' "But it is a special occasion. From now on, every day is." Regan felt the surreptitious graze of Tyler's fingers at her waist, fighting the urge to cuddle in closer. Working side by side was going to be a challenge.

"You sweet-talker," Regan whispered with a blush. She was about to address their working-lover conflicts, but half the office was descending on the highly regarded pastries.

"They weren't sold out yet?" Ethan asked, almost knocking Regan off her feet to get past her, grabbing and shoving a chocolate-covered buttermilk donut in his mouth.

"Obviously not," Tyler replied with good-humored sarcasm. Donna returned just in time, placing the napkins in Tyler's hand as if bestowing an expensive gift.

"Just in time." Tyler handed Ethan several napkins, barely avoiding a mountain of crumbs on the carpet.

"You must have been there early. I never get there in time."

"Ethan, try getting up an hour earlier. Come to the gym with the guys and me, and you can be there while there are still donuts."

"I gather these are a big deal?"

"Regan, where have you been?" her brother challenged. "The Donut Vault and Stan's have the best donuts in all of Chicago. But at the Vault, when they run out, they close. 'Sorry. Done for the day.'"

"Maybe I better try these famous donuts," Regan said, reaching for a sprinkle-covered donut and breaking it in half. She automatically offered the other half to Tyler, who inhaled it.

"Mmm, this is so damn good," Regan said with a bite of donut still in her mouth, the rest hovering just beyond her lips. She stood there savoring the sweetness of the sprinkles and frosting of the moist cake; her eyes closed so she could focus on the flavors. She had forgotten how delicious a donut could taste. It was Tyler. He made everything brighter, sweeter, more.... She finished the last bite and reached for another without thinking. Ethan gave her a strange look.

"What happened to you, Ree? I can't remember the last time I saw you eat a donut or any dessert."

"Hmm? I walked a lot this weekend."

Looking from Tyler to Regan, then back to Tyler, who avoided making eye contact, Ethan asked again, "So you're inhaling donuts? Not worried about fitting into a wedding dress anymore?"

"Don't you have work to do?" Regan snapped at her brother. She strode away like a ship under full sail, but she caught the remainder of her brother's conversation.

"Did something happen?" Ethan asked Tyler. "Or is it my imagination?"

"I have no idea what you imagine, Ethan, so I can't say."

With that cryptic reply, Tyler grabbed another donut and headed down the hall to his office. He was rapidly catching up with Regan, who was stalled outside her office picking up messages. Ethan was mumbling about significant changes while escaping with the box holding the remaining donuts and heading to the other side of the building.

Regan entered her office without looking back at Tyler. She could hear his footfall despite the thick carpet and knew he would follow. Perhaps she could steal a kiss before the workday began.

What am I thinking? I have to be able to separate business and pleasure. Just remembering how much pleasure made a hot blush rise in her cheeks. Maybe she should have a stern talking to with herself. It was time to think about LHRE, not Tyler.

"Step into my lair," Regan suggested to Tyler, hoping for two more minutes alone before switching to all-business mode. When his office phone rang, Tyler swore under his breath, and she knew she had lost her opportunity. Tyler stepped into his office and firmly shut the door, but not before Regan heard him growl, "how'd you get this number?"

From inside her bookshelf-lined office, Regan could hear Tyler raising his voice, although the words were too muffled to understand.

She considered going to stand outside his door to figure out what he was saying.

"Nice," she chided herself, ashamed that she considered eavesdropping. She settled behind her desk, leafed through the pile of messages, and punched the intercom.

"Donna, please get Mr. Blackstone on the phone for our 9:00. And ask Ethan to join me if he is available."

"Right away," the efficient assistant responded. Within moments, the call was ready. Ethan was settling in across from her, eager to listen and learn. In the moments before she connected the call, Regan heard Tyler, his raised voice tense and furious from behind the thick walls.

Tyler lowered his voice, finally cognizant of his surroundings. "I can't drop everything and walk out of the office now." He listened to his caller, pacing the space between the door and window.

"I need to get back to you. I need more time to get the money together," Tyler hissed into the mouthpiece. "No one could raise that sum in such a short period."

I'm going to wear a hole in this carpet or strangle myself on this phone cord. Tyler threw himself into one of the armchairs facing the desk, trying to still his anxiety. In only moments, he was back on his feet, pacing the window to the door path again.

"Give me until Friday," he demanded, frowning when he heard the response. "Not Wednesday. Friday. I need the full week."

Tyler's face was etched with frustration and anger. "Alright," he responded in a clipped voice, "end of day Wednesday." He returned the phone to its cradle, wondering again how they had traced him to his new job, despising this added sign of their desperation.

Reaching past the office phone to grab up his cell phone, Tyler hit a number on speed dial, listened impatiently to the ringing at the other end and drummed his fingers on the desk.

"Haley, hi. How are you? It's Tyler. Is my father available?"

"Hello, Tyler. I'll see if he is taking calls." Wouldn't that be just great if his father wouldn't talk to him? It wouldn't be the first time. Tyler's fingers drummed harder.

"To what do I owe this honor?" Tyler heard the chill in his father's voice but, after a deep breath, plowed forward.

"Father. Thank you for taking my call." Tyler's warm enthusiasm was obvious moments earlier, with the assistant muted to a zombie-like cadence with his father. "I wasn't sure you would talk to me."

"I wasn't sure myself," came the reply.

"Mother spoke with you, correct? You know what is happening?"

"She did. Why didn't you come to me when this first started?"

"Would you have helped me?"

No response. "You shouldn't have involved her. I suspect you already know that. You are a grown man. Where are your balls? You should have come to me yourself."

Tyler remained silent. He had expected this. It was only the truth. He never should have put his mother in the middle, but he was at a breaking point. She had seen him suffering. She could always read him like a book. When she had asked how she could help, Tyler had cracked and told her everything, as if he were still a child running to mommy. When she offered to speak with Emmett, he could have said no, but he didn't. Maybe he should have. His father was being so aloof.

"This is a highly unusual request, Tyler. How did you allow yourself to get into this mess?"

"You know how." Tyler took a calming breath to control his exasperation and began pacing again. "Would you have tolerated the publicity? I did it to keep the shame away from you and Mother."

"Don't put this on us," came his father's angry retort. "It was your irresponsible behavior that started all of this. We did everything we could to keep things quiet. Now, after all this time, you want this from us? Do you think that's fair?"

"Would you be saying this if it was Denny?"

Tyler heard his father's exasperated sigh before he answered. "Denny would never have put us in this position, Tyler. You were always the reckless one."

Tyler cringed at the harsh words. One dreadful night, but in his father's eyes, it had been a pattern of unacceptable behavior. He had expected some put down, a remark comparing him to his saintly brother. He might need help, but he didn't have to listen while his father berated him.

"Yes, well, I didn't call for another lecture, Father, I called for the money. Will you help me or not?" He held his breath, waiting to see if his pleading calls to his mother had paid off.

"I will not. You got yourself into this mess. You get yourself out. And leave your mother out of this, you hear me, boy? If I hear you've involved her again, I will make things way worse for you. I promise."

"Thanks a lot, Father. I should have known I could count on you," Tyler made the wisecrack and hung up the phone without a goodbye. He missed being able to slam it. Defeated, he fell against the back of the chair like a rag doll and sat like that for a long moment before dialing another number.

"It's me," he stated flatly. "Forget the money. I'm in."

One disaster down, one to go.

Chapter Thirteen

When Tyler rejoined Regan in her office, he looked ten years older. There was sadness in his eyes that she could not remember seeing ever before, hopelessness, as well as a tension radiating from his body.

He appeared to listen as she and Ethan completed their client call, but he added nothing to the conversation and Regan could tell he wasn't paying attention.

"We'll be back in touch after we get those estimates," Regan told the client, winding down the call. "Ethan will follow up by the end of the week."

She nodded at her brother to assure that he jotted down the follow-up assignment, exchanged pleasantries and farewells, and ended the call.

"OK, Ree, I will follow up with him on Friday," Ethan confirmed, gathering his notes and preparing to leave her office.

"Sooner if you can. We like to exceed expectations," Regan corrected. She flashed a broad smile at the two men before her. Ethan returned it with a grin of his own and left the office. Tyler remained unresponsive and mute.

"What's going on?" Regan prodded, touching his arm to get his attention. "Has something happened?"

"What?" Tyler asked, coming out of his daze with a start. "No, nothing happened. Just another unpleasant call with my father. Nothing new."

"Yeah, I could hear your anger through the walls. It's not like you to raise your voice to your father."

"Sorry about that. I didn't realize I was that loud." Tyler apologized, ignoring her observation about the Winthrop family dynamics. He was lying. In all the years she had known him, Tyler had never dared to raise his voice to his parents. Never. He was hiding something from her.

"Ty, it's me. Talk to me. Tell me what's going on. We are a team here, and together we can solve anything."

"Regan, nothing is going on. Let's focus on work, okay? We need to push this weekend out of our heads and get a job done. That's what we are here for. That's why your family is paying me a lot of money. Bring me up to speed on the call with Bluegate Development."

Regan stared deep into Tyler's eyes, trying to fathom his mood. He was dark, mysterious, and wholly shut to her until, finally, she began discussing work. She would try again later, perhaps when his emotions weren't as raw.

Tyler was focused now, moving quickly through the Bluewater project, his ideas for a new rental strategy, and finally to his proposal for expanding East.

"East?" Regan asked, completely flummoxed by the suggestion. "After the last few days, I thought we would scrap those plans. I won't be moving, after all, so why do we need an East Coast program?"

"I think you should still pursue that government opportunity, Ree. And you might still want a relationship with your senator." Regan was stunned. What shit was Tyler spouting, and why? "It was a weekend, Regan. No one changes their life just because of a weekend of hot sex."

Regan recoiled from Tyler's words as if he had slapped her. Pain coursed through her body and confusion muddled her brain. She must have misunderstood what he was saying?

Tyler was still talking. Regan was having trouble following him. Who was this man? He was like Dr. Jekyll and Mr. Hyde, and Regan wasn't sure which character she was dealing with at the moment.

"I know we said a lot of romantic words to each other over the weekend, but get real Regan. You can't just destroy all your plans. You have a fabulous opportunity in Washington, you said so yourself. I would never deny you that chance. What kind of man would I be if I did?"

"The man who loved me. The man who only yesterday announced that he wanted to spend his life with me." Regan heard the wobble in her voice, stood and walked to the windows, turning her back on Tyler, watching the boats skim along the lake while she regained her equilibrium.

"What kind of joke are you playing here?" she demanded.

"No joke, Ree. C'mon, we are both adults. We had a great time together, like always, but now we need to get back to reality. Your life is in DC; mine is here. We run a company. We do important work together. Did you honestly think I would let you mess up this chance for me to be CEO? You know me better than that."

"I don't know you at all," Regan felt her ire building. "This man in front of me is a cold, calculating stranger. I don't have a clue what happened in the last hour. I only know that Tyler Winthrop walked into this office this morning and now some selfish asshole is standing here in his place."

"Nice, Ree. Selfish asshole? I'm not the one who fucked around with an old flame all weekend while I was engaged to another man."

Regan itched to slap Tyler's smug face. "I am not engaged, damn it, and you know it." He was stabbing a knife in her heart and twisting it. "You also know I had every intention of leaving Brandon once and for all. But now..."

"Leave a rich senator who owns half the East Coast because of a one-night stand? I gave you more credit than that."

"Why are you doing this, Tyler? What happened?" she begged. "Tell me the truth." What was with this sudden about-face? Something dreadful must have happened when Tyler talked to his father. He was pushing her away too hard, too fast. It had to be something else. She could not believe that the weekend had meant nothing. It was transparent between them for the first time in years. They were destined to be together. Why the hell was he playing this game?

Even now, even as he was putting up a sky-high wall between them, even as he was breaking her heart into a million pieces and shattering her dreams, she found him irresistible, confirming that she was right about them. If she could love him at this moment, she would love him always.

Tyler's hair was lush and dark, cut long enough to roll back from his face but short enough to stick straight up haphazardly, an unforced look that rock stars had been trying to perfect for years. She could tell he had been running his hands through it, probably in frustration. One tiny lock was falling forward now, not entirely resting on his forehead. She itched to fix it, to touch him. But one look at his firm, determined jaw stopped her. His gaze was cold and hard, aloof.

Regan understood that they were under pressure, that Tyler was working too hard and worrying too much. Signs of both were etched on his face in the form of dark circles and creases just starting to form between his nose and mouth. But there was something else there now too. Fear maybe?

"Please, Tyler," she tried once more. "Tell me the truth and stop trying to push me away. We can get through this together. I am here for you. Just talk to me."

"Regan, you always did have an overactive imagination. Nothing is going on," his voice was flat, his stance closed to her. He stood with his arms crossed, close to the door like he wanted to make a quick escape. "Make your plans for DC. I've got things covered here. Go live your life and let me live mine."

She had no time to respond or fall apart. Tyler turned on his heel and exited the office without a backward glance. She watched his long angry strides take him further from her through the tears that were forming. She watched him blow past his office, heading for the elevators, where he repeatedly punched the button with his fist until the doors finally opened and he disappeared from view.

Fine. Go. Get out and good riddance. You might treat me like our relationship doesn't matter, but you won't get rid of me being your boss that easily. I will get to the bottom of this. You can't avoid me forever.

Chapter Fourteen

Regan's eyes were bloodshot and rimmed in magenta. Her nose was as red as Rudolph's, and she looked like she hadn't slept in a week. She hadn't. She had lovingly relived those two glorious days with Tyler repeatedly, rehashed every word, every look, every touch.

Then she revisited his horrible words in her office last Monday, trying desperately to figure out what changed between them and how it could all go so wrong, so fast.

He had never given her a clue. One minute he was sending her nerve endings dancing, bringing her donuts and promising forever, the next he was cutting her loose like a deal gone wrong. In truth, he treated his contract negotiations with more respect.

Regan recognized that her friends were treading lightly. They were outside, sitting on her extensive patio, the summer sun an orange and pink glow setting low on the horizon. The distant sounds of sirens, traffic, and construction, the typical background of the city that they all learned to tune out, was a faint rumble from the lofty penthouse. Only Keeli had commented on the beauty of their surroundings, never one to take for granted the luxuries that the others expected as their due.

Even Keeli's admiration of the place had made Regan tear up, remembering Tyler's first impression of her outrageous abode. Everything her friends said made Regan cry or scream, although she was exhausted from doing both. Being as understanding as best friends could be, they were trying to soothe Regan while still forcing her to move forward. She had to get past bemoaning her weekend with Tyler. She had cried over it five times longer than it had lasted.

"I agree with you, Ree. Something was definitely going on. But if Tyler won't share the truth with you, then you have to move on," Missy told her for the umpteenth time.

"I agree," Sloane added. "If he can't be open and honest, why would you want him?" Sloane flicked her thick hair over her shoulder in emphasis, pinning Regan in her direct gaze, daring her to shed even one more tear. "And if whatever he is hiding is so awful, you are better off without him."

Regan wished she had Sloane's toughness and resilience. Regan had believed herself to be strong and independent, but not compared to Sloane. If Tyler could completely throw her for a loop, she questioned everything she understood about her success and her role in the world.

"I know," Regan whispered her reply. "I know," she repeated in a stronger voice. She would keep saying it until she believed it.

"You've had a week, Ree," her friend and co-worker Charlotte reminded her. "You have to decide about DC before you run out of options. I think you should at least go on the interview, regardless of what you decide about Brandon. You've earned this chance, Regan. You've worked so diligently for it."

Charlotte knew just what to say to remind Regan of her hard-won success at the top of LHRE. Regan straightened her shoulders and lifted her chin a little higher at the words. "And you know it would be better for office morale if you and Tyler were in different cities for a while." Defeated, Regan slumped once more.

"You're right," Regan acknowledged the truth of Charlotte's statement, her voice tired and scratchy from crying. Charlotte was sensible, smart, and, as the chief financial officer, Regan's right hand at the office. "I know the tension at work has been awful."

"The tears were worse than the tension," Charlotte confessed gently. She tucked an errant strand of hair behind her ear nervously and handed Regan another tissue as she watched the tears threatening to spill over again. "We all feel terrible for you."

"Does everyone know?" Regan questioned Charlotte, raising her head in alarm. Her tears were forgotten.

"No, of course not. The staff only knows you are miserable about something. Of course, everyone can see that Tyler is acting like a complete shithead. Even Donna seems to have lost interest in him."

"Don't say that about Ty," Keeli piped up, returning from the kitchen with a fresh bottle of Pinot Grigio. "I just know he is hurting too."

"Did Wyatt say anything?" Regan was too quick to query, hungry for answers.

"Sorry, Regan, I did ask, but Wyatt can't explain it either. He had a conversation with him a while back where Tyler admitted he loved you and that he was going to fight for you. According to my husband, this weird behavior has been going on for a few months, but according to Wyatt, Tyler has been getting worse. Lots of text messages at all hours that Tyler won't explain, but that always seem to leave him angry or tense. It's not like Tyler to keep any secrets from Wyatt."

"Especially after the blowup that the boys had when they found out Alex was keeping secrets," Charlotte added, a delicate blushing pinking her cheeks when she remembered how the secrets both she and Alex kept from one another almost destroyed their relationship. "Remember what a mess that was?"

"Charlotte is right. They have been obsessed with honesty ever since then. Wyatt would tell you if he knew something, wouldn't he?" Regan asked Keeli, a bit too suspiciously.

"He would tell *you* if he knew anything," Missy scolded.

"Sorry Keeli, of course, Missy is right. I am..." Regan felt the tears forming in her eyes again and blinked to hold them back. "I need to stop obsessing." She got up from the comfortable lounge chair and paced between it and the balcony ledge. "I'm just a wreck," she boldly confessed to her friends.

"You are not, Regan. You are a beautiful, brilliant woman. You have just been dealt a blow to the heart. You'll recover. You need to go to that job interview and leave this all behind," Keeli corrected her friend, pouring her a large refill and flashing her a smile. Regan turned from looking out at the sky and took the glass from her sister-in-law. "Go back to Brandon, Ree. He's a catch."

"Keeli's right," Charlotte seconded. "I know him, Regan. He is a catch. You could love him if you closed the chapter on Tyler. Brandon is serious about you. I have never seen him pursue a woman the way he has pursued you. Give him a chance."

"Give him a chance," Keeli parroted. "Tyler has had hundreds of chances to be with you, and he has blown them all. Give it up."

"I know." Regan let the tears fall. Her friends didn't understand, they were logical, and the situation was anything but. They had not spent their lives learning to appreciate this cryptic man. They had not enjoyed a weekend wrapped in his arms, feeling the passion between them, listening to Tyler's rich descriptions of their future together. Tyler loved her, but something was pulling him away, something more important to him than their love.

Her friends were right. Brandon loved her too, in his way. He might not be as romantic as Tyler, but perhaps if she gave him some encouragement...

"I could use the change of venue for a few days, I guess," Regan told her friends, deciding the issue on the spot after fighting the idea for days. "The job does sound fantastic. I should at least go find out more about it, right?" She looked to them for reassurance.

"Right," her friends agreed, nodding their heads and offering convincing smiles. Only Missy stayed quiet.

"Missy?"

"You should go, Ree. It's just that I will miss you terribly," her sister admitted reluctantly.

"I can go see Brandon and figure that out, too," Regan continued.

"You're making the right choice," Sloane pushed, considering the conversation over.

"I hate to leave LHRE with Tyler." Regan hesitated once more. "I deserve to be at the helm. I earned it." Her friends nodded their agreement. "Still, anything is better than sitting here wondering."

"No kidding," Sloane announced in her blunt way, standing up and moving toward the sliding glass doors to the apartment. "Okay. We're done crying. Let's get you packed."

Chapter Fifteen

Tyler sat on the edge of the large leather wing chair, unable to relax back into its comfort. He looked around the room again, like a panoramic camera, shifting his eyes from the impressive desk in front of him to the view of the lake beyond, then scanning the walls of leather bound law books, the priceless artwork, the tastefully chosen rugs and furniture. The room was large, elegant and intimidating, as it was meant to be. For Tyler, the room represented scolding and lectures over a thirty-year period. He could not remember one happy moment in the space.

This day would be no different. He was here as the supplicant, begging his father in a way he had promised himself he never would. His father still used the tuition bailout against him in every argument, a source of shame he could never shake. Being here again went against every fiber of his being.

He knew his mother hovered nearby, protective and loving, perhaps more nervous than he was himself. He also knew she had summoned his father nearly ten minutes ago. His father was playing power games, keeping him waiting. Not a good indication of how things would play o ut.

Finally, the door gave a well-oiled click behind him, moving on its nearly silent hinges before he heard the footfall of his father's perfectly shined shoes on the hardwood floors, then the rug. Would he take the matching chair beside him for a conversation, or sit behind the desk for an interrogation? Tyler would know shortly.

Tyler finally scooted back into the recess the high-backed chair created so that he appeared relaxed and at home when his father assumed the large desk chair across from him. *Well, now I know where I stand.*

"I know why you are here, and I thought we already discussed this, Tyler. Is there more to be said?" His father's voice, well-modulated, only hinted at his blue-collar, East Coast roots. Emmett Winthrop had surpassed his father's success. His father had risen far above his own father, who had climbed on the shoulders of his sire. Emmett's great-grandfather arrived in Boston and worked on the docks until his hands were raw, and his back was bowed, but finally, he owned four ships. The family had come far, and far up, since then. Young Emmett had been educated in Boston's top schools, his father ensuring that Emmett had access to a stellar education and connections with the right people despite his background. He sold his father's business for a small fortune not long after graduating from law school and moved to the Midwest, leaving his past behind and forgotten. He established himself as a high-priced lawyer, purchased a home in the appropriate upscale suburb, married the socialite, Marion Field, and built the ideal upper crust life.

In all the subsequent years, only one incident had threatened to mar Emmett's perfect life and encroach on his elite status. Tyler had created that opening and Emmett's substantial fortune had made it disappear. *Until now.*

Tyler heard the ambivalence of a wealthy man in the dismissive words of his father's greeting and realized how much of this battle would be uphill. His mother had told him to ask again, in person.

She hadn't promised anything, but Tyler had expected slightly more warmth.

"Father," Tyler inclined his head slightly in greeting, acknowledging his father's initial salvo. "Nice to see you, too. How have you been?"

"Cut the crap, Son, what are you here to discuss? Your poor mother has been pacing all morning," he admitted. "You must be in some serious trouble if you are daring to ask again."

"I am, Father," Tyler confessed openly. "I tried to keep you out of this – hell, I have tried to get myself out of it. I don't blame you for turning me down last month, but I am asking again. I hate to admit it, but I think I have made things worse, if that is even possible."

"Well then," his father said, softening slightly now that his son had relinquished the upper hand. "Tell me the situation. It can't be as bad as that mess you got into in high school. After all, I don't see a judge present this time."

Tyler tried to laugh at his father's feeble joke, but he almost choked on the effort. At that moment, his father grasped the severity of the problem.

"It's the money, right? For a girl? Gambling? Tell me what's going on, and we will deal with it as we did all those years ago."

"It is the money, Father, and a whole lot more."

"May I come in?" Marion Field opened the door after a quick knock. "I can't wait in the hall wondering any longer." Emmett flashed an impatient but indulgent smile at his wife and motioned to the empty chair next to Tyler. Marion, slim and elegant in unwrinkled linen pants, a soft pink cotton sweater, and peep-toe flats, quickly took the chair and grabbed her son's hand in a surprisingly firm grip. She gave it a reassuring squeeze before turning her full attention to her husband.

"Has he told you yet?" she asked anxiously.

"He hasn't had a chance, Marion. But he was about to start. Tyler, you now need to explain why your mother knows everything and I don't, after my last warning on the subject, so add that too, please."

Tyler nodded guiltily, took a deep breath and began. "You would know, Father, if you had been willing to talk when I called." The sharp tone was not lost on the senior Winthrop, who scowled at his son. Tyler realized he was off to a bad start and started again in a quiet voice. "It all stems back to that summer after high school, Father. The summer you thought you paid off the right people to make a story go away while you let me rot in juvie. If the story had come out then, perhaps we wouldn't be here now."

"That's not fair," Marion piped up defensively. "We thought we were teaching you a lesson."

"A badly needed lesson, frankly," Emmett added. Tyler felt the bile rising in his throat. He was sick of hearing about his mistake, about needing a lesson. That lesson had inflicted permanent damages his father couldn't imagine. He needed their help too much to fight over blame. Leaning forward in his seat, looking his father straight in the eye, he confessed his problem.

"I learned plenty of lessons that summer," Tyler continued sadly. "Just not the ones you intended. For example, now I know way more than I ever would have known about blackmail."

"Blackmail?" His father formed a perfect 'O' as he leaned back in his chair, astonished.

"Yeah, Dad. I've been blackmailed for years to keep our dirty little secret. I've spent most of my earnings to keep them quiet, and a healthy percentage of my trust fund. Only now my blackmailers want me to help them embezzle from LHRE through a software hack or pay them a quarter of a million dollars. I finally realize that they won't stop there.

If I pay them now, they will just come back again. I am sinking here. They want payment this week, and I don't know what to do."

Tyler fell back against the leather chair. He looked relieved now that he had finally told his father the truth. Emmett, on the other hand, looked furious.

"You idiot. You paid them all these years and said nothing to me?"

"Emmett, anger management, dear. Our son is coming to you for help," Marion filled the uncomfortable silence. "Try not to lose your temper with him."

"I'm not angry at you, Son," Emmett said, visibly struggling to ratchet down his fury. Impatience remained in his voice as he reiterated, "I wish you had come to me sooner. When I get my hands on those thugs, I plan to rip them to shreds."

"Good luck with that, Father," Tyler responded with a tinge of sarcasm.

"What did you tell them? How much time have we got? Who else knows?"

"Father, slow down. I can't answer all your questions this fast."

"Marion, get us a drink. We're all going to need one. Make mine a double, please."

"Mine too, Mom." Tyler was astonished. What had caused this sudden change in his father?

"Thanks, Dad. Your support means the world to me." The relief in Tyler's tone was palpable.

"No one, and I mean no one, attacks my family," Emmett announced.

Marion returned with ice and a bottle of Oban. "Did I miss anything?"

Her question made Emmett chuckle, presenting the men with a moment of much-needed levity as they fixed their drinks and settled back in their chairs.

"Okay, so we have less than a week to provide some response. That's going to be tough. I will contact the FBI – they won't be monitoring our phones, will they?"

Tyler shrugged his shoulders. "I only know the blackmailers threatened to bug mine." They were all business now, working as a team. This man who had almost hung up on him only days ago was suddenly on board to help him resolve a problem that had seemed overwhelming. Tyler felt the vise grip on his stomach loosen. His father was leading the charge. Things seemed less dire; he felt less vulnerable.

"First the FBI, then Wyatt, then that lawyer friend of yours."

"Wyatt," Tyler gulped in alarm. "Why do I need to bring Wyatt into this?"

"Wyatt's the software guru, and he knows the LHRE systems. We can use his knowledge to trace anything they might do or – God forbid – have already done. He can work side by side with the FBI, speeding things up." Emmett was like a whirlwind of action. With a powerhouse like Emmett on his side, Tyler believed they might beat this thing. "Call him now. Don't tell him anything. Just invite him for a drink."

"Here? He'll be in the city. He's not going to come out here now."

"Damn, I hadn't thought of that. It's too late tonight anyway." Emmett punched the desk in frustration. "It has to be tomorrow. After that, we are out of time. Why did you wait so long?"

"I didn't wait, Father, I did call you. I tried to solve it myself. I couldn't. I have been negotiating with them for more time. These shitheads always win."

"I would tell you to watch your language, but shitheads describe them perfectly. Come on," Marion continued, enjoying the surprised look on her son's face, "let me get us dinner, and we can come up with a plot to beat the crap out of them."

Chapter Sixteen

"It was incredible," Regan gushed for the fourth time in as many minutes. "I met people I read about in newspapers. They talked about meetings at the White House. It was incredible."

"Was it incredible?" Missy laughed. "You hadn't mentioned that."

"I'm sorry. I know I am repeating myself, but I feel like... Pinch me, Missy. I keep wondering how I got here. What did I do to deserve this chance?"

"Are you kidding me, Regan? You studied your ass off for six years, worked like a dog climbing your way to the top of a Fortune 500 company, and then you succeeded there. You might be overqualified for this job."

The words were just the reassurance Regan needed. Regan had spent five long hours with undersecretaries and directors grilling her. Since then, she had second-guessed every answer she gave them.

"Overqualified? It's CDFI for heaven's sake. HUD. We're talking about the US Government, the Treasury Department. Think about it, Missy, I could be working in a department created by Alexander Hamilton, living in Washington and making a difference in people's lives all over the country."

"Yeah, you said all of this before, Ree. Come off that cloud now and tell me what the hell you would be doing. I have never even heard of CDFI."

"It's cool, Miss. They work alongside the private sector in distressed communities to inject investment dollars where they are badly needed and unlikely to be found. Think communities in Chicago where violence is awful, and no businesses want to invest. With my help—me, Missy—we could get grocery stores, drug stores, restaurants, and retailers to open in those neighborhoods and turn them around. It would be amazing."

"That would be amazing, Ree, and you would be perfect for this job. You have the connections in the business world, the philanthropic background, and the financial knowledge. Brandon chose well for you."

"Oh shit, Brandon. Missy, I was supposed to meet him fifteen minutes ago. I have to run. Love you." Regan hung up without waiting for Missy's response.

Running a quick comb through her hair and finding the pumps she had kicked off when she returned from the interview, Regan ran out of the door with her arm already raised to hail a taxi.

Touching up her makeup in the cab, Regan wished she had changed into a more feminine blouse. At least her suit wasn't severely wrinkled, and the Prada shoes were appropriate. It would have to do.

Regan easily spotted Brandon sitting at the bar chatting up a cable news reporter who was hanging on his every word. If this had been a movie, he would have had a dedicated light above his head to represent his aura, to show he was the golden boy.

He had that something special, alright. Regan could feel his pull from across the room. He was better looking than anyone around him, better dressed, more confident. He radiated confidence, wore it like armor. It was magnetic, drawing Regan into his circle just like everyone else.

If she briefly compared him to Tyler—better groomed but less sexy—it was only natural. It had been less than a month since she'd lain in Tyler's embrace and it would take a while longer to forget him altogether. They had communicated via email and only about business. It helped her stay angry, but it didn't help her let go.

Their eyes meeting, Brandon gave Regan a megawatt smile, extricated himself from his groupie, and moved swiftly to her side.

"Well," he said as he bent to give her a perfunctory kiss on the lips, "are we celebrating?"

"It's too soon to celebrate, and you know it. But I think it went well."

"And what about you? Do you want the job?"

"It would be tough to turn it down. I could do outstanding work there, meaningful work."

"Let's go to our table, and you can tell me all about it," Brandon said, signaling to the hostess with a nod of his head. She moved instantly to usher them to a table, leaving Regan wondering if the young brunette had been watching Brandon the entire time. Or was she just good at her job?

Regan rehashed her meetings as Brandon pestered her for details. She consumed drinks and dinner with little awareness, still talking about the different people she met and the opportunities the job would present.

"Do you want dessert?" Brandon asked.

"Oh my god. I blabbed through our entire dinner. How was your day? How mortifying that I have been so selfish."

"Don't be ridiculous. I wanted to know everything. I love your enthusiasm; it's contagious."

"You know me well, Brandon. CDFI was exactly the right place for me."

"I just made a couple of phone calls, Regan. When I told them who you were, about your background and credentials, you could have had your choice of jobs. You still can."

"Let's just see how this turns out," she laughed.

Brandon took her hands across the table, carefully repositioning her wine glass first. "I am sure it will turn out perfectly. And, when it does, Regan, I think you should plan to move in with me. We can announce our engagement right away, now in fact, and you can move into my place. If you prefer, we can house hunt for a new place—a fresh start."

"Brandon," Regan pulled her hands from his and began twisting her napkin under the table. *Breathe. She was making a big decision. Choose wisely.* "Brandon," she began again, "I don't even have the job. Maybe we should wait until we know for sure?" It sounded feeble, even to Regan's ears, and she knew Brandon wouldn't accept her excuse.

"Regan, I love you. You know I love you I have never pursued a woman the way I have pursued you. From the beginning, I have known you were the one for me, but I have been patient, friendly, platonic most of the time—which believe me, I hated. I have played the waiting game for you, for my career, and for the paparazzi. I am done waiting. I want to marry you, spend my life with you, have dazzling careers and a family with you. I am asking you to marry me, Regan."

If the napkin had been paper, it would have been in shreds by now. Regan could feel her heart racing, threatening to explode in her chest. Could she pass up the chance to build a life with Brandon, because it was clear to her that he was serious? His timetable was now. He was finished biding his time. She had to commit now or risk losing him forever.

"I thought we would have more time together before this happened. I have only been back in DC three weeks, Brandon. We were going to spend time together, see how it worked out. Are you absolutely sure this is what you want?" *Good, put it back on him.*

"Regan, you have been in and out of Washington for weeks since Tyler took over, granted not full weeks, but these last three weeks have been virtually around the clock, long enough for me to be sure. I want you by my side, Regan Howe. I want you to be my wife."

"Well," she dragged out the word, "if you are sure, then yes, Brandon, I will marry you."

Regan sat there in a daze, unsure even now that she was doing the right thing but determined to leave the past behind and greet her future. Brandon was taking her right hand from her lap, tugging it gently until she released the hapless napkin and twined her fingers in his. Only then did she realize that he was slipping a giant, glittering diamond on her ring finger.

"What the..." Regan caught herself before she said the wrong thing. "When did you? I mean, Brandon, this is stunning." She looked at the large diamond, pear-shaped and heavy, not at all what she would have chosen for herself, but it was obviously costly and beautiful. "It's... I am at a loss for words."

"Well, I only need to hear one for the rest of the night. Yes. Just keep repeating yes, and we will do fine. We'll announce it to the press after we call our families."

"Yes."

"Do you want a new place together?"

"Yes, please. Although you have the nicest bachelor pad of any senator I know, that isn't saying much."

"Spoken like a true real estate mogul."

Finally, Regan felt the fog lifting, so that she was able to laugh and joke with Brandon about planning their futures. So what if the emotions she was feeling didn't jell with what she had imagined as a young girl dreaming of love? She wasn't that young girl anymore. This was logical and smart, just like her. Regan shook off any remorse and admired the giant diamond again, pleasing Brandon enormously.

"It's a family heirloom," he explained. "I had it reset to be a bit more modern. I am so glad you love it. I knew you would."

Brandon had already written a press release—she felt a certain *je ne c'est quoi* when he told her that. Why had he been so confident in her reply when she was so uncertain? She resented feeling like a sure thing, but she shook it off. They were not kids. He had not taken advantage of her. To the contrary, he was a perfect gentleman. They had been on this path for a while now, and if she had made a brief detour, she learned it was a dead end, encouraging her to turn around and return to the right track quickly. There was no need to bother Brandon with that lost weekend with Tyler.

"We'll go to Chicago for that golf outing and..."

"Ooh, Brandon. Do you think we could wait until then to tell my family? It would be wonderful to share the news with them in person."

"I hadn't planned to wait that long."

"It's a week. I think we can wait one more week, don't you?"

"Of course, Regan, whatever you like," he responded, kissing her knuckle above the sparkly ring. "After all, what can happen in a week?"

Chapter Seventeen

It was a perfect day for a golf outing and attendance, and revenue, exceeded everyone's hopes. The Howe Art Museum Young Adult Board of Directors had been a brilliant idea for attracting a younger donor group. Twenty-something's crowded the course, most of whom had never donated to the museum before.

"I have to hand it to you, Missy," her husband Stephen said as he stepped in to drive one of the last of over 90 golf carts heading out for the day. "This is a much bigger success than I would have figured."

"What can I say?" Missy replied, turning pink at the compliment, "I just figured if we created a board of young people, they would attract other young people."

"A lot of them have parents who are donors, but it looks like both age groups opened their wallets. So this is all net gain. Nice work."

Stephen planted a long hard kiss on his wife's lips, causing her to look around to make sure no one noticed. Her embarrassment just caused him to do it again, until Regan, who was standing nearby, told them to "get a room."

"Just who made these pairings?" she asked again for the third time that morning. "Who thought to put Tyler with Brandon?"

"Yeah, sorry about that, Ree," Stephen told his sister-in-law. "We weren't thinking about the connection at the time. We just thought he would be a good business contact for LHRE."

"And he will be. You're right. Forget I even asked."

Almost as if their conversation had conjured them up, Wyatt and Keeli stepped out of the clubhouse in front of Brandon, Tyler and two other men.

"You're with us," Tyler told one of them as the other moved to join Missy and Stephen. Wyatt walked along with him, kissed his wife goodbye, and hopped into the empty golf cart.

"That leaves us," Tyler announced to Brandon, Regan and the other gentleman, Nathan, who was CFO of a new construction company that LHRE was hoping to do business with in the future. *I guess they really were only thinking about business connections.*

Tyler looked entirely at home in his golf clothes, long legs looking fit and tan, white golf shirt open at the throat. Regan checked him out from head to toe, visualizing every inch of skin underneath his attire, earning a bewildered scowl from Brandon.

"Nice to see you again," Tyler said, grabbing Brandon's hand in a firm shake. "You have been a busy man. I have seen your new ads on TV. Not wasting any time, are you?"

"Name recognition can only help. I've heard a lot about your work, too. Thanks again for taking over at LHRE. I needed Regan with me in DC."

Needed? It was strange phrasing, in Tyler's opinion, and certainly not the word he would have chosen.

Relieved that the awkward introduction was over, Regan took her first full breath of the morning. The hostility was evident, palpable, but both men were behaving like gentlemen. It would be fine.

"Let's get this show on the road," Nathan called to them now, causing the small group to split between the two carts. Brandon went with Regan, of course, wrapping a firm grip on her elbow and steering her to the passenger side of his vehicle before stepping behind the wheel and taking off.

At the first tee, there was still a small line of people waiting to drive their first ball of the tournament. Tyler and Wyatt stepped off to the side, away from the golfers and spectators, Wyatt's arm around Tyler's shoulder. They were very chummy, too chummy for Regan's peace of mind. Wyatt knew what Tyler had done. She was his sister, for god's sake. Why wasn't he tougher on Tyler? And what were they talking about, anyway?

When they returned to take their place in the line, both men looked grave and thoughtful, like co-conspirators. Regan was about to wander up—looking casual and disinterested, of course—to ask what they were discussing.

"You're up, Regan," Brandon called to her, interrupting her plans. "Come hit a hole in one, honey."

Honey? He never called Regan "honey." He knew she hated when men marked their territory, yet here he was doing it. That didn't bode well for the afternoon.

Her thoughts on anything but golf, Regan sliced her ball deep into a patch of woods far down the fairway.

"Tough luck, Ree," her brother sympathized as he took his place at the men's tee. Of course, he hit a perfect drive, dead center and very long, gaining the applause from the crowd and the adoration of a few teenage girls. Wyatt had that effect on girls—women, too.

Regan realized she had not even seen Brandon's drive, but of course, he was proud to inform her that it was far beyond hers, near Wyatt's.

"Your brother is good, Regan, but I think my ball maybe closer to the green than his. We'll make up for your shot, don't worry."

She was worried, but not about the game. She didn't know what to do with all her nervous energy. Golf was not a sport where she could take extra swings to release her anger, so it just simmered below the surface.

"How dare Wyatt betray me like that?" she mumbled.

"What'd you say, Regan?" Brandon asked, momentarily taking his eyes off the course and swerving slightly.

"Huh, oh. I thought I was talking to myself. That was such a bad shot."

"Let it go. You'll be back on the green in no time. You need to concentrate." Brandon proceeded to give her tips on her swing as the golf cart moved down the path, all of which she tuned out.

"Thanks, Bran, I've got it from here." Regan almost leaped from the cart before it stopped, stepping into the woods in search of her errant ball. She quickly found it under Tyler's foot.

"What the hell do you think you are doing?" she hissed at him as she looked around. No one was nearby to hear or see them.

"Regan, I had to talk to you. You need to trust me again and for just a little longer. I swear I am going to fix this thing and then I am coming for you. Brandon better be long gone by then. You once told me you'd end it with him to be with me."

"Well, you once told me you'd love me forever," she retorted, then covered her mouth, wishing she could get the words back. She had revealed too much.

"I meant it. I do. I will. I swear. Just trust me, please."

"I ca-can't, Ty. I just can't anymore. You have done this to me one too many times. I'm marrying Brandon. We're engaged."

"You're engaged? When the hell did this happen?"

"Last week."

"You need to break it off, Ree. You need to wait for me. I promise you I will be there for you. I swear. I need you, Ree. I love you. I always have. Give me a chance to—"

"Regan, did you find it?" Brandon asked. They could hear him approaching through the thicket. Tyler moved away quickly, but not before giving Regan a beseeching look.

"Who was that?" Brandon asked, watching a broad set of shoulders retreat through the woods.

"My brother. He couldn't resist teasing me about my slice."

My, my, that lie just slipped right off my tongue. What are you doing?

"Sorry I missed him. I have wanted to have a chat with him. Oh well, take your shot and let's get you back on the fairway," Brandon said, offering to help guide her swing.

Passing on the offer, Regan swung at the ball with all her might, finally finding an outlet for her frustration, and needing it more than ever.

Chapter Eighteen

"It's gorgeous," Keeli gushed. "It's so beautiful that I can almost forgive him for not buying it from me."

"Sorry about that. It's an heirloom, reset at Tiffany's."

"Yes, of course," she replied, retaking Regan's finger and studying the ring more closely. "I would guess it is about nine carats and the color is superb. It's a wonderful ring. He has good taste."

"You don't think it's a bit too much?" Regan asked in a low voice. "I always pictured something simpler."

"What could be simpler than a huge diamond solitaire," her sister asked, approaching to stare at the diamond ring, "a US Senator and what will be the wedding of the year?"

"It is huge, Missy, isn't it?" Regan asked, ignoring her comments about the wedding.

"Ostentatious is the word I think you're looking for," Missy said as the three women laughed together.

"When will you get married? Where will you get married? Here right, not DC?"

"Oh Keeli, I have no idea. I guess I need to start thinking about all those things. Brandon would like a winter wedding, sooner rather than later, but I would prefer waiting until next spring at least."

"Let's head into dinner, everyone," Julia Howe called to her family. "I don't want anything getting cold."

As the family moved toward the dining room, Brandon detained Wyatt near the family room door. "I've wanted to talk about funding for my next campaign," Regan heard him saying. She slowed down just outside the double door and leaned against the wall.

"Your campaign?" Wyatt asked. "What about it?"

"Well, I want to get a leg up on my rival as soon as possible, curb any primary challenges and head for a win with plenty of money in the coffers."

"You have family funds and a good fundraising team, right?"

"That's true, I do. My staff will run the grassroots campaign, of course."

"Of course," Wyatt agreed, as if he had expertise in politics.

"But I was thinking about hooking the big fish, those donors that will put me on the map. I have ambitions, you know. I wouldn't mind a run at the White House someday. With Regan beside me, and your family money and network behind me, there is no reason I couldn't make that happen."

Wyatt just nodded his head, and Regan could see that Brandon had his complete attention. "I have the Hockney name in my favor. I'm young and rapidly building a reputation as a leader, getting on the critical committees. In a few years, I should have a straight shot."

Regan was riveted to her spot, hearing for the first time about Brandon's goals and ambitions. "Regan is a key component to my continued progress. Good family, smart, pretty but not too threatening to the women voters—don't get me wrong, I actually do love her—she is perfect for a first lady. And of course, her name opens doors." Regan was kicking herself for trusting this man. When would she learn to go with her gut? But the idiot was saying more. When would he stop bragging about himself? *What on earth did I think I saw in him?*

"Now that we will be family, Wyatt, I thought we could discuss infusing my campaign with a healthy dose of Howe money. You could have an important appointment in exchange. A role in the administration down the line. And if people know you are backing me, or if you make a few strategic introductions, we will be swimming in campaign contributions. There is more than enough money, Ivy. Come on, you know it." Brandon was speaking casually, but Regan could hear the desperation in his undertones.

"This is neither the time nor the place," Wyatt responded, ice in his voice.

"No. No. No, of course not. It's time for family dinner. I just wanted to plant the seed, get the ball rolling. We can talk later," Brandon said, slapping her brother on the back before walking into the dining room. He never noticed Regan pressed against the wall behind him.

Fury simmered in her veins. What a fool she had been. Brandon had been using her all along. "Don't get me wrong, I actually do love her." Was she some pathetic dog to whom he was throwing a bone? She suspected Wyatt's anger would rival her own. As he came around the corner, she stepped away from her hiding place. The look on his face confirmed her suspicion. Wyatt was livid. He looked like he wanted to kill someone.

"Don't rush into anything, Ree," he commanded. "Don't marry this arrogant, ambitious, money-grubber."

"Brandon's rich, Wyatt. I don't know why he's asking you for money."

"Who cares why? He is, and in the vilest way, as if we owe it to him for taking you off our hands. He sees you as an advantageous pawn in his game."

"I'm nobody's pawn, I promise you," she assured him.

"You better not be. Wait for Tyler to fix things."

"You just told me not to be someone's pawn. I have waited for Tyler my whole life. For what? I can't trust him either. What's different now?"

"Everything. You can trust me, Ree. Everything is different."

"Trust me. That is all men ever tell me. Trust me while I stab you in the back, trust me while I walk out on you with no explanation, trust me while I steal the job you want..."

"Hey, that's not fair."

"No," she agreed sheepishly, "that wasn't fair. But it's all I ever hear. Marry me, wait for me. Trust me. I am all out of trust."

"I'm your brother, Regan Howe, not some random man. I am telling you to trust Tyler and delay this engagement as long as you can. Better yet, give him back that rock now and say sayonara."

"C'mon you two," Ethan called from the dining room doorway. "Mom is waiting for dinner on you." The siblings flashed each other a guilty look, exchanged a swift hug, and moved quickly to the dining room.

"I mean it, Ree," her brother said just before they entered the room, "Tyler is going to fix this."

"Sorry," Regan mumbled as she slid into her seat beside Brandon at the table. Her mother immediately signaled, and the family quickly loaded their plates with the feast hot off the grill.

The burgers and hot dogs seemed incongruous against the pristine tablecloth and sterling silver serving pieces. Ketchup and mustard had been removed from containers and placed in lovely glass bowls, but the barbeque was a barbeque, nonetheless. Missy's children were biting into one end of their hot dogs and dripping ketchup from the other.

Ethan was running his teeth down an ear of corn like a beaver, but somehow talking at the same time.

"So does this mean you are done with LHRE for good?" he asked Regan. "How soon can I be in charge?"

"Don't talk with your mouth full," his mother scolded.

"And don't rush me out the door," Regan added. "Do you think you're ready to take over?"

"Well..."

"Exactly," Regan responded.

"He needs to assume control at some point, Regan. After all, we'll be married soon. He won't have you to lean on then," Brandon told the room at large. "We announce the engagement later this week, and if you can get everything organized, Julia, I'd like a winter wedding."

"Brandon," Regan cut her mother off before she could respond, "My mother and I both think a spring wedding would be nicer."

"Yes, spring," her mother concurred, barely masking the confusion in her voice. "And I need the extra planning time, Brandon. You men don't always understand that." She looked over at her daughter, who offered a subtle nod and smile.

"Yes, it takes months and months to plan a wedding," Julia latched onto her role as the mother of the bride, playing it for all she was worth. "Especially a big important wedding like this. At least a year or more."

"You know, Bran, now that I think about it," Regan picked up again, beaming down the table at her mother, "if we are waiting until spring, I think we should hold off on the announcement. This time of year, it could get lost in the August recess. I think you want it to go out when the Senate is in session, don't you?"

"Good thinking, Regan," Wyatt continued. "The Howe-Hockney merger—I mean wedding—is big news. You want that to hit the press when you're in session. Right, Brandon?"

"Absolutely," Brandon agreed, completely missing the sarcasm in Wyatt's tone or the way he had just been manipulated.

"It is rather like a merger, isn't it? My daughter is marrying a United States senator," her father beamed with pride.

"And a scion of New England society," her mother added. "You will be like Jackie Kennedy, sweetheart. And just as pretty."

"Oh, Mom," Regan blushed.

"Let's hope," Brandon tossed in on a weak laugh, "I don't end up like Jack."

Chapter Nineteen

Everyone was tiptoeing around the office, afraid to attract the attention of either Tyler or Regan. It had been a while since both had been in the office on the same day and the entire staff had appreciated the reprieve. The tension today was palpable.

"You have to face him sooner or later," Charlotte reminded Regan gently, being the lone soul willing to confront the CEO. "He's in the office next door. If nothing else, you'll have to pass by it to go to the ladies' room."

"I'll hold it," Regan responded stubbornly. "Why doesn't he go to some meeting, or at least shut his damn door?"

"Why don't you put on your big girl pants and stomp in there and remind him who's in charge here? It's still your company, Ree. You can fire him if you want."

"Not anymore. Not without board approval," Regan shot back. "But they would approve it if I told them to." A sly grin bared her teeth, and she sat a bit taller.

"That's better," Charlotte responded reassuringly. "He doesn't bite, Regan. You have been emailing for two months without an altercation. You run a business together. Just stick to LHRE business, and you'll do fine." Without another word, Charlotte lifted her growing bulk from the chair, rubbed her lower back instinctively, and moved toward the door.

Regan felt ashamed. "How are you feeling, Charlotte? What a self-absorbed friend and boss I am. I should have asked sooner. Please forgive me."

"No problem. I am feeling huge since you asked. And nervous."

"Nervous?"

"The doctor says everything is fine, but Alex is a wreck and he's turning me into one too. I can't wait for this little girl to be born so we can both get a good night's sleep."

"Not too much longer for the delivery, but don't count on a good night's sleep for about 20 years," Regan teased. "You'll both do great."

"You will too," Charlotte responded, gesturing with a hand toward Tyler's office. "Just get it over with."

The women left Regan's office together, but Regan stood nervously outside Tyler's door when Charlotte continued down the long corridor to her office.

"He's free if you want to go in," Donna offered from behind her. Although Donna was Regan's assistant, Regan knew she watched every move Tyler made. It looked to Regan like she was in love with the man, infatuated. But maybe she simply didn't trust him. If it was the latter, how would Donna handle it when Regan was gone, and the assistant worked for Tyler full-time? If it was the former, she was headed for disappointment. Regan considered saying something, but what? Donna would have to find a way to manage her personal feelings. Regan pushed the thought away; she had enough problems without taking on Donna's.

"Thanks, Donna," Regan responded, rapping lightly on the frame of Tyler's office door with her knuckles before proceeding into the room without hesitation, covering her trepidation.

"Hey there," she began as she slid gracefully into a chair across from him.

"Hey there, yourself," he responded. "Welcome back." His eyes rested first on her face, then went straight for her ring finger. Tyler frowned, then schooled his features.

"I thought we might catch up on things," Regan offered, feeling her heart ready to beat out of her chest. Tyler looked breathtakingly handsome. He had tossed his suit jacket casually over the back of the sofa and rolled up his shirtsleeves. His forearms were tanned and strong. His hands rested calmly on the keyboard of his computer, but he must have been running them through his hair, which stuck up in front as if styled that way. "If I'm not disturbing you."

"What kind of things?" He was not going to make this easy, she realized, shifting in the chair, gripping the arms a bit too forcefully and trying again.

"Perhaps you can bring me up to speed on a few pending deals and the strategy you have laid out for downstate?"

Regan watched as Tyler's hands tensed. She was mesmerized watching the hands that had worked magic with her body. He moved to pick up a pen and began fidgeting before responding in a sarcastic tone that snapped Regan back to the present. "Happy to, boss. How long have you got?"

Regan pondered the question. How long did she have? Weeks? Months? How much longer was she supposed to wait? Shit, Tyler expected an answer. What was it they were discussing?

Regan forced herself to concentrate on work, ignoring the questions racing through her brain. "I can meet for an hour right now. If you need more time, let's table this for later. I am here all week."

"All week? Wow! How will your fancy senator survive that long without you?"

Now Tyler was just childish. "Tyler..." Her voice was stern, but she had no other words. What could she say that wouldn't either sound like scolding or begging?

Regan crossed and recrossed her legs in frustration, then rose to pace the room. She stopped to gaze at the view and settle her pounding heart.

Why were they talking about work when she craved answers about the two of them? She was dying to look Tyler in the eye and beg him to tell her the truth. Instead, she was pretending to be engaged to one man when she was in love with another.

"Yes, boss?"

His expression was closed, his voice derisive. Was the son of a bitch making fun of her or hiding his own confused emotions? Tyler was so good at hiding his feelings that even after all this time, Regan couldn't be sure. She just knew he was keeping her at arm's length.

Regan briefly considered challenging him, but when she turned back to face him, their eyes locked. She saw something there, pain or confusion, a signal to go easy on him.

Regan took the easy way out for them both by sticking to work. "I am trying to be civil here, trying to discuss business and get a few things done," she announced, moving closer so she would tower over him as they spoke. It was a little thing, but all she had at the moment. His vulnerability left her shaken and unsure. If she just stayed in CEO mode...

"Would you please cooperate? And stop calling me 'boss.'"

"Of course, boss, let me just get the files." Tyler rose to his feet, their shoulders brushing—was that intentional? – then loped out to Donna's desk with that cowboy stride of his. The lingering scent of his cologne and his skin played at her nostrils, creating a familiar longing.

He returned too quickly, while Regan was still regaining her equilibrium. He stopped next to her, dropping the files on the desk in front of her. Leaning over her, Tyler opened the one on top of the pile. She had lost her brief height advantage, and he was too near.

"What are you doing? Are you playing games with me? You're standing too close."

"You didn't think this was too close two months ago," he reminded her in a low, growly voice. "You thought it wasn't close enough," Tyler bent his head to whisper in her ear. "If you'll recall."

Regan felt the heat of his body through their layers of clothes, the moist warmth of his breath on her neck. Her body responded instantly, swaying close for more before she resisted, pushing at him weakly. "That was then. That was a different Regan and Tyler. Things are different now."

"You were a temptress then, Ree, and you still are. You always have been." Tyler stepped back, but only inches. "But you're engaged to that senator. I guess that makes you an off-limits temptress."

"That's right," she replied in a clipped voice. "Off limits."

Tyler stood behind her. She could feel him there, but not see him. What was the infernal man doing? He wasn't moving away, that was for sure. She inhaled his scent deep into her nostrils and leaned her head back until it brushed his shirtfront. That small touch was all it took. Their two months of separation disappeared; the heat rose between them without a word. Regan felt the dampness pool between her legs, holding her breath, waiting, always waiting for Tyler.

"You sure as hell didn't behave like you were off-limits, Regan," Tyler mumbled under his breath, leaning his head in closer until she felt his warm breath slide down her collar. "Not when you were wearing that dress."

In an instant, Regan relived the feel of his hands on her skin, removing the Marchesa dress, fussing over the corset briefly before exposing her naked body. Was that two months ago? It felt like minutes as she sat still as a statue, listening to Tyler, sensing his body behind her. She felt his eyes boring into her and remembered the heat she had seen flare in their cocoa depths that night. Finally, she turned to look at Tyler. Regan could see that same heat now, his desire evident. She felt the passion pulsing through her body as he leaned closer.

"That's right, my temptress. I am yours. I need you to focus on this feeling and be patient a little longer," he whispered, his breath sweet on her flushed cheek. "Remember this moment; right now. Remember how good we are together?"

Tyler's voice was hypnotic, his dark eyes holding her gaze until he shifted. His lips were resting lightly against the skin behind her ear, caressing there so that his breath traveled, sending sinful signals to her body as the moist warmth whispered along her spine.

"Tyler," came her hoarse response, asking, begging for more with just the sound of his name.

"That's right, Ree. You are mine. You were always mine. You will always be mine." His handsome face came into view, his eyes locking on hers until she was certain he saw into her soul. His lips hovered millimeters from hers. She could already taste him as her mouth lifted slightly to meet his.

"Excuse me, Regan, there's a call for you." Donna's voice came from the door, quintessentially professional. When Regan met her eyes, she saw disillusion and hurt. Regan knew what Donna had seen, confirmation that Tyler was not available to her. The poor girl was in love with Tyler. What a fatal mistake.

It was a mistake for Regan, too. She pushed at Tyler's chest to give herself space. The man was a snake charmer. She walked to the windows, her back to him, catching her breath and hiding her embarrassment from her assistant and friend. Regan gave herself a mental scolding for getting herself into this situation, for hurting Donna, and setting herself back two months.

Without a word, she turned on her heel and stormed out of Tyler's office, entering her own with a hard slam of her door. You are here to work, she reminded herself, and only to work.

Regan's phone began ringing. Taking a deep breath, she answered the phone in a calm, professional voice that belied her agitation and frustration. "Hello? Yes, this is Regan Howe," she responded to the voice of the unknown stranger. "Yes, I'll hold."

Twitching her skirt into place, Regan sat tall in her executive chair and fidgeted with the pen resting on the desk. Regan's heart was hammering in her chest, even harder and louder than it had pumped only minutes earlier. She didn't think that was possible.

"Regan," came the voice of the Undersecretary of the Treasury. "How are you? I've been trying to reach you here in Washington. I thought you were living here already."

"I am still commuting a bit, sir," she explained, standing and pacing in her agitation.

"Well, no matter. You'll be here soon enough, and that's what matters. I wanted to call personally—although the official offer will follow. I know we interviewed you as an advisor to the Director of the CDFI, but I have just learned the Director is leaving. We would like to offer you his position. Would you be interested in running CDFI? It's a bigger, more consuming position, but I know you can handle it."

Regan dropped into her leather chair, feeling it tilt back under her weight. She swiveled to look at the Chicago skyline. It was the moment Regan had longed for—and dreaded. Did she want to give up everything here? Give up her chance with Tyler? Regan would have to decide not only about the job but her personal life as well. It meant she would be starting over.

"Regan?" The undersecretary's voice interrupted her musings. "I am asking you to serve your country."

"Yes, sir." Regan rose to her feet reflexively. "It would be my honor, sir." She stopped herself from saluting the empty office, feeling foolish for standing as if the man could see her. It just seemed like such a patriotic moment. She would be working for the US Government. The idea sent a shiver of anticipation down her spine.

"Good, that's what I wanted to hear. We'll see you in DC by the end of the month."

The click of the phone broke through the fog, leaving Regan stunned. She trembled with excitement. She had done it. She had the job. No, she had an even better position, a fantastic opportunity as top dog. Who should she call first, Missy or Tyler?

Tyler. He would be so proud of her. He was always so supportive of her accomplishments.

Tyler.

Regan dropped back into her chair as her legs gave out from beneath her. Tyler! Oh my god. What had she done?

Chapter Twenty

Regan settled into her new position quickly, focusing on the work and avoiding the politics. Brandon, however, loved all the publicity, making the round of Sunday morning talk shows and finding a way to announce that he was half of the newest Washington power couple. She, not Brandon, was in demand for the shows, but each time she turned one down, he managed to find the spotlight instead.

"I wish you would stop talking about me on the talk shows," she begged him again, for at least the tenth time. "Talk about the what you are doing, Brandon. Leave me out of it. The way you keep highlighting our relationship makes it sound like I got the job only due to our involvement. And we aren't engaged. I asked for more time to think about it, and you know it."

"CDFI and the undersecretary know that you earned the job, Regan. That's all that matters. I'm not trying to make you look weak. It's good for both of us to be seen as a power couple." Why did he make her feel like she was in the wrong every time she asked him to stop doing something? She thought of Ty, who didn't always come clean with her, but who never put her in a bad light in public.

"Still, I would prefer you refrain, and I have asked you politely."

"I'll cut back, Regan, but all publicity is good publicity, as the saying goes." Regan shot him a withering look. "The talking heads are inviting me because of you," Brandon continued, undaunted. "You are the news, your job, your move to Washington, and our engagement. That is the personal interest story that people want to hear."

"But Brandon," Regan blew her hair from her eyes with an exasperated sigh, "it's a false narrative. There is no engagement. You have to stop spreading these rumors. I know you are the consummate politician, but try to slow down about us. For me. Please. The more you push for this, the more you push me away."

They were sitting on the leather sofa in her townhouse, sipping wine. Brandon had come from another news show—damn those 24-hour feeds—although she had told him to go straight home, that it would be too late to visit. It was almost midnight, but he was showing no signs of leaving. Instead, he made her regret opening the door. She understood that something was holding Tyler back, but he was the man she loved. It was time to cut and run from Brandon.

"I'll try," Brandon agreed. "I am doing it for us."

"Well, I've told you how I feel," Regan said. "It's late, so I don't want to argue with you."

"Me either," Brandon agreed, wiggling his eyebrows in a bad Groucho Marx imitation. "I can think of much better ways to spend our night."

Regan avoided making eye contact. "Not tonight."

Brandon turned to her, pointing an accusing finger. "It's always, not tonight, Regan. I can't remember the last time you let me stay over. First, it was exhaustion from the move and the packing and unpacking. Then it was the new job and staying focused. What's your excuse this time?"

Regan resisted an exasperated sigh. They had been having this same argument repeatedly since her move. "Please don't get angry with me about this again, Brandon. I want some space. You need to give me some time to consider our future together, and the sex complicates things for me." Regan twisted a paper napkin between her fingers, dropped the shredded mess onto the coffee table, and drank a deep swallow of Rombauer Chardonnay. "You are pushing me, and I don't like it," she finally confessed.

"What the hell are you talking about?" Brandon raised his voice to her, taking the glass from her hands and carefully placing it on the table. "Look at me, Regan. I don't understand how we got to this place, but I don't like it. We have been planning a life together. I am going to marry you within the year. We are going to move into a place of our own. You are going to run CDFI. I am going to get a spot at the convention or even on the ticket. Then, we are going to run the campaign of a lifetime. We are the couple to watch in DC right now. Our families are rich and powerful, our names are synonymous with rank and privilege, and we are gorgeous together."

"We, we, we, except this is your plan, Brandon, not mine. Not to mention, that was anything but a romantic proposal." She was exhausted physically and with this conversation. It came out in her voice.

"Don't get snide, Regan, it doesn't become you."

"I'm just tired, Brandon. Let's table this discussion for the weekend."

"But, honey, we have been tabling it." Regan cringed. Brandon rarely called her pet names, but she hated them all. "It's been too long, and I have all this adrenaline from doing the show. I could be hot tonight. Superman."

Regan wanted to laugh. She had experienced her personal Superman, but he wasn't Brandon. "Maybe, but I am sending you home tonight. I warned you I was exhausted, remember? I told you to go straight home."

"I wanted to be with you," Brandon whined. "I always want to be with you. You used to want to be with me, too."

"I do, Brandon, just not tonight." Why didn't she seize the moment and end it? Regan was exhausted, frustrated, and unable to face a fight.

Brandon cajoled, but eventually gave up and moved toward the door. Regan followed, trying to hide her visible relief. Since she had moved to Washington, she had avoided nights with Brandon, except for their attendance at public functions. Proximity was not helping their relationship. She couldn't erase her memories of Tyler's touch.

Brandon took her into his arms now, and Regan had to brace for his kiss. "I miss you, Regan. We don't have enough time together. I want to be able to hold you close." His touch was gentle as he took her in his arms. Brandon's kiss was skillful, his tongue probing her lips, softening against her until she sighed and opened her mouth to him. His hands roamed her back, slipping under her silky blouse. She allowed him to cast a spell over her and leaned into the kiss.

Just because he wasn't Tyler didn't mean he wasn't pretty damn good. Regan was unfair to him. She had relinquished Tyler for Brandon and needed to put her money where her mouth was. In this case, on his mouth.

Regan sighed against Brandon's lips and opened her mouth to his tongue. He accepted her invitation with alacrity, pushing her against the door, caging her with his body. He pressed himself against her from lips to thighs, leaving her in no doubt of his desire.

"C'mon baby," Brandon said. "Let's go upstairs. I'll make it so good."

Regan hated when he called her baby, loathed when he made demands on her time when she asked him not to, and she cringed when he whined and persevered. She hated when Brandon ignored her wishes. His current insistence left Regan cold. He may as well have thrown a bucket of ice water on her. "Give it up, Brandon. Go home."

Regan felt guilty for insisting that he leave. Still, she shoved Brandon out the door. Why was she sorry? For asking him not to come over in the first place or for making him go? For not wanting him the way he wanted her? She wasn't certain.

Regan only knew she was relieved to be alone. She listened as his footsteps receded, turning out the lights and leaning against the door with a long, frustrated sigh. Regan was a smart woman. She made tough decisions every day and yet she could not let Brandon go, nor could she commit.

She found her wineglass using the glow of the streetlamp outside and dropped exhausted onto the sofa, wondering once again how she got herself into this mess.

Washington was exciting, new, and bustling with culture, events, and parties. Regan loved her new job, although she missed her old life and her family. The work was challenging. She loved her team, and after only one month, it seemed as if she was making a real difference.

The move would have been ideal if it had been with Tyler, but it wasn't. He was in her former office now, the official and sole head of Lyons Howe, until the board found Ethan competent to take the helm. Tyler had been in the position half a year already, and she reluctantly admitted he was doing a fantastic job.

Six months. No wonder Brandon was impatient. She had been pushing him away even as he believed she would marry him. Enough time had passed. It was reasonable for him to expect an answer from her. When she wasn't tired, when he didn't ignore her wishes, he was attentive and kind. He loved showing her off and sharing his town. They had fun together.

And he wanted to marry her, commit to her for life. Tyler offered her nothing to compete with that. Although Regan resisted, eventually even she was forced to relinquish her girlish dreams of a future with Tyler Winthrop. She had the memories, including an incredible weekend right out of a steamy novel. Those would have to hold her for a lifetime since Tyler offered nothing more. Her head told her to walk away, but her heart...

After a few weeks in DC, she had stopped calling Tyler with business excuses, feeling transparent and exposed in her efforts to connect with him. It hurt when he treated her with nothing but professionalism. She missed the innuendo, heat, and tension between them. It died the instant she told him she had accepted the DC job. He had been thrilled for her as she had known he would be, but from that moment on, there was a wall between them. The teasing, flirtatious Tyler, asking her to be patient and full of promises for the future, disappeared. In his place was a competent CEO with overwhelming anger.

Heading up to the bedroom after refilling her wineglass, Regan recalled the hurt on Tyler's face and his words when he had learned of her plans. She would need bottles of wine to numb herself from those memories.

"What about us?" he cut straight to the chase. "You are choosing Brandon, after all of this?" Tyler buried the hurt in his eyes and the defeat in his voice beneath a fiery display of temper. "After the way we kissed, the way we touched, I was just an easy fuck for you?"

Regan cringed at the hurtful words. He knew just where to thrust the knife. "Tyler, that's not fair. You knew how things stood. Hell, that's why you have this job."

"I have this job because I came to fight for you, to win you back. Now, you're going to give up and let this man run your life? Because that is what Brandon is doing, Ree, he is taking over your life."

Regan recalled the way Tyler had paced the large office, his stride eating up space. "He's vacuous, Ree, using you for your brains, your poise, and personality. If he didn't have money…"

"Stop right now, Tyler. That's not fair to Brandon or me."

"Like I give a shit." Tyler stopped pacing and faced her. "He's using you. I know it."

"Brandon loves me. He is not using me. He could have his pick of women, but he chose me."

"He doesn't love you the way I do. I love you, Ree."

"Why tell me that now?" Regan demanded, refusing to allow the words to penetrate. "It's too little too late. You've had years and years to make this right between us, but nothing. You gave me nothing."

"I couldn't, Ree. I thought you understood that."

"And now, what can you give me now? Are you offering me a future, a life together, marriage?"

Tyler's face crumbled, and he turned away from her. "Not right now," he mumbled, "but I am working to get there…"

"Enough with the buts, Tyler. There is always a but. I am done with buts." She motioned to her door, and he moved slowly toward it, as if the weight of the world was on his shoulders.

"Ree, I need more time," he begged.

"Well then, there you have it," Regan announced. "I will be leaving in ten days. That's how long you have for me and work. Let's plan to transition everything by then."

Later that day, those three words finally seeped into her brain. He loved her. Tyler still loved her. He came back to fight for her, but then he gave up, leaving her more confused than before. He pulled her close, then pushed her away. She cried buckets, but stuck with her decision. Tyler might love her, but after all these years, he was still hiding secrets and asking for time. Always more time. He would never marry her. There would be no happily ever after in their future, and she didn't understand why. He promised to tell her everything, then remained silent.

So, she had returned to DC, if not quite to Brandon. Had she hoped Tyler would follow? He hadn't, forcing her to face reality. She wanted a family, to build a future with a wonderful man who made her laugh, who wanted her and never failed to say so. She tried to convince herself that Brandon could be that man. After tonight, Regan worried about committing to him. Brandon's hands and lips were terrific. The man was handsome and sexy as sin. He was smart and funny, destined for great things. He would be any woman's ideal. Except Regan's. He wasn't Tyler.

When he touched her, Regan compared Brandon's touch to Tyler's. Same with his kisses, or the feel of his skin. When Tyler called her pet names, she melted. When Brandon did it, she cringed. At the end of a great day, it was Tyler she wanted to talk to, not Brandon.

And damn Tyler for his accusations, but Regan was starting to sense that Tyler was right about Brandon. Despite the lovely packaging, the gift was disappointing. Brandon appeared to be using her. First, there were the rounds of talk shows and parties where he put her on display, constantly telling people they were engaged, and consistently adding Regan's lineage to his remarks. He was pedigree dropping, and it was unattractive.

Recently, Brandon had begun bringing up fundraising and money. Until the last few weeks, Regan had blamed Tyler and his insidious seed of doubt, but she could no longer deny that the only person Brandon was interested in was Brandon. She didn't doubt that he loved her, in his own way, but he loved his political ambitions more. It was eating at her and driving a wedge between them. She replayed his actions repeatedly, looking for another angle, hoping she was mistaken, but each time, she returned to the same conclusion.

It had started gradually. On Regan's phone calls home, Brandon would chime in: would she please remind her family that he was having a campaign fundraiser? Might they attend or send a small donation? That quickly expanded to requests that they host fundraising events, or underwrite ad campaigns. He was asking for expenditures that amounted to small fortunes.

"What about talking to your family?" she had suggested one night when they were leaving for a campaign benefit. He came from money, after all, and every time she was with his family, they made it clear that they supported his ambitions. He had been complaining all night that the take would not be big enough. "Couldn't you underwrite this yourself, Brandon, or ask your folks?"

"Are you saying you don't think your family should invest in our future?"

"That is not what I am saying, and you know it." Regan took a deep breath to reduce the sharpness in her tone. "But you have been asking them for quite a lot recently, and I have not seen you tapping your resources."

"You're right," he conceded. "I will call my parents tomorrow."

But when that scenario happened a second time, and then a third, she started to hear Tyler's words in her head. How she wished he had never said them.

Going through the motions, getting ready for bed, Regan tried to block all the arguments of the last month from her mind. She had moved to Washington for the job, but also thinking she would build a life with Brandon. Instead, she was finding fault and looking for a way out. Time to admit he wasn't the man for her.

It wasn't his fault Regan presented the opposing position. She had not given him a fair shake. Brandon loved her, she told herself again. He was anxious to marry her. So, he was ambitious. That was no crime. She needed to focus on why she found Brandon so attractive in the first place and get back to that place. Regan vowed to push Tyler from her mind and be more patient with Brandon, to approach her relationship with Brandon with an open mind. She would give him every chance before she gave up on him.

Only she couldn't. The kisses were passionate, but started to make her skin crawl. And the spin Brandon put on their relationship—she knew she couldn't trust him. She needed to call it quits.

Slipping into a silky camisole the color of a shiny penny, Regan slid between the sheets and lay in the darkness, waiting for the wine to dull her senses and allow her to sleep. She felt the slippery material brush against her nipples and thought of Tyler's fingers, gentle sometimes, sexy and rough other times. She missed those hands and the magic they could do.

Stop thinking about him. It's just the fabric, the wine, and Brandon's kisses, Regan convinced herself. Stop, stop, stop thinking of Tyler.

Regan started breathing as slowly as she could, concentrating on her deep breaths, working to clear her mind. Her phone pinged from the bedside table. She picked it up expecting to see a thoughtful text from Brandon to say a final goodnight. It was a final goodnight, alright. But not the one she expected. It was from Tyler.

"Can't stop wanting you. Come home to me. Please."

So much for not thinking about Tyler. He was toying with her. After a month of silence, he was back inside her head. Who was she kidding? He never left. With texts like this, Regan was back to square one, fighting her mind, her body, and her treacherous heart.

Chapter Twenty-One

"This is incredibly embarrassing to admit, but I drunk texted your sister last night."

"Oh, jeez," Ethan remarked. "Anything I should know about?"

"It's bad enough she knows. No way I am repeating it to you."

"Then why even tell me, Ty?"

"Good question, pipsqueak. Forget I mentioned it." Tyler fussed with the few items on his clean desktop to cover his embarrassment.

"I will if you stop using that annoying nickname. I outgrew it years ago."

"Only in your mind," Tyler laughed. He pushed back in the executive chair, resting his feet on the edge of the desk. The two men had started a habit of meeting over coffee every morning, shooting the breeze and discussing the work of the day. Tyler might tease Ethan as if he were still the kid from his childhood, but once they got down to business, he treated him with the respect he was earning.

"Let's get to work."

"So, you're not going to tell me what you wrote? Please tell me you told her you want her back. I can't stand Brandon. Go fight for her."

"What?" Tyler's head shot up at the statement, all ears. "You never told me that before."

"Yeah, I think I did. Or I at least encouraged you a hundred times to go after Regan and bring her back home."

"Ethan, I can't do that." Tyler heard the resolution in his voice. Despite the text—he wasn't drunk this morning. "I would never come between Regan and her dream job." Now, interfering with her and Brandon was another story.

"I think you can, Ty. I think she's just waiting for you to rescue her from the clutches of that pushy S.O.B."

"There is nothing wrong with ambition. The man is a go-getter." Tyler contradicted everything he had said to Regan. "You can't survive in politics otherwise. It's how he got where he is."

"It's how he got my sister," Ethan interrupted, dropping his voice to a whisper. "Between you and me, Wyatt thinks it's about the money."

"Anyone would want Regan. She's smart, funny, loving, and besides, Brandon's family has tons of money of its own," Ty countered.

Ethan was whispering now. "Brandon keeps hitting us up for campaign funds, making Wyatt suspicious. Now he's convinced it's a sham. The Hockneys had money at some point," Ethan confided, "but Wyatt has been doing some digging, and he thinks that they have depleted their coffers. Brandon's not the only politician in the family, remember, and each of them has taken loans against the personal fortune to run expensive campaigns. I'm just sayin'." Ethan sat back in the chair, slouching and stretching his long legs out in front of him. As he sat back, Tyler leaned forward, fully engaged.

"It's just the campaign. Running for office costs a fortune," Tyler argued, hearing the uncertainty creeping into his voice. "He's covering everything else, right?"

"Well..."

"Spill, pipsqueak," Tyler commanded.

Ethan cringed at the title but spoke up. "He wants their new house in her name, not his."

"They found a place?" Tyler felt a fist crushing his heart. They were moving in together.

"Maybe, but she is dragging her feet, Ty. I think she is waiting for you to save her."

"I am not some white knight, Ethan. Trust me on that one. Not even close." Tyler began rearranging the few items on his desk unconsciously until Ethan put them right back.

"Cut it out, Ty."

Tyler couldn't contain his energy, but he stilled his hand and began pumping his foot behind the desk instead. Ethan couldn't see the nerves coursing through his blood, but Tyler feared they would explode from his veins. He couldn't let this man hurt Regan, but he was in no position to intervene. Not yet.

"Yeah, that's what my folks say, too." Leaving that statement hanging, Ethan oozed from the chair, opened the office door and asked Donna for a refill on his coffee. She gave him an evil eye, but she came into the office, grabbed the carafe, sent a longing look Tyler's way and sashayed out to get them a fresh pot. Her clothes had become increasingly revealing since Regan had left, and so were the moon eyes she made at Tyler. He needed to have a talk with her and straighten her out before she crossed a line, and he had to let her go.

"Why were your parents talking about me?"

"Who said they were?" The half-smile lifting Ethan's lips gave him away, so Tyler just turned a hard stare at the younger man and waited for him to cave. It took less than fifteen seconds.

"Okay, okay," Ethan plopped back into the chair, extending his hands as if to ward Tyler off. "They have been talking about you a lot.

With Wyatt, to be honest. About when you would return to Lyons Solutions, about whether you had changed and could be trusted. What do they mean by that?"

Did they know? Tyler had suspected that Wyatt's dad knew about his long-ago misdeeds in high school, but he couldn't know he'd been funding the Russian mob for years, could he? Tyler felt his objection to the relationship with Regan stemmed from the knowledge of his early escapades, but no one ever said anything. Had Wyatt known too?

"I don't know what they mean, Ethan," Tyler lied smoothly. After all, he had years of experience lying to people's faces. Just thinking about it made him feel sick. "Maybe you could just ask them."

"Well, whatever it means, they think you could stick around here another year and then go back to Solutions, but that's if things speed up. You might lure Regan home."

Tyler slammed his palm on the desk. "Damn it. You guys need to stop trying to bring Regan back. She's so happy in her job." Tyler lowered his voice, his mind already calculating how to win Regan without costing her an enviable career opportunity.

"It's not the job," Ethan said as Donna knocked and reentered with the coffee. The conversation lagged as she lingered over the mug on Tyler's desk, displaying just enough cleavage to tempt a lesser man. Tyler discreetly looked away. With a disappointed sigh, she placed the carafe on the sideboard, ignoring Ethan entirely, and left in a huff.

"That girl's got it bad for you, Ty. Anyway, where was I?" Ethan poured himself the fragrant brew and started to pace the office. "Oh yeah, it's not about the job. Wyatt said something about delaying a home purchase, and an engagement announcement to give you time."

"To give me time?" Tyler felt the rapid thud in his chest. Had the Howe family had a change of heart? Were they on his side?

"Yep, I am sure they said 'to give you time.' Wyatt has been bitching about Brandon since the golf outing, and even my mom is dragging her feet on a big society wedding now. My father said you had 'turned a corner.' Wyatt said not quite, but he thought you were close. What the hell are they talking about?"

"Ethan, take your coffee and get out," " Tyler commanded, not unkindly. Tyler shouted for Donna to get Wyatt on the phone. "Now."

Ethan yanked the door open, and Tyler could hear him laughing as he moved down the hall. Donna told him Wyatt was on the line.

"How much do you know?" Tyler began without preamble.

"Not enough. You ready to talk?"

"I think I am," Tyler admitted, not even asking why Wyatt knew what he was discussing. "How long have you been waiting for me to call you?"

"Twenty years, Ty. I have been waiting twenty years for you to trust me. It's about fucking time."

"It's not about trust, Wyatt. We can't talk on the phone. Ditka's, half an hour. We may as well eat."

As soon as they saw each other, Tyler spoke up. "I think they might have my phones tapped. Wyatt, this might get dangerous. Anything you know could be dangerous."

"Danger is my middle name, my friend."

"How much time have you got?" Tyler asked, feeling the weight of the world lifting from his shoulders.

"Well, that depends. An hour? A lifetime? How much time do you need?"

Chapter Twenty-Two

J onathan Chen slipped into the leather booth quickly, checking over his shoulder one last time before settling nervously and turning to his companions.

"I don't think anyone followed me, but I don't know how to be sure."

"If you didn't see anyone, we're good," Tyler explained. "These guys aren't subtle, and they would stick out like a sore thumb in this place."

This place was Ditka's steakhouse, a room of hushed voices and dimmed lighting. Tyler had Donna call his father and lawyer to meet him here the moment he made the arrangements with Wyatt. If he were going to spill his guts, he would rather only do it once.

The four men were in the last booth against the far wall. No one sat beside them, and it would remain that way. Tyler sat with a perfect view of the entrance. He would know if anyone entered, and except the servers—all of whom Tyler had vetted already—anyone trying to eavesdrop would be noticeable.

"Okay, now that we've played Sherlock Holmes, can we get down to business?" Jonathan Chen asked kindly.

"What's your rush, Chen? You bill hourly," Tyler teased him.

"Oh yeah," the small Asian lawyer answered with a grin, "take all the time you want."

"Seriously," Tyler continued, "Jonathan's right. We have a lot to cover. Here's what I know so far. The guys I went to jail with…"

"Excuse me?" Wyatt's jaw dropped.

"Oh, did I leave that part out? More on that later," Tyler responded cryptically. "Juvie, Jail, Europe. They're almost the same."

"Tyler, you aren't helping," his father scolded. "Just bring them up to speed now."

"Okay. So, at the end of high school, I stole a car with some kids. We were going to take it for a joy ride and return it, but it was a Ferrari. That's why we wanted it, of course. Got caught, after all. Who would notice a bunch of kids crammed into a bright red Ferrari speeding along residential roads? We were idiots. My folks thought it would teach me a lesson if I spent six weeks in the slammer. They forgot they were imprisoning me with the same guys that convinced me to steal a car. My parents hushed it up by saying I went to Europe. I went along with the lies in exchange for my college tuition. How'd I do, Father? Adequate summation?"

"We weren't the bad guys, Tyler. You were heading in the wrong direction," his father preached parentally.

"That explains so much," Wyatt sighed. "So much. You could have told me."

"It was a choice. Betray you or betray my parents, Wyatt. Not a lot of good options there," Tyler admitted offhandedly, doing a poor job of covering up his hurt. "Anyway, these guys are blackmailing me now. Well, they have been for about sixteen years."

"Sixteen years?" Jonathan exclaimed, turning to Emmett. "When you mentioned this and asked me to come to this meeting, I had no idea it had been going on that long."

"Yeah, sixteen years of escalating demands," Tyler clarified. "I should have cut them off at the start, but I was a stupid kid. Then they explained I was supporting the Russian mafia, effectively committing treason by paying terrorists, that I could end up losing everything, so I shut up and kept paying."

"What did the police do?" Wyatt asked, dumbfounded.

"Nothing. I didn't involve the cops, protecting the family name and all that. I just paid what they asked."

"You paid them? For sixteen years?" Wyatt exclaimed, before being quickly shushed by his companions. "How could I not know this?" he whispered.

"Well, I had hoped nobody would know. That was the point of paying." Tyler's frustration was painfully clear in his tone. Wyatt's face was thunderous.

"You should have told us years ago," Wyatt accused.

"I said the same thing," Emmett echoed.

"At least you are telling us now. So, what do you need?" Jonathan got straight to the point.

"Well," Tyler took a deep breath, and after a pregnant pause, continued. "They want more than I can afford. Now they want me to embezzle funds from LHRE."

"What?" Wyatt's indignation threatened to curtail the conversation.

Tyler spoke up quickly, hoping to assuage Wyatt. Doubtful he could. "These guys are big time now, hooked in with Russian hackers. Thugs. They were small fry twenty years ago, but they have grown into dangerous men. The guys I knew are not smart enough to run an operation like this alone; someone must back them. It's ugly, and I am up to my ass in it."

"Just admit you went to jail," Wyatt suggested. "Then they have nothing on you."

"It was juvie anyway, right?" Jonathan asked. "That file has been expunged by now, anyway. Wyatt's right. If you have no record and nothing to hide, they have nothing to use against you."

"They have all the payments, like I said. And my life. They are threatening to kill me, or someone I love," he flashed a downtrodden look at Wyatt, "and I believe they would."

"We've been to the FBI," Emmett continued when it became apparent that Tyler was too emotional. "They want Tyler to play along in exchange for immunity. He knows the little fish in this group, but the Feds want the ringleaders. Tyler can lead them right to them."

"Isn't that risky?" Wyatt queried, blanching.

"Of course," Emmett responded. "Worst of all, of course, is that everything will come out. All that money will have been for nothing."

Tyler's head sunk low against his chest. The embarrassment and shame were overwhelming. He had kept this secret for nearly twenty years at great expense, financially and emotionally. And he had paid a painful price with Regan. He couldn't think about losing Regan now. It would break him.

"So why tell us after all this time?" Wyatt challenged, his tone accusatory. It would take Tyler a long time to regain his trust.

"I wish I could say it was just because it was long overdue, but the truth is I've only hurt myself until now. Going forward, I can see that will change. And Ivy, I need your help. I need you to put software markers in the LHRE files. I know you can do it, Ivy. Trackers for the customer files, I will hand over to them. We will scrub them, of course, but they will look legit. They have to look legit. And Wyatt, your hooks have to be flawless. None of us can get caught. The situation is life and death. I cannot stress that enough. The FBI has folks ready to help you, but you have to be very careful. You cannot meet with agents where anyone might see you. From now on, you are looking over your shoulder at all times."

Wyatt's face was pale and stern, but he nodded in agreement.

"In case you are being watched," Emmett added.

"Our phone call today may have tipped them off. Be careful."

"What do you need from me?" Jonathan asked now.

"An airtight immunity agreement, so none of us gets charged with conspiracy, hacking, embezzlement. That's your job."

"I'm on it." Jonathan shot back. "You guys are never boring." The remark garnered a weak laugh from the group. "You have involved me in the most interesting cases of my career. The most lucrative, too. Undoubtedly my best clients." The foursome laughed, grateful for a moment of levity.

"OK," Tyler said, calm now that he had confessed everything and Jonathan had injected a bit of humor. "That's it. Let's eat. Lunch is on me. Let's dig into the details."

"Were you pissed?" Wyatt asked Emmett. "I forgot to ask."

"Only that Tyler didn't come to me sooner."

"Yeah, I know that feeling."

"I'm sorry, Ivy, Dad. I honestly thought I was protecting you."

"Well, it explains why you've been dragging your feet with Regan," Wyatt acknowledged. Tyler had been expecting this conversation in the restaurant. "You aren't the kind of guy to pull her into a mess like this. I appreciate that."

"I'm surprised he pulled you in," Jonathan said, sliding copies of non-disclosure documents to everyone. "These are dangerous men we are dealing with; they are out for blood."

"Well, actually, money," Tyler corrected sarcastically.

"Glad you can joke about it." Jonathan laughed. "Let's get to this."

Two hours later, Jonathan had a sheaf of handwritten papers in front of him. He stretched and asked for one last cup of coffee.

"So where are we? Is that everything?" Wyatt queried.

"I think we have a plan," Emmett answered, scanning the papers he was reviewing. "The sooner this is over, the better."

"We have a good plan," Tyler reassured them, scanning the nearly empty room once more before speaking. "Right. To summarize, Wyatt, now that you are on board, we have some options we didn't have before. We will use your computer skills and the data center at Lyons Solutions to plant a tail in the real estate code."

"You mean tracking code, right? I will inject some self-erasing code based on the persistent threat evidence we get from the forensics team. Then I can bypass the intrusion detection system and first responding code that would kick out the hackers and, with Tyler's help, create the fake accounts at LHRE. After that, we'll be in business."

"I have no idea what you just said," Emmett admitted.

Wyatt laughed. "Sorry about that. Force of habit, I guess, but in plain speak, I said that we have a plan. We will execute it and have our sting ready to go."

"You make it sound simple," Tyler warned. "Nothing about this is simple, Ivy. These are sophisticated hackers."

"You are right, Tyler. It's good to have your reminders about how reprehensible these people can be," Emmett concurred.

"It's also good to see you and Ty in a room together for a change," Wyatt added.

"Don't patronize me, Wyatt. I have always loved my son. I just thought he had disappointed his mother."

"And his friends."

"Guys, I am right here. Please don't talk about me like I'm not," Tyler interjected. "I was saving all of you from being blackmailed."

"Lot of good it did you," Jonathan stated, matter-of-factly voicing what all of them were thinking. "OK, gentlemen, let's lay a trap."

Leaving the restaurant, Wyatt and Tyler said farewell to Mr. Winthrop at the entrance to the parking garage and walked into the first bar they passed. Tyler dialed Donna to inform her he would not return to the office that afternoon while Wyatt ordered them each a scotch. With drinks quickly in hand, they walked to the darkest corner they could find and dropped into the booth.

"I think this will work, Tyler. Jonathan is excellent."

"He better be, for what he costs me."

Wyatt laughed, "Yeah, there is that." The friends sat in silence, savoring their scotch for a full minute before Wyatt broke the silence.

"Once this is over, you'll go after her, right?"

Tyler didn't have to ask who 'her' was, and he didn't look up from his drink. "I think it will be too late," he mumbled into his glass.

"I don't, Ty. She's dragging her feet. She keeps postponing the wedding, arguing about announcing an engagement. I think she's waiting for you."

"I had my chance, and I blew it, Wyatt. Shit, I had dozens of chances and blew them all." Tyler's head dropped lower over his glass, and his shoulders slumped in defeat.

"Get your ugly mug out of that glass and look at me," Wyatt demanded.

"What are you, my father?" Tyler asked, but his head came up and his eyes locked on Wyatt's.

"If I was, I swear I would tan your hide. Regan loves you, Tyler, and you love her. You two are right for each other. She may have thought she could marry Brandon, but she can't go through with it. If she thinks she can, then you need to save her from herself."

"What if she doesn't want anyone to save her, least of all me? What if she is happy?"

"We can all tell that she's not. And none of us are okay either. You have a chance here. Missy was right, Ty, when she suggested throwing you two together. Use it, damn you. Come up with excuses to contact her. Dream up a problem she has to help you solve."

"She has that CDFI job, Wyatt. It's a great opportunity for her. I can't spoil it for her."

"Man, you have it bad. Listen. I don't want to ruin the job for her, just the engagement. The guy's a sleaze. I have been looking into him. He wants to be the VP on the next presidential ticket, and he's lobbying hard for it. She's first lady material—connections out the wazoo, smart as a whip, pretty as a picture."

"Got any more clichés in your bag of tricks?" Tyler asked. He ran his hand through his thick hair, pushing it back from his forehead, again and again, his frustration obvious. "She chose him."

"He chose her. She went along with it because she couldn't have you. She's rethinking it. He wants her money, Ty, and ours. He keeps hitting me up for dough and trying to structure deals to borrow from her. Something is fishy there. It's time you stepped up, damn it."

"I thought the Hockneys were rich and powerful."

"I thought so too, and I cannot find an obvious problem," Wyatt admitted, stopping to take another sip from his glass. "But I know I am right."

"You just have a gut feeling? He's going to be your brother-in-law, Wyatt. You need to let it go."

"I heard you drunk texted her last night," Wyatt announced, his perfect teeth clear in a knowing smile.

"I am gonna kill your brother."

"My brother?"

"Yeah," Tyler said. "Didn't Ethan tell you?"

"No, why would he know? Missy got it from Regan."

"Regan told Missy?" Tyler perked up. "What else did she say?"

"Oh, so you aren't disinterested after all?" Wyatt punched his friend lightly on the shoulder. "Go get her, Tyler. The past is the past. We will catch these sons of bitches and put them behind bars. Your reputation may suffer slightly, but you were a kid then. You're an adult now. Act like one, tell Regan the truth and go get the woman you love."

"It was never about me. As long as I could continue to practice law, I didn't care. But my parents, Wyatt. I never wanted to embarrass them. Denny was always the perfect child, and I was the screw-up. I never wanted to taint Regan or any of you."

"Denny was never perfect, and you did pretty well for yourself," Wyatt argued. "You need to let go of the family drama. You need to let go of the guilt."

"You're right," Tyler whispered under his breath. "You're right," he said louder, polishing off his drink. Tyler sat in silence, letting the scotch and the words sink in. It was time to shit or get off the pot. He loved Regan, and he was running out of time. "So some dirt from my teenage years comes out. I'm nearly forty."

"Yeah, my friend. You need to be marrying my sister and starting a family."

"Well, alright then," Tyler said, slapping Wyatt on the back as he stood to leave the bar. "I'm going to go get started. Meanwhile, you can pay the bill." He heard Wyatt grumbling all the way to the door.

Chapter Twenty-Three

T houghts of Tyler had been haunting her since that text. A month had passed, and she was finally going to see him again. Regan's heart skipped a beat at the thought, just as it had every day this week, just thinking of being with her family for Thanksgiving, being in the same city as Tyler.

Brandon had been at his most charming since she had hinted they were through. So charming that she caved on him accompanying her home. She tried not to examine her motives for letting him come. She gave in to his constant demands and allowed him to join the festivities in Lake Forest.

Brandon was trying hard. She had to concede that point. He had grilled her on the family traditions, attire, and assured her he was ready for the annual pre-dinner football game. She was concerned that he was a bit competitive, but when she thought of her brothers, she stopped worrying. They would eat him alive.

Besides, she had no time to worry about how Brandon would fare when she was concerned about her own survival. Initially, it was texts every three or four days: "Sorry to bother you," they would begin.

Then Tyler would ask some question about an old negotiation or some Lyons Howe Real Estate problem. Nothing personal—at first.

But after half a dozen fundamental questions shuttled back and forth, the texts got a bit friendlier. Perhaps they began with something like "I hope you are happy in DC," or "Is Washington treating you well?" Nothing romantic, but they exuded a bit of warmth. She tried not to read too much into them. Until two weeks ago.

Suddenly, the discourse moved to a whole new level. After answering Tyler's questions, Regan might get a kiss emoji, or a "What would I do without you?" Sometimes Tyler would say he was thinking of her without a work question, just out of the blue. Then, this week, he texted several times to say he looked forward to seeing her or that he was counting the days.

Counting the days, that was what Regan had done, and now it was day zero, the day before Thanksgiving. She was pulling up to her parent's home in the limo, Brandon by her side. He was chattering away about meeting with her father and brother about the campaign—money again—while she was thinking about long, magical fingers and a pair of curvy lips.

Would Tyler stop by tonight or show up after Thanksgiving dinner tomorrow? He used to hang at the house all the time, but she didn't know anymore. She had been away most of the year, and she felt a bit like a stranger in her family home.

"It feels odd," she shared her feelings with Brandon as they turned into the driveway. "Like it's not home anymore."

"Of course," he responded, taking her hand in his. "DC is home now."

"But don't you think it's sad?" Regan searched Brandon's face for some sign of empathy. "Do you feel like this when you go back to Rhode Island?"

"What are you talking about?" he dismissed. "Of course it's not sad, Regan. It's progress. You are leaving your family to make your home and family with me." Regan bit her lips to silence further questions. She'd more than hinted the wedding was off. And how could Brandon be so unfeeling, so matter of fact, while she felt a little piece of her past dying? Couldn't he understand her longing for what was?

"Where is your empathy?" Regan wiped a stray tear from her cheek. "I am feeling nostalgic, Brandon."

"I'm sorry, Regan. I don't mean to sound callous, but while you are mourning, I am excited beyond belief at the idea of our future. Don't you get that?"

Regan turned to look out the window. They had no future, and he refused to acknowledge it. She needed to stop evaluating Brandon's behavior. It was what Regan did these days, examining what he said, what he did, and finding fault, pulling further and further from him, until she could barely recall the loving feelings she'd once had for him. The more she resisted him, the more persistent Brandon became. It was a vicious cycle.

Regan silently vowed to give him the benefit of the doubt these next few days. It was now or never. She had dragged this on too long when she wasn't serious about marriage. Lake Forest offered a respite from DC meetings, work, and politics. Regan could see Brandon completely relaxed, having fun within the bosom of her loving family. When she traveled with him to Rhode Island, Regan had enjoyed the time away from their demanding jobs. She had relaxed with him, laughing and joking. He was more romantic when they were away from DC. Before she pulled the plug irrevocably, she owed him this last chance.

Yes, it would be better here in Lake Forest. He would do well with the Howes, she was sure. He was polished and well informed. During meals, they would have interesting conversations about the direction the country was taking, and Brandon would charm her mother with his good manners and good looks. Once she saw him in this setting, Regan was confident she could make a fully informed decision. Their relationship would be on track again by the time they returned to Washington on Sunday or they would be finished.

Muddying the waters was the possibility — the certainty — of seeing Tyler. They were scheduled to meet Friday afternoon to discuss LHRE business. If it remained strictly business, Brandon might stand a chance. But Regan feared that she would tumble into Tyler's arms. She had thought of nothing else since the night of his last text, dreamt of nothing else, wanted nothing else.

She needed to stop wanting what she couldn't have and learn to appreciate what she did. Tyler had to let her in, or let her go. Her emotions were so raw and confusing. If only Tyler wanted her; if she could trust him to stay by her side, to share the secret that kept them apart. But if he could not. Regan was determined to forget him and build a life with or without Brandon.

Sure, she could do without both men. If she couldn't have Tyler, maybe there was someone out there who was better suited for her. That idea had crossed her mind more than once when Brandon's little quirks annoyed her. But she wanted a family, and Regan trusted Brandon to be a devoted husband and father. She couldn't minimize the importance of that. She had seen him interact with his family, saw how much he valued them, valued home. They shared common values and similar goals. Could it be enough?

Regan's thoughts returned to the present as the limo pulled to a stop and the door opened on well-oiled hinges. The driver reached in to help her from the car, then went to get their bags from the trunk. Her nieces toppled out the front door and into her arms, followed at a slower pace by Missy.

"You rascals," she scolded. "I told you to wait until Aunt Regan got inside. At least let her get out of the car." She made eye contact with Regan and started shaking her head as if to admit she never stood a chance.

"Did you bring presents, Auntie Ree?" the girls were asking, falling over each other to get to her first. Hugging them both, she gave them a non-committal answer and reminded them they had to behave, getting exactly the response she desired.

"But we were very, very nice," the eldest insisted while her sister whined, "I was super-duper good, Auntie Ree." Rubbing their heads and hugging them close, Regan had a nostalgic moment.

"Missing all this chaos?" Missy queried with a laugh. Reaching around a child clinging to Regan's leg, she hugged Regan before bestowing a perfunctory kiss on Brandon's cheek.

"Welcome to Chicago and our crazy Thanksgiving," she said to Brandon.

"Thanks, Melissa, it's great to be here. Reminds me of home."

"Please call me Missy. Everyone does." Scooting her daughters away, she walked arm in arm with Regan into the house.

Motioning behind her to make sure that Brandon was following, Regan allowed her sister and nieces to pull her along. Stephen, Missy's husband, stepped into the doorway as soon as they passed through it, greeting the politician with a hearty slap on the back.

The two men fell deep in to conversation, and Regan cringed when she heard Brandon discussing campaign financing. Did the man have a one-track mind? Discussions of money were grating on her nerves. But when she looked at Stephen, he looked engaged and interested. Taking a deep breath, Regan convinced herself she was oversensitive. She joined the crowd gathered in the family room.

"Girls," she leaned over her nieces sprawled on the floor in the center of the pandemonium, "can you turn off the cartoons for Auntie Ree-Ree? Pretty please?" she begged, hugging her mother warmly and kissing both of her powdery cheeks. Missy quickly took control, insisting her children turn off the cartoons and go upstairs to watch in the spare bedroom. They shot out of the room like lightning, quieting things down substantially.

"Now I can hear myself think," Regan announced.

"You have been away from the ruckus too long," her sister chided, handing Regan a perfectly mixed, perfectly chilled martini. "Here, this will help. Liquid courage," she told Brandon, handing him a glass.

"Don't need it, Missy," Brandon assured her. "But I'll happily take the drink." Missy laughed and winked at Regan.

Score one for Brandon. Regan smiled as she sipped the cold liquid. Spotting Tyler chatting with Wyatt across the room, she gulped her drink, setting off uncontrollable coughing. Brandon patted her back, repeatedly asking if Regan was alright until she told him not to fuss. Regan moved toward Wyatt, hoping Stephen would keep Brandon occupied a few more minutes.

The two men went silent as she approached, exchanging a knowing look between them. "Talking shop?" she asked, hugging her brother. She was not sure whether to embrace Tyler or not. Things felt awkward, especially with Brandon present. The seconds of hesitation passed and then it was too late, so she just nodded in his direction.

"We were," Wyatt admitted. He looked over at Tyler and Regan, watched a secretive look pass between them with disappointment. "But we can happily change the subject."

"No need on my account," Regan assured them. When did everyone become so secretive? It made her uncomfortable. Had so much changed in so little time?

"We don't mind. Tell us about your new life in Washington," Tyler suggested. He spoke politely, like a casual acquaintance. Regan felt ice settle in the region of her heart with an accompanying sadness that threatened to overpower her.

"No, you'll hear enough of that later. I guess I'll leave you to it."

If the men were surprised when she retreated so quickly, they didn't show it. They immediately fell back into their discussion, voices low, heads bent close together.

Regan returned to where Brandon was still discussing campaign costs with her brother-in-law. "Give the man a break," she told Brandon, sliding her arm through his and standing close. "You are here for Thanksgiving, not a fundraiser."

"But I can do both, Regan," Brandon objected, completely missing the point.

Regan took a more direct approach. "Not today, Brandon, please?"

She steered the conversation to art—in particular, Stephen's upcoming photography exhibit at the Howe Museum. Missy chimed in, her passion for the museum evident. "It will be amazing. You can see it while you are in town. It promises to be a boon for the museum, attracting a younger audience, and hopefully a new donor base."

"How come Missy gets to talk about money, but I don't?" Brandon pouted. Regan dropped his arm, turned on her heel and headed out of the room mumbling, "It's completely different, and you know it."

Frustrated with the lack of warmth she felt so far, Regan wandered down the hall to her father's inner sanctum, hoping to rekindle some family connection. She knocked lightly, entering before she got a reply. The sight of her father, seated behind his massive desk but dozing in his leather chair, made her smile sadly. His health and stamina were not what they used to be.

Closing the door softly, without disturbing him, she went to the kitchen. The staff was getting the giant turkey and trimmings ready, her mother overseeing all with the authority of a four-star general. Thanksgiving at the Howe's was a full-blown production. This year, including the children, there would be almost twenty people.

Today might be dangerous in the kitchen, but tomorrow the family would merely turn on the oven and enjoy the day.

"Can I help?" Regan asked, although she knew the answer.

"It's all under control, dear," her mother responded. "Sloane and Randall are coming tomorrow with the baby. We will need to dig the high chair out of the basement. Could Brandon help with that?"

"I can't wait to see them. Who else is coming?"

"Just Tyler's parents. It will be cozy—family—the way it should be. Brandon's family must be disappointed that you did not go to them for the holidays."

Regan could not squelch the emotions moving across her face. The concerned expression on Julia's face told Regan she was doing a lousy job of hiding her feelings. Her mother's words confirmed it.

"What is it, honey? Talk to me." Wrapping her arm around Regan's shoulder, Julia led her daughter away from the commotion, where cries were going up to start practicing for the annual football game.

Leading her into the dining room, the table already set with a Brussels lace cloth and napkins, fine china and the good silver and crystal, she pulled out one large chair and motioned to Regan to sit in another.

"We won't be disturbed in here," Julia began, "so tell me what's going on."

"I want children," Regan began, her chin wobbling as the tears fell down her cheeks. "I have always wanted this," she motioned around the room, hesitating in the direction of the family room.

"You're crying because you want children?" her mother asked, confused.

"I think I am making a terrible mistake, Mom. I don't love Brandon. But I do want a family, and I am not getting any younger. Brandon is perfect."

"He may or may not be perfect, Regan, but that is not the question you need to be asking yourself."

"I don't understand." Regan wiped her fisted hands over her cheeks to dry them, only to have more tears follow. "If he's perfect, I should just marry him, right?"

"The question, my love, should be 'is Brandon perfect for me?' My strong mother's intuition tells me that I know the answer to that one. And it's a resounding no."

"Not so resounding, Mom. I am so damn confused."

"Are you? These tears don't look like tears of happiness. What makes you hesitant about Brandon?"

"He'll be such a good father, Mom. I have seen him with his family. He is loving, devoted to his nieces and nephews and close to his parents."

"Family is important, Regan," Julia agreed.

"And he has been so supportive of my goals. He helped get me in front of Congress, helped me land this plum job. He is always talking about our Harvard educations, our accomplishments."

"And yet," Julia countered, "he asked you to give up your CEO job to move to Washington."

"Well, it wasn't like his job could move, Mom."

"True," Julia conceded, leaning back in her chair. "Not without giving up his political ambitions."

"Brandon is his political ambition, Mom. He wears his aspirations like a custom-made suit. His father was a senator; his grandfather was a senator. It is in his blood."

"His father also had to forfeit his position because of another woman, Regan. Brandon is a handsome man. He's been around the block. I am not suggesting that he would cheat on you, darling, just asking if you have discussed it with him."

"We haven't been quite that open," Regan admitted, picking up a fork and twirling it nervously until her mother took it from her hand and placed it back on the table. "He has given up all his other women, Mom. He understands that politics and sex are a lethal combination. He is always there for me."

"You don't make that sound like a good thing. Regan."

"I worry that he is there for political expediency. I project the right image, and it's good for his career to be married. And there is the money."

"This sounds like you are suspicious, honey, not like you are in love. You have a lot to consider here." Julia leaned over and took her daughter's fisted hands in her own, smoothing them out, turning her left hand over to admire the massive engagement ring resting on Regan's finger. She'd meant to leave it in D.C. "He certainly knows how to pick out a ring."

Regan laughed half-heartedly. "Brandon is certain, Mom. He knows he wants me. He wants to shout it from the rooftops. The sooner we get married, the better. He is that sure we are perfect together."

"Isn't there, perhaps, someone else you think might be perfect?"

"I know what you're thinking, but Tyler doesn't want me." Or did he? There were those texts. There was that magic weekend together. But he sent her away without a second thought. "He let me go, Mom,"

Regan blurted as the tears started fresh. "And you and Daddy don't like him. You haven't liked him for years."

"That's not true." When Regan opened her mouth to argue, Julia put a soft finger scented with expensive hand lotion over her daughter's lips. "You need to hear me out, Regan." Her mother leaned forward in the upholstered chair and removed a piece of imaginary lint from the table. Finally, she spoke up. "Your father convinced me when you were still in high school that Tyler was in some sort of trouble. Wyatt knew nothing. We grilled him, so we know that. But your father was certain, certain enough to convince me with no proof. We expressed our disapproval, but fortunately, Tyler went away for the summer and then left for college. The problem, as far as we were concerned, was solved. You two went your separate ways."

"But you said nothing to me, Mom. Why didn't you say something?"

"You were young, Regan; young enough to rebel. You know how teenagers can be. Tell them they can't have something, and they will do anything to get it."

Regan nodded her head in agreement. "I think that would have been me," she admitted. "I was sure I was in love." Regan flashed her mother a bright smile and wiped her tears for the last time. She forgot her self-pity in her absorption with her mother's tale.

"Was he in trouble?" Regan queried. "Why tell me this now?"

"Wyatt has been closeted with your father today, and he has been calling all week. Something is up, and it has to do with Tyler."

"What?" Regan asked in alarm. "What's happened to Tyler? Is he alright?" Julia squeezed Regan's hands in hers to offer reassurance.

"He's fine, honey. He'll play football like a rambunctious teen."

"But what's going on? Do you know?"

"All I know is that your father seems to want you at the helm of LHRE and back here where you belong."

"I have a job I adore, Mom, and a fiancé who makes his home and his life in Washington. How can I come home? Is there a problem with the business? I thought Tyler was handling everything."

"It's not the job, sweetie, it's you. Your father believes you belong with Tyler, not Brandon. Whatever obstacles stood in his way before are gone."

"But..."

"No buts, Regan. We will not be the excuse you require. You need to examine your true feelings and listen to your heart."

"I'm trying, Mom."

Rising from her seat, signaling that the conversation was over, Julia hugged her daughter. "I better check on things in the kitchen." She exited the room, leaving Regan no more confident of her mind—or her heart—than before. Regan had more questions. Everyone seemed to be in on the secret but her, and the sound of Tyler Winthrop's shouts from the yard, permeatin the background of her life.

Chapter Twenty-Four

"I'm not keeping you from any Christmas shopping, am I?" Tyler asked, resisting the urge to place his hand on the small of Regan's back to usher her into his office. The hug at the doorway had been awkward enough, although they had gotten along fine yesterday.

"Not at all. You know me. I hate the crowds. Black Friday or not, I'll wait or go online. What about you?"

"I'm fine, still recovering from your mom's dinner." Tyler patted his flat stomach with a satisfied grin. "It was amazing, as always."

"It was good, wasn't it?" Regan responded, carefully smoothing the skirt of her perfectly tailored suit before sitting at the small conference table near the window. "I think she used a new stuffing recipe."

"I think so, too. Good thing we play football before we eat. I am too stuffed to move after," Tyler confessed, pouring her coffee and adding a touch of cream, precisely the way she liked it. Did Brandon know how she took her coffee?

"What a terrible game." Regan stared out the window, sipping her coffee, chatting comfortably but avoiding making eye contact. Good, she was nervous. Maybe that meant she cared.

"Terrible? How can you say that? We won by three touchdowns," Tyler laughed.

"We won by three touchdowns and four injuries," she corrected. "That was the toughest game of touch football I can recall. Did you guys have to be so rough on Brandon?"

"He threw down the gauntlet with all his bragging. What else could we do but take him down a notch or two? You know how competitive Ivy, Randall and I can be."

"I do," Regan conceded, "but both he and Ethan are limping today. Missy has a huge bruise on her arm, and Stephen has a swollen hand. You guys were brutal."

"Maybe we were a tiny bit overzealous," Tyler admitted. Regan laughed and raised her head from her cup at last. Don't stare, he warned himself. She will know everything if she looks into your eyes.

"So where is your senator today? Was he okay with sharing with you?"

Regan blushed at Tyler's question, a rosy pink stealing across her perfect complexion. So she was feeling it too. There had been an undeniable pull between them all day yesterday, although they were never alone. She finished his sentences; he laughed at her jokes before she got to the punch lines. They were simpatico' just as they had been when they were a couple, and it felt natural.

"He's hanging out with Charlotte. She's showing him the sights and catching up. They haven't talked much since she and Alex visited."

"That was ages ago."

"Exactly, so this was ideal. Char wanted them to have time together, and we needed time, too." There was that blush again. "Maybe we should get down to business."

"We are waiting for your brother. He should have been here by now."

"Oh." Was that disappointment in her voice? "Ethan is joining us? I hadn't realized, although it makes perfect sense."

"Not Ethan, Ree. Wyatt is joining us. I asked him to help out today."

"Wyatt?" Her confusion was obvious. "What does Wyatt have to do—"

"Sorry I am late," Wyatt announced, dropping his heavy coat on the couch then throwing himself onto the leather cushions with a sigh of relief. "Traffic was a bitch."

Donna entered the office on soundless ballet slippers, giving Wyatt a thorough once over, taking his coat, and hanging it in the coat closet. She offered him coffee and did her cleavage-exposing pour, to Tyler's amusement. All the time, Regan looked to the two men for explanations that didn't come.

"Mom outdid herself, didn't she?" Wyatt began, as he made himself comfortable. He accepted the coffee with a dazzling smile that sent Donna into a tailspin, then lounged back with it cradled in his hands, crossing one long leg over the other. "I thought that meal was her best."

"Stop with the small talk," Regan commanded as the door closed behind the assistant. Turning a steely gaze on her brother, she asked, "What the hell are you doing here?" Looking back at Tyler, she added, "What is going on?"

Tyler fidgeted with the papers in front of him, looking at Wyatt to take the lead. His friend indicated this was all on him. There would be no help from Wyatt's corner. Tyler took a deep gulp of air and started speaking. "Well, Ree. There is something we figured you should know, but it's a long story..."

"A really long story," Wyatt added with a broad grin. "A twenty-year story."

"You want to tell it?" Tyler shot at his friend. Wyatt shook his head. "Then shut the fuck up and let me."

"What is going on with you two? Seriously, do I need to be here while you two duke it out?" Regan made as if to rise from her chair.

"Okay, I apologize." Tyler lowered his voice. "But this is not easy for me, Ree, so just sit down and listen."

"I'm all ears," the blonde muttered under her breath. Still, she settled back in the chair and pinned her attention on Tyler.

"This all starts right before I graduated from high school," Tyler began. "Remember how I said I wanted us to be together, then I disappeared for the summer, then we decided to break up?"

"You decided," Regan corrected in a hurt voice. "As if I could forget."

"I didn't go to Europe that summer," Tyler continued, eyes focused in the distance as if he saw it all again reflected in the office window. "I wish I had been touring Europe, but I was in juvie, Regan. I was in jail."

"Tyler, that is not funny," Regan blurted, looking to her brother to correct his friend. "You're not joking," she added in a stunned voice after seeing the looks on the two men's faces.

"I wish I were. I spent the summer from hell hanging out with a highly unsavory crowd that got caught joyriding with me in a stolen car."

"But why would you steal a car? You could have had any car you wanted. Besides, you had the Harley. You loved that Harley."

Regan's voice rose with each question, looking at Tyler as if he had sprouted a second head. "This makes no sense."

"I was seventeen, Ree. It didn't have to make sense. I met a bunch of guys when I was riding. We smoked a little weed, we stole a few cars, just for fun."

"Yeah, you thought it was just for fun," Wyatt interjected. "May I remind you that those guys were selling the cars, not abandoning them as they promised?"

"OK," Tyler continued. "I was young and stupid. I thought we were driving around and then ditching the cars somewhere they could easily be found. It turns out that these guys were hardcore thieves, Ree. Several went to prison; some went to juvie with me."

"But how could I not know this all these years? How could you keep this from me? Why tell me now? Why does it even matter anymore?"

"My dad covered it up then. He was ashamed of me. He made up the Europe story, and I went off to Cornell thinking I had paid my dues. Ha, what a laugh that is."

"You did pay your dues, man," Wyatt spoke up. "That should have been the end of it if your father hadn't been such an asshole."

"Watch it, Wyatt. You're speaking about my father. He did what he thought would benefit me." Tyler rose to pace the room, coming to stand behind Regan before he continued. He didn't want to see the pity on her face when he continued. "Maybe Wyatt is right. My dad may have been more concerned with the family name than with my safety. Maybe he was a complete asshole, dying of shame as if this was about him. He went on and on about the disgrace that had befallen the family, comparing my downfall with perfect Denny and his achievements. He made me feel like complete shit and made me promise never to let anyone know."

Regan swiveled in her chair to see Tyler's face. "So I ask again, why are you telling me now?"

"You know how secrets come back to haunt you?" Wyatt questioned cryptically.

"That's it exactly," Tyler continued, resuming his seat, anxious now to look Regan in the eye. He didn't see pity, just interest. Telling her this much had already lifted a weight off his shoulders. The words spilled from him easily. "When the news never came out about me, the guys figured I had covered it up, and they began blackmailing me to keep my secrets."

Regan nodded her head to keep going. Tyler leaned toward her in response and continued his story. "It started as soon as I got to college. They threatened to hurt people I loved, including you, Regan. So I broke up with you, believing they would think you no longer mattered to me, and I paid."

"You knew about this?" Regan interrogated her brother. "You knew and never said a word to me?"

"He didn't know, Regan," Tyler admitted. "I told no one."

Wyatt raised his hands as if to protect his hands from a punch. "I found out last month, so back off, tiger."

"You didn't even tell the boys?" Regan turned back to Tyler, astonished. "No one?"

"No one. I put my head down, finished school, my MBA and law school, and made those quarterly payments like clockwork. Until they got too big..."

"And too dangerous." Wyatt completed the sentence.

"Which is where you come in, I'm afraid." Tyler watched the color drain from Regan's face and with it his hopes for their future together. She was appalled by what he had done and where it had led. "The gang is big now, and highly sophisticated. They don't want a few grand now and then, and they have the goods on me because of where the money I paid went. They are hackers who want millions. And they want it from LHRE."

Regan sat so silently and stoically that Tyler was sure she had not heard what he said. "They want it from LHRE," he repeated quietly.

"I heard you, Tyler. I am just processing the fact that we are talking about destroying everything my family and I built to cover up a stupid mistake you made when you were seventeen. Why is this even up for discussion? Twenty years ago you pulled a teenage prank, went to juvie and did your penance. So what? Let people talk. Who the hell cares?"

"It's not that simple, Regan," Wyatt spoke from the couch where he was no longer lounging. In fact, he looked like a cat ready to spring. "Now it's pay or die, Ree."

"And I would die, sweetheart, if I believed it would protect you. But it won't. They have targeted you, Regan. That's why I am telling you now."

Chapter
Twenty-Five

Regan suspected she was being tailed immediately upon her return to Washington. It took less than a day to notice the shadow and another day to eliminate congressional assignees as possible tails. That left either the bad guys or a protection detail. They didn't look threatening to her, so she assumed Tyler had hired them. Of course, what did she know?

She had been numb since her meeting with Tyler. And scared. For herself, sure, but especially for Tyler. What he was doing was dangerous. If he got caught, these people would kill him. How on earth could this have happened to a kid from Lake Forest, born with a silver spoon in his mouth?

Focusing on work as much as possible, and avoiding Brandon, for his good as much as hers, she dug into her job and stayed busy. The weeks passed until she gratefully acknowledged the approaching Christmas holiday. The DC party circuit had been torturous. She wondered about every strange face. Were they the bad guys? Were they friend or foe? Add to that, constant pressure from Brandon to announce their engagement and set a date, and Regan's nerves were frayed to breaking.

Finally, the recess forced Brandon to return to Rhode Island for meetings with constituents and town halls that he could not avoid.

She was thankful for the reprieve. The Hockneys had welcomed her for a weekend visit early in December and pressured her to return for the Christmas holidays, but a significant fundraiser in Chicago and the excuse of some vital LHRE work provided ample reason to decline. Which brought her to this December day; Regan, along with at least one of her protection detail, was on her way back to snowy Chicago.

Unable to tamp down her excitement about being home, Regan longed to be back in her apartment, and her calendar was filling with social activity, a girls' night out, the Children's Hospital event, and, of course, Christmas with her family.

The butterflies in her stomach had nothing to do with seeing Tyler, she assured herself again. That boat had sailed. He had told her his sad tale, pulled her into the periphery of the proposed solution, and promised to keep her safe.

Safe. Damn it. While that was reassuring, it was not the promise Regan wanted to hear from Tyler. Did she want him to profess love? Regan understood he couldn't while in the middle of this mess, but was that even what she wanted? Regan, the woman who ran a major government agency and a multi-billion-dollar business, could not get a clear reading on her own life. What kind of intelligent woman got herself engaged to one man while still longing for another? Who in their right mind traded a handsome, powerful US Senator who loved her and wanted to marry her for a man who could end up in jail, or worse?

But of course, that was the issue, Regan reminded herself for the thousandth time. What was her right mind? She was away from Brandon, and within Tyler's radius for the next nine days. She vowed to decide during that time.

Wrapping her coat tightly around her before she even exited the jet way, Regan moved quickly through O'Hare despite the Christmas crowds clogging the walkways. She spotted her limo driver standing at the bottom of the escalator, her name in block letters on his sign. The driver took her bag from her shoulder and walked with her to the baggage carousel to await its matching pieces.

As they walked, Regan scanned the crowd looking for anyone suspicious, quickly finding the goon who followed her everywhere. Definitely protection, although with his jacket pulled up around his ears, his earpiece was less noticeable. She watched as he made eye contact with two other men and a woman. Four people to protect her. Things must be speeding up. Her pulse did too.

In Washington, it was easier for Regan to forget the threats to her safety. Here in Chicago, surrounded by strange faces moving past her quickly, it was easier to remember. She took a look at her limo driver through new eyes. Was he one of them? How could she be sure?

She pointed out both pieces of luggage coming toward them on the carousel, their red 'priority' tags fluttering. Ah, the perks of flying first class, she thought as her phone chirped.

"Chckd out drivr," the text from Wyatt informed her. "Go str8 to offc. Ty will brief u then get u home." Regan felt a vice release from her heart at the words. She had been more concerned about the driver than she realized. One less thing to fret about. Ty was waiting. Regan's excitement was palpable.

Her bags loaded on the cart, Regan and her entourage exited the airport. She was impatiently inching into the city through holiday traffic, happily ensconced in the warm comfort of the limo, wondering how her security detail knew where to go when her phone rang.

"Everything ok?" Tyler's voice sent shivers up her spine. It had been only a week since they last spoke, but she never got enough of his honeyed tones and that way he had of making even a business discussion sound sexy.

"A-okay," Regan replied, laughing at her detective-movie lingo.

"I am waiting for you with bated breath," Tyler told her, his voice dripping sex appeal and stopping her heart.

"Is anything wrong?" Regan was delighted when her voice sounded reasonable to her ears. She felt breathless.

"Only that you aren't here." She felt her heart start beating again in double time. "I'm anxious to see you with my own eyes, safe and sound."

So it was just about her safety. Again. That was all they ever discussed. Tyler wouldn't share what they were doing to protect her. Tyler wouldn't see her alone while she was in town unless it was business. God forbid anyone might think Regan mattered to him. Did she matter?

"I want to get to my apartment at a reasonable hour, Ty. I have a girls' night, and I want to change before I go out."

"You'll have plenty of time, Ree. But I need to know where you ladies are going. You understand."

"But I don't know where. Sloane made reservations."

"No problem," Ty reassured her. "I'll check with Randall and see you shortly."

He disconnected without a goodbye. All business. Not what Regan had hoped. Stop it, Regan Howe, you are an engaged woman. Stop wishing for what you will never have and learn to love Brandon. He's terrific, and he wants to marry you. Regan repeated those words in time to the tires turning on the roadway, watching the skyline grow larger, swelling her heart with pride. She loved this city.

Tyler was standing on the sidewalk without his coat, the wind buffeting his dark hair. He stepped forward to open her door. When he helped her exit the car, she felt the comfort from his touch spread through her whole body. His face was more etched with concern than she remembered, but his smile was warm and welcoming. He gave her a perfunctory kiss on the cheek and ushered her into the building as he took her bags from the driver.

Once the elevator doors closed behind them, Tyler was a different man. He took Regan's face in his chilled hands and demanded her kiss. He leaned into her, moving his mouth over hers, snaking his tongue between her teeth, drawing the breath from her body. She couldn't help but respond to his urgency, his passion. She felt her body urgently pressing against his, her mouth open to his as a small moan of pleasure escaped from her.

He pulled back as the doors opened, bending to retrieve her bags and following her down the corridor as everyone stopped their work to welcome her back. Walking down the hallway, greeting everyone, Regan wondered if anyone else could see what she was feeling. It had happened so fast. Tyler had been a man possessed. If her heart wasn't pounding, and she didn't feel the moist readiness between her legs, Regan might convince herself that she had imagined the whole episode.

The man was a chameleon, suddenly professional and aloof. What the hell was she supposed to think? She was moving past her former assistant when Donna cornered her. The women caught up quickly while Donna reassured her that she had prepared the apartment for Regan's arrival.

"That's great," Regan said, paying attention with half her mind, while admiring Tyler's retreating form with the other half. "It will be so much nicer staying in my place." She listened and nodded at the appropriate times as Donna told her when the cleaning staff would arrive, what groceries were in the kitchen, the temperature at which she had set the thermostat until Regan wanted to scream with frustration.

"I'm sure it is all perfect. Thank you for handling this for me." Regan's tone was final and dismissive. The conversation was over.

At last, Regan followed Tyler into his office and shut the door behind her. He was staring into her face, waiting for her reaction, she supposed. She stood with the safety of his massive desk between them.

Just what was her reaction? She had kissed him back. She couldn't deny that, and he wouldn't buy it if she tried. But she should scold him, tell him she was engaged, all the clichés about overstepping his bounds. Regan stood there, examining her feelings, staring at his handsome face, doing nothing.

"Cat got your tongue?" Tyler prompted, those soft lips tilting up into a smug smile. It was the catalyst Regan needed.

"What did you think you were doing back there? I do not understand what has gotten into you all of a sudden. I am an engaged woman, Tyler." They both heard the words coming from her mouth, while Regan hoped Tyler couldn't recognize how much they lacked conviction.

He moved from behind the desk, prowling toward her like a lion with its prey in sight. He had undoubtedly heard her vacillate. Damn.

"Are you Regan? You haven't set a wedding date. What are you holding out for?" He was standing too close. Regan took a step back, only to find the door behind her. Tyler lifted his hands to either side of her head, caging her. "I'm fighting back, Ree. I see an end in sight to everything that kept us apart, and now I want you where you belong. With me."

Regan's temperature steadily climbed as she felt his warm breath on her face. He smelled of coffee. *If I fixate on the coffee...* Regan tried to think about dark roast as his head bent closer, but her traitorous mind could only think of those lips claiming hers. And then they did, and she thought of nothing else. She simply responded.

Regan's arms circled Tyler's waist, pulling him tight against her. She felt the muscular weight of him pinning her against the door as his mouth descended to touch her lips gently, begging permission for more. Her response, her mouth pressed to his, her tongue flicking along his bottom lip, signaled her okay to take more, and he did.

Tyler leaned into her until his elbows rested against the door and his lips molded to hers. He sucked her lips, then licked the edge of her teeth and finally invaded the honeyed warmth of her mouth, swallowing the sigh of pleasure that escaped her as she sank into the kiss. It had been six long months since he had kissed her like this and she was savoring every sensation, every touch.

When she was dizzy with longing, her body clinging to Tyler's like a lifeline, he raised his head. "That's more like it," he whispered, his voice husky with desire. "But we have business to discuss. You have a girls' night to get to, and I plan to do this in a better place. And all night."

His words roused Regan from her stupor like a face full of ice water. She couldn't have Tyler thinking they would pick up where they left off, not while she was engaged to Brandon.

"Ty, you can't expect us to be together while I am here."

Regan scooted out from under Tyler's embrace and moved across the room to look out the windows. "I love this view," she mumbled under her breath, ignoring her pounding heart and confused mind. "I love this city," she said as she turned around to face Tyler. "But I live in DC, where I am engaged to another man, Tyler. That hasn't changed."

"Not yet, Ree, but it will. I promise you. It will."

"Don't make promises about things you can't control, Tyler. We have a long way to go to rebuild the trust between us, for starters."

"But I have told you everything." Tyler strode across the room, grabbing Regan's elbows and turning her so she couldn't help but make eye contact. "I have bared my soul to you, Ree. Don't you understand why I did what I did all those years ago?"

"I understand you were young and stupid, Tyler. And you stayed stupid, paying blackmail fees all those years. But, still, you aren't sharing everything."

"That's not true," Tyler challenged.

"Goons, you put a goon squad on me night and day and never thought to mention it?"

"I told you I would protect you, remember?"

"You're thinking defies logic sometimes, but there is so much more. Look at our history. Don't you understand how much you pushed me away? How you broke trust with me over and over again? I have another life now. So do you. We don't magically find our way back to each other."

A knock on the door caused the couple to jump apart. The guilt must have been evident on Regan's face from Donna's response. "I'm so sorry to interrupt," the assistant said, blushing. "You have a call on line one, Tyler, and they are very insistent on speaking with you."

A look of understanding flashed between the couple. Regan retreated to the sofa, curious about this call and questioning her behavior, how quickly she had fallen into Tyler's arms. Tyler moved with purpose toward the desk phone. "They have started calling here instead of my cell," he explained to Regan. "More brazen. More invasive. When the FBI went to tap the phones, they found them tapped already. These guys are ruthless."

Regan nodded her head in understanding, but she didn't understand at all. She could sense the fury coiled in Tyler's body, but his voice was calm as he answered.

"Tyler Winthrop." He hesitated, listening intently, then punched the button to put it on speaker. "... protection detail won't help, Tyler. You should save your money, call them off. Just get this done and the girl will be fine."

"The girl better be fine, or all bets are off," Tyler responded in a tight, clipped voice.

"Are you on speaker?" The accented voice on the other end of the call rose in alarm. "Who's listening, Tyler? Oh, it's her, isn't it?" The voice turned oily and smooth. Regan felt a shiver of disgust.

"Hello, Ms. Howe. Lovely to make your acquaintance."

Tyler shook his head, warning Regan to say nothing. She wasn't sure she could have found her voice, anyway.

"We are so looking forward to getting to know you better, dear. I am excited about our upcoming time together. My boss and I find you very lovely. We are already fighting over you."

The menacing voice had precisely the effect it wanted. Tyler's fist slammed into the desk, and his voice rose in anger. "Keep your fucking hands off of her, you prick. I am working on your solution. I still have a month. Leave Regan alone."

"One month, Tyler, and the time will fly. Can't wait to meet you, Regan." The phone clicked, the sound loud in the quiet office. Regan felt the sweat pooled in her armpits and between her breasts. How had Tyler endured this for so long? Just a disembodied voice brought images of a serpent squeezing the breath from her. Regan began to sob

"Oh honey, don't." Tyler rushed to the sofa, gathering Regan in his arms and rubbing her back. "It will be fine, I promise," he repeated in a soothing voice until she quieted in his arms and pulled back.

"I'm sorry," she said in a shaky voice.

"Why are you sorry? This mess is my fault," Tyler rebutted.

"I just wasn't prepared for the reality, I guess. That man sounded so repulsive."

"He is repulsive, and so are his cronies, but next month, they will be deported and go to Siberia or go to jail. Either way, they can rot in prison until they trade it for hell."

"Promise?" Regan sounded like a little girl and resolved to buck up. "You better make good on that promise," she said in a stronger voice.

"I will," Tyler replied with complete conviction. "With the help of you, your brother, my father, the FBI and Jonathan Chen, we will pull this thing off. In the meantime, you keep the goon squad." His smile was reassuring and devastating to Regan's equilibrium. How could she feel lust under these circumstances?

"Agreed." She returned his smile, determining to be as brave as Tyler. "Now, let's handle those contracts so I can go have my girls' night."

"Agreed," Tyler replied, turning all business in a split second. Who was this man with so many moods and faces? Did she truly love him? She knew she lusted for him, but did she trust him? She needed to decide before she turned her whole world upside down.

Chapter Twenty-Six

The noise level at Maple & Ash was typical of a Chicago hot spot on a Friday night, but it disappointed Regan that she needed to shout. She wanted to connect with these women, her posse, as she liked to call them because they always had her back.

"Do you think we could finish this round and find someplace quieter?" she ventured.

"I love that idea," Missy stated as Keeli bobbed her head in agreement. "What do you say, ladies?" Regan queried the remaining women.

Confronted by Missy's hard stare, Charlotte and Sloane conferred before Sloane answered. "I thought we were going to eat here."

Charlotte concurred, scanning the room. "But we can go if you prefer, but we need to wait for Clarice and Joanne to show before we move on."

"Did I hear my name?" Clarice strode across the bar, her dress short and tight over large breasts and a rounded behind. Her sister Joanne followed three steps back, slim-built and dressed like a conservative businesswoman.

After they exchanged hugs all around, they agreed to one more round before dinner elsewhere. Sipping exotic cocktails, they caught up on the latest news. Sloane showed off pictures of her baby Sutton. Clarice passed her phone around the table to show photos of her most recent success. It was a giant sculpture installation filling the lobby of a new Lyons Howe office complex, receiving high fives and congratulations from all.

"Was this your doing, Regan?" Sloane couldn't help but ask. "I see your hand in all this."

"Actually," Missy corrected, "You see my hand. Stephen and I wanted to do an exhibit of Clarice's work at the Howe Museum. We figured this would build some buzz for it."

"Smart move," Sloane conceded. "It's something I might have done."

"Nothing like turning this into a compliment for you," Charlotte teased, making the women laugh. Sloane just held her head higher.

"Well, I'm the best," she defended.

"We all know it, Sloane," Keeli acknowledged, always the peacekeeper. "That is why I hired you."

The women had come a long way from their days fighting over the same man. Now that Sloane was happily married to Randall and working as the president of Keeli's jewelry business, she acknowledged she didn't have to prove anything to this group. "Sorry, ladies, a force of habit. I always feel under attack."

"Not here," Joanne piped up in her soft voice, "you are among friends tonight."

"Speaking of," Regan finally interjected, "I don't get enough time with you guys. Can we go someplace we can hear each other?"

"Why don't I just get us a suite at the Peninsula and we can order in?" Sloane suggested.

"I love that idea," "That's brilliant," and "I'm in" chorused around the table.

"But I wore this dress for our big night out," Clarice argued.

"Then make the most of it, honey, cause we are leaving in ten," Missy commanded.

"Yes, ma'am." Clarice downed her Lemon Drop in two gulps. "If you'll excuse me, I need to go grab some male attention now so I can brag about it to my husband later tonight." She sashayed to the ladies' room, her friends laughing as she went.

Regan felt as if she had come home. Watching Clarice work the room while listening to Sloane trying to cover her insecurities, Charlotte having her back and Keeli keeping the peace, it was just like old times. She could never replicate her Chicago friendships in Washington, DC. Here, they knew each other; they had a history together, good and evil.

Still, they supported each other, rescued each other from tough situations and themselves. Regan needed that kind of straight talk from the people who loved her unconditionally. She wanted their input to sort out her feelings. The quiet of the Peninsula Suite would be perfect.

"We could go to my place if you prefer," Charlotte offered. "Alex is with his dad in California this week. We would have the place to ourselves."

"Nah. Let's go trash a hotel room instead," Missy suggested, garnering surprised looks from her friends.

"As if you have ever trashed a place in your life, Melissa Howe."

"Ah, Ree," Missy complained, "Let me live the fantasy. Please?"

Sloane reserved the room, Keeli ordered steaks for all and Clarice called catering to deliver enough liquor to put them under the table.

No one considered the short notice for such demands, knowing the luxury hotel would fulfill their every wish.

"Do you realize how spoiled you all are?" Joanne blurted out finally, unable to contain herself. "We'll just get a suite, and cater appetizers, and order dinner from a restaurant where you have to wait months to get a reservation and order enough alcohol for a large bachelor party," she accused in a judgmental voice ticking each point off on her fingers.

The women stopped what they were doing and looked at Joanne, abashed by her scolding. There was silence at the table for a full ten seconds before Keeli responded.

"Hell yeah! We are rich, powerful women and we rule. Regan is the CEO of a massive conglomerate, and she's marrying a US Senator. Doesn't get much more powerful than that." Keeli pointed at her sister-in-law with pride, then held up Regan's left hand so the women could admire her giant engagement ring.

The women never tired of admiring the rock on Regan's finger. Regan allowed the oohs and ah's to swirl around her, the noise closing in like a thick fog as her brain shut down. She couldn't think with all this attention. She felt the tears falling before she was conscious she was crying.

"The hazard of being among your genuine friends," she offered with a watery smile. "You can let your emotions go."

The women fell upon their friend with concern and grabbed their coats to leave the bar. "Let's get out of here before she loses it completely," Missy warned. "I think it's going to be a gusher."

Walking the distance to the Peninsula in their impractical heels, the women happily fell upon the couches and kicked off their shoes immediately upon entering the suite. The bar was set up, the ice hardly melted. Flatbreads, sushi and other bar-bite appetizers covered the coffee table, delicious aromas rising from the platters. The seven women dove at the food like linebackers after a hard practice. When the dishes were empty, and Missy was whining about how long it was taking to get their steaks, Keeli turned to Regan at last.

"OK, Miss watering pot," she said, gently. "Spill."

The women quieted and settled with their drinks to get comfortable.

"It's Tyler, right?" Missy prompted when Regan sat silently. "I've been expecting this."

"Of course you have," Regan finally spoke up. "You set this whole thing in motion, knowing full well that I still loved him."

"Actually, I wasn't sure about you. I just knew Tyler still loved you," Missy corrected, earning a surprised look from her older sister.

"But Brandon," Sloane stated. "That man is such a catch. And he loves you, too. For god's sake, Ree, Brandon is the one that asked you to marry him. Tyler has been dragging his feet for an eternity."

"She's right," Charlotte agreed. "Why give up a terrific man you know wants you for one that may or may not want you?"

"Oh, he wants me," Regan corrected. "He has always wanted me."

"Wait," Clarice piped up from the far corner of the sofa, where she sprawled with her legs draped over her sister's thighs. "Are we talking want as in sex or want as in marriage and babies? Cause, girl, those are two different things entirely."

"She has a point there, Ree," Sloane piped up. "Are you thinking that a confirmed bachelor like Tyler is going to walk down the aisle? I don't see that happening."

Regan nodded and cried harder, prompting Clarice to pour her another drink, while Keeli and Joanne set up the dinner that arrived. Regan was grateful for the chance to calm down. When she finally had a plate of sirloin in her lap, a cloth napkin draped to protect her Proenza Schouler dress, she took a deep breath and started talking.

"I need you guys to help me through this," she confided. "Look at me. I am a grown woman, a woman who made tough decisions at LHRE and now at a critical federal agency day in and day out. I cannot decide between these two men.

"Tyler has good reasons for dragging his feet," she continued. When the women bombarded her with questions, she put her hand up and shook her head. "They are his reasons, and I am not at liberty to share them. If he wants you to know, you will, but you won't hear it from m e."

"What if I bribe you?" Clarice teased, lightening the mood for a moment.

"Nice try." Regan smiled, took a few bites of her food, and continued. "Ooh, this is delicious. Good choice, ladies. Anyway, here's the thing. I have always loved Tyler, but I stopped trusting him when he broke my heart. Trust is critical for me."

Charlotte had the good grace to blush as she said, "It should be. It's critical to any relationship."

"Well, now Ty is asking me to trust him and doing everything he can to earn that trust."

"Like what?" Sloane challenged.

"Don't be bitchy, Sloane," Keeli tossed out.

"Not bitchy, I swear," Sloane corrected. "Believe me, I know when I am bitchy. I am just asking. What has he done to undo years of hot and cold, and decades of lies? It's not an effortless task."

"I have been working side by side with him for months, and I would trust him with my life," Charlotte spoke with passion.

"He has been coming clean about so much," Regan told her friends. "Explaining the unexplainable and taking me into his confidence. I have to admit he had some good reasons for his behavior and his secrecy."

"You know you are just making us want to pump you for informa-tion." Sloane pinned Regan with a hard look, then her face softened, and she laughed. "We realize you can't say anything else. Although, Ree, you know we could keep any secret you told us."

"I just can't," Regan told them again. "Trust me on this one."

"OK," Missy grew impatient with the digressions, "can we get back on track? You have learned to trust Tyler, who you have loved forever. And he has told you he loves you, right?"

"That doesn't justify casting Brandon aside," Charlotte piped up. "I have known Brandon my whole life. He will be in the White House someday, Regan, and he will need a woman like you by his side. He's handsome and brilliant."

"Weren't you just defending Tyler two minutes ago?" Clarice asked. "I think you have to take sides here, Char, or you are no help to Regan. For me, Ree, go to the White House. It's a no-brainer."

"But that's just it. I have this niggling doubt about Brandon. He is perfect, but maybe not perfect for me. I feel no warmth from him, just need. He needs me to move, and he needs me to accompany him to these political events. He needs my family to support his campaign..."

"What?" Missy asked.

"Didn't Wyatt say anything to you, Missy? It's all he talked about after Thanksgiving weekend," Keeli interjected. "Brandon kept cor-nering him about funding the campaign. It was as if he was desperate for the cash."

"Exactly," Regan added. "He's been the same way about Howe money going into purchasing 'the perfect house for a senator' in Georgetown."

"But that makes no sense," Charlotte corrected. "The Hockney family is the richest family in Rhode Island. Hell, they are the mod-ern-day Kennedys."

"Are you sure?" Joanne asked in her soft voice. The women quieted to hear the youngest of the women. Alex's assistant was reserved. Her friends understood that she only spoke when she had something significant to add. "Weren't they heavily invested in that New England furniture venture that went under last year? I believe the profile on the business in *The Boston Globe* last year stated that they were the most prominent investors."

"Why were you reading *The Boston Globe*?" Clarice attacked. "Oh, never mind, Alex was investing, right?"

"Alex was looking at property in Boston for the bakery expansion," Charlotte explained. "He has been thick as thieves with Don and Jake about the new operations."

"Is it possible they lost their fortune?" Regan asked in a dazed voice. "Is he just after my money?" Hurt laced her words. She stopped eating, placing her plate on the coffee table. The food she had enjoyed moments earlier now repulsed her. Regan began pacing the room, hugging an expensive silk throw pillow against her chest. "He's just another man after my money?"

"Stop that Regan," Sloane spoke up. "I am sure he adores you. How could he not?"

"That's so sweet, Sloane." Regan smiled weakly at her friend. "That means a lot coming from you."

"Yeah, I know you way better than Sloane does. I certainly think he could be after your money," Missy teased. The women laughed, breaking the tension. Regan, realizing she was holding the pillow, hurled it at her sister, only to miss, knocking the plates from the coffee table to the rug below.

"OMG! I thought we were joking about trashing the room," Keeli laughed.

"I will not jail for you," Clarice told Regan, holding her sides as she laughed at the chaos the small pillow had created.

"And I am certainly not cleaning up after you," Sloane added, earning her a throw pillow in her face from Keeli.

"Damn, girl, where did you learn to throw like that?" Clarice asked.

"Brothers," was Keeli's laughing reply.

While the laughing and joking continued, Regan bent to pick up broken plates and, taking a towel from the bathroom, scooped up the mess on the floor.

"Feel better now?" Missy asked her sister.

"I do, actually," Regan confessed. "Still completely confused, but better."

"I love both men, Ree," Charlotte announced to the room. "I may be the only one who hasn't already taken sides. Here is what I suggest. First, you need to discover the financial situation for the Hockney family. If, in fact, they have lost their fortune, then you need to confront Brandon. You cannot marry him, thinking he is just using you."

"Maybe just put the marriage on hold?" Sloane proposed.

"How much more can she drag her feet?" Joanne asked. "What does your heart say, Regan?"

"Yeah, and how the hell is the sex?" Clarice asked, sending the women into peals of laughter as a blush climbed Regan's cheeks.

"Fantastic," she admitted.

"With which one? Or is it both?" Clarice leaned forward, pumping her friend for information.

"The sex is good with both, if you must know," she admitted, "but it has that forbidden quality with Tyler that makes it so damn hot."

"Or maybe it is just hotter, period." Sloane offered.

"You, my friend, are trouble," Regan pointed to Sloane as she spoke.

"Always was. Never pretended to be anything else."

"Isn't that the truth," Keeli confirmed. "You tried to ruin my life without a second thought," she reminded her friend, but without malice.

"And you ruined a perfectly gorgeous Elie Saab gown," Sloane shot back.

"Hey, that was an accident, and you know it," Keeli stood to emphasize her words, placing her hands on her hips in a defiant stance.

"And it was years ago, and it is water under the bridge," Missy reminded the ladies who were spoiling for a fight. "You are friends now, remember?"

"I remember," Keeli admitted, shamefaced. "Hug and forgive me, Sloane?"

"Oh, please, don't go all mushy on me," Sloane told Keeli, but she hugged her friend tightly.

"OK, back to Regan's problems," Joanne suggested. "The admin in me can't help it," she announced, holding up a small notepad she had scribbled all over. "I did a pro/con list."

"You're joking," Clarice asked, grabbing the paper from her sister's raised hand. "She's not joking. Tyler: live in Chicago, shared a love of real estate, history, passionate sex. Those are the pros. Cons: broke your heart, trust issues."

"What did she write for Brandon?" Charlotte asked.

"Pros: proposed marriage, a great job in DC, possible White House run, smart," she read.

"Wait a second. Tyler is just as smart," Missy and Regan corrected in tandem.

"OK, strike smart, continuing with pros then, great sex, and that rock on your finger. Cons: takes you away from Chicago, possibly using you for your money."

"Both lists are missing the important stuff, Ree," Keeli spoke up. "Nothing personal, Jo," she apologized to her friend.

"What's missing? I think the White House might override everything else," Clarice reminded Regan again.

"Seriously, where is the personal stuff? Which one makes you laugh? Which man supports your goals and dreams? Whose shoulder can you lean on? Who treats you as a partner? Is one more demanding than the other? Is one more helpful? Which one can you see yourself beside when you grow old?"

"Oh, Keeli, you are wise beyond your years," Joanne admitted. "Without those, my list is worthless."

"So, Ree?" Missy asked. The room was silent, all eyes on Regan.

Regan stood still, looking at her friends without seeing them, allowing the questions to run through her brain as the answers came back at her repeatedly—Tyler, Tyler, and Tyler.

"I've been an idiot," she admitted at last to her friends.

"Tyler," Missy stated. "It's always been Tyler."

"Always," Regan confirmed. "He is the hero in all my fairy tales, the man beside me when I envision success, failure, family. Oh God, family. I can't imagine having children with anyone but Tyler."

"Looks like you have an engagement to break," Sloane stated.

"Yes, I do." Regan agreed, nodding her head, a light coming into her face as if a weight lifted from her shoulders.

"I admit, I can't wait to have you back in the office full time," Charlotte told Regan. "But Brandon will be heart broken."

"He'll get over it. So many women want a man like him. He'll find one quickly enough. Oh shit, what about my job? I love my new job, and I can make such a difference. I wanted to improve urban housing accessibility. How can I give that up?"

"You gave up your CEO job," Missy reminded her sister. "And that was the job you wanted more than any in the world. I know, I watched you beg and cry, dealing with Father about it. Come back and do the job you were born to do. You can use the Lyons Howe Charitable Trust to do good works."

"She's right," Charlotte agreed. "You belong at the helm of Lyons Howe. Come home, Regan. We will all welcome you with open arms."

"Even Tyler?" Regan asked uncertainly.

Her friends smiled, laughed, and responded in unison. "Especially Tyler."

Chapter Twenty-Seven

R egan called and texted Brandon repeatedly. He was not responding. She wasn't alarmed. He often fell off her radar when he was back in Rhode Island. He overbooked his short time at home and staying in touch with Regan sank to the bottom on his to-do list.

But now, knowing what she wanted, Regan couldn't wait to take action. She couldn't tell Tyler how she felt until she officially broke it off with Brandon and returned his ring. It wouldn't be fair to either man. She was going to see Tyler in a matter of minutes, so her immediate concern was how to balance her emotions.

She settled for sending a text that wasn't exactly a dear John, but was more outspoken than her earlier messages. "I have been trying to reach you. We need to have a serious conversation. I think it is time for us to reconsider a future together. I know it's the right decision for me." It would have to do until they actually spoke and issued a joint press release, calling off the engagement.

Lyons Howe was a sponsor at the Children's Hospital fundraiser. Tyler would be at the table with Regan all evening, looking dashing in his tuxedo, pulling her every heartstring. She just wanted to fall into his arms and begin her life with him. But there was the work at CDFI, and it was important.

Regan spent much of the day on a call with her right-hand person at CDFI, Maureen. With just a bit of probing, Regan ascertained that she wanted the promotion to Regan's position and would take it if offered. Regan felt confident about recommending her to the undersecretary and Regan would leave CDFI, knowing she had left the agency in skillful hands.

Of course, it would require approvals, everything in Washington did, but at least Maureen would be assigned the Interim Director position, getting her foot in the door and allowing Regan to leave without feeling she turned her back on the agency.

It turned out that people in Washington eyed Regan's position as temporary anyway, viewing her as nothing more than an extension of Brandon. Her job was seen as a well-played step toward Brandon's inevitable run for office. They all imagined Brandon in the White House, with Regan as the perfect little lady by his side. She bristled at the idea.

Why couldn't he be the ideal little husband at her side? No one, least of all Brandon, could envision that. She suspected that in a deprecating way, Brandon had encouraged the perception of Regan as a helpmate who was first lady material while downplaying her ability to be a strong business leader.

Tyler had no problem being her second in command; her 'First Husband, if that had been her ambition. He was a partner in every sense, always supportive of her goals and aspirations. What a fool she was to have looked elsewhere. She would never be happy with anyone else. It was Tyler for her.

They still had massive hurdles to overcome. The security detail was a constant reminder of past lies and current danger. Regan had faith, though. The best in the business was working on the solution and there were no more secrets between the couple. In just weeks, it would be over, and they could be together.

But she had to break up with Brandon first. Not that she could handle that now. Regan entered the Casino Club ballroom, admiring the décor and the size of the crowd. This fundraiser would be a success, raising needed funds to help attain the hospital's lofty goals. Since Sloane was on the board, she was sitting with the handsome, enigmatic guest of honor, Grant Harris. The famous doctor had been missing in action for a few years. Since his return to medicine, he was setting the world on fire. It promised to be an exciting night.

Regan pasted a smile on her face and braced herself for an evening touting the hospital and LHRE. Tyler would meet her here, taking some of the pressure off and helping her sell the corporate message.

Regan glided across the rotunda floor, circling the dance floor, admiring the flowers and elegant table settings; interrupted constantly by friends and business associates. Growing frustrated, she focused on Tyler, standing at the table they had purchased. The gauntlet kept growing. People who wanted a piece of Regan and her possible place in the White House. Tyler looked up and locked eyes with her. Her heart raced as he insinuated himself through the crowd, growing closer.

Damn, he looked good. The man could be a model for the classic tuxedo, his broad shoulders and long legs showing it off to advantage. Regan felt the breath leave her lungs and a smile lift her lips. He loped toward her, undeterred by the crowd determined to keep them apart. His eyes focused only on her.

The business woman in her had a brief second of concern. Tyler was dismissive to those who stopped to chat, but she studied him as he managed to acknowledge the most philanthropic of Chicago's elite while still covering the distance between them.

Finally, Tyler wrapped a hand around her arm and inched her away from the curious hangers on. "You look stunning," he whispered, blatantly checking her out, pausing on the cutouts at the waistline of her silver sequined dress before returning to lock his chocolate brown gaze on her blue one. "Gorgeous."

Regan stood dumbfounded and elated. Here was the old Tyler, the Tyler that wore his heart on his sleeve. His love for her radiated from his expression as his head tilted to hers and he brushed his lips across hers.

When Regan leaned into him, Tyler stepped away. "Careful to keep it chaste, Ree. Business partners, nothing more," Tyler warned. "Anything else might attract attention, from the press that we don't need."

The kiss broke her stupor, his lips warm and full of promise even in the too-short time they connected with hers. She reached up to move a small lock of hair from his forehead, needing an excuse to touch him. "Understood."

The electricity vibrating between them was palpable. How she would get through the night without constantly touching and kissing him was beyond her, but he seemed to be toeing the line for them both.

He took her arm, and they moved slowly through the crowd, stopping as a team to speak with influential leaders, dropping hints about deals to be made and properties that were available. They finished one another's sentences, operating together like a finely oiled machine, while their fingers or bodies collided surreptitiously.

"How long do we have to stay?" Tyler whispered in her ear as they moved away from the CEO of a huge construction company that loved to hear himself talk. "I can't make small talk all night when I need to be touching you."

Regan considered scolding the incorrigible man but found she agreed too much to argue. "We have to make it to the introduction of the honoree, and then we can sneak out."

"OK. I will try to control myself until then, but maybe we shouldn't sit next to each other." Tyler's smile was wicked as his brow rose suggestively.

So much for staying away from him until she spoke to Brandon. Regan felt her ability to fight this man's charm slip through her fingers. Her blood was hot, her breath coming fast, her body hungry for his, and he had hardly skimmed his fingers over her. One serious kiss and she knew she'd be a goner.

If she hoped to retain what little composure remained, fate was working against her. The last two seats available at the Lyons Howe table were side by side. Tyler gave Regan a knowing smile, his eyes all but promising indecent behavior. Regan tempted him with her grin, knowing he would take it as an invitation.

Tyler pulled a chair out for Regan, admiring the long length of leg that was visible as the slit in her Akris dress slid open high on her thigh. He pushed her chair in, leaning forward with lips against her ear, and said, "Nice view."

Regan turned to her right to greet the Turners and Felts, two of her best clients with their spouses, admiring the women's dresses, commenting on the room and the crowd to hide her flustered emotions. She transitioned between small talk and business issues, while her heart fluttered uncontrollably. She was smooth, the bent of her thoughts going undetected by all but the incorrigible man seating himself beside her.

Tyler took the seat beside her, the scent of his body taking her back to the night when they had first made love. The memories swamped her, forcing her to ask her companions to repeat what they said. So much for holding it together.

"We were looking forward to meeting your fiancé," Mrs. Felt repeated, the words hitting Regan like a gut-punch. Why did everyone insist on calling Brandon 'hers'?

"He is back in Rhode Island, Mrs. Felt. He is with his family, taking advantage of the holiday recess."

"When is the wedding?" Mrs. Turner asked, scanning Regan's hand for the engagement ring she no longer wore. Regan mumbled something about things being uncertain. Fortunately, Mrs. Turner didn't seem to care about Regan's vague reply.

"I was concerned the early snow would keep people away tonight," Regan changed the subject. "But what a crowd. It's gratifying, isn't it?"

"With the new building, the hospital outreach has been fabulous. They are honoring that famous Dr. Grant Harris, too, now that he has returned to work. Such a sad episode that was, but talk about making lemonade from lemons. His new procedures are making news all over the world."

"It will make a huge difference in the lives of children," Regan agreed, looking across the room toward Sloane's table, expecting to see the handsome doctor sitting there. No sign of the elusive man, but Sloane caught her eye, motioned toward Tyler and gave Regan a thumbs up. Regan quickly dropped her head, hiding her deep blush. Could Sloane read her mind or was she just so obvious?

She must be obvious, Regan decided, when she felt Tyler's strong hand slide along the edge of her dress opening, stopping just short of the apex of her thighs where she was rapidly growing damp. He was looking away, speaking earnestly with the couple beside him, a lawyer from their board and her husband.

Looking above the table, no one would guess he was thinking of anything but work, but his fingers told an entirely different story. They were stroking a languid pattern along Regan's skin, caressing higher with each pass, growing indecently close to her now soaking panties.

"Not sure I will make it to the speeches," he leaned over to tell her calmly, as if he were asking her to pass the salt. "Can't we at least excuse ourselves and find a corner?"

Regan turned her flaming face to his in shock, only to realize he was teasing her—in more ways than one. "You need to behave," she scolded.

"Do I? I'm getting a completely opposite vibe, Ree, and we both know I can read you like a book. Whatever has happened, I like it. Hell, I love it." Before she could absorb his words, he had turned away to continue talking to the lawyer's husband about the Blackhawk's chances for the Stanley Cup. How could he do that when she couldn't think of anything but his hand on her... Idiot, two can play that game.

Regan shifted in her chair, lifting the hand resting quietly in her lap and sliding it across Tyler's lap. It came to rest lightly on his crotch. She got an immediate and gratifying response. Tyler faltered as he discussed the hockey team's schedule, turning to catch her eye and give her an evil look. She watched him hold back an audible hiss.

Ah yes, all was fair in love and war. Regan had a self-satisfied moment fondling Tyler's expanding erection before she became aware of Tyler's fingers reaching higher and caressing her in ways she couldn't possibly ignore. She gasped, drawing attention from those around her.

"I just realized..." What excuse could she give? Her mind was mush.

"Yes, I see them too," Tyler said, speaking to the table at large. "Will you excuse us a moment? We need to say hello to someone. We can't be rude." The vague excuse seemed to satisfy those at the table as Tyler stood to help Regan from her chair and led her away, arm wrapped around her lower back.

"What are you doing?" Regan hissed at Tyler.

"Finishing what you started," he responded, gazing at her with longing. She felt his hand spread across her back, touching the bare skin low on her back and sending fire racing through her veins.

"What you started, you mean," she accused.

"Can you blame me, my temptress?" he asked, motioning to her body. "You can't sit beside me looking like that and expect me to keep my hands off of you. Let's get out of here."

The double doors of the large room shut behind them. "But we can't go..."

"Stop worrying about what people will think, Ree. Just feel," Tyler commanded, placing his finger across her mouth to shush her. "Give me your coat check ticket. Did you Uber?"

As if on autopilot, she nodded yes and handed him the ticket. Tyler quickly bundled her into her cashmere coat and led her to the door. The valet brought the car in minutes, and the moment they were tucked into the car, Tyler was speeding away on Lake Shore Drive.

"Do you need anything? We are going to my place."

It was a stupid question. Regan needed a toothbrush and clothes. Otherwise, she would have to do a walk of shame tomorrow morning in a shimmering silver gown.

Ignoring all of that, Regan blurted the first thing that came to mind. "I need to break off my engagement."

"That goes without saying," Tyler told her, reaching for her hand in the dark interior and rubbing his thumb over the back of it. For Regan, it was the reassurance she needed from him. He understood her situation, and he was promising he would be there to support her.

"You'll need a new job," she added.

"Yeah, that goes without saying too," Tyler agreed, pulling into the garage under his South Loop apartment building and gliding into the tight parking space with ease.

He jumped around the Tesla to open her door while Regan gathered the skirts of her long gown. Tyler reached in to help her exit the vehicle and pull her straight into his arms. She went willingly, lifting her face to his for the kiss she had craved all night. As soon as she felt his lips on hers, warm, sexy and demanding, she sighed into his mouth, leaned into his body and allowed the electricity to flow from him all the way to her fingers and toes.

God, she wanted this man. She wanted his touch, his mouth, this magic he made just by being near her. How had she been stupid enough to think she could be happy with anyone else? She felt it in every fiber of her being. She was home.

Chapter Twenty-Eight

Even if Wyatt hadn't shared the bits and pieces of conversation Keeli confided in him from her girls' night out, Tyler would have known things had changed just by looking at Regan when she stepped into the ballroom. Even without the light in her eyes, the come-hither smile and the telltale blush, that dress would have given everything away. She intended the provocative dress to send Tyler a message.

The sequined gown shone like a beacon in the room, catching and reflecting the lights from above, making it impossible to take his eyes off of her. All modesty from the front, the dress was almost backless, with those cutouts just calling to him to slide his hand into the naked waist of the dress. The fabric clung to her slim curves. She had never looked more desirable, forcing him to wipe a sheen of sweat from his skin and concentrate on controlling his erection.

Her skin felt like silk under his fingertips, tempting him until he was almost indiscreet under the table—almost. But when he felt her hand slip into his crotch, he knew he was lost. If he didn't get her out of that ballroom, and fast, he would come in his tuxedo pants for all the world to see.

Damn, she put him on edge.

Not sure how he had survived as long as he had, Tyler was thrilled he had her alone at last. He could jump off that edge and take her with him. And he planned to do just that, for the rest of the night and all day tomorrow. The real world could wait. The next twenty-four hours belonged to them.

Tyler resisted divesting Regan of her coat on the elevator, settling for wrapping his hands around her cheeks and in her hair, holding her tightly and kissing her senseless as the car took them up forty floors. Once the apartment door closed behind them, and the deadbolt clicked soundly into place, her coat was history as he glided his hand down her back and under the waist of the dress. Tyler pushed her gently against the door, trapping her willing body and lowering his head to claim her mouth. Without breaking the lip-lock, he shrugged out of his coat and tux jacket, hearing them swoosh to the floor behind him
.

Tyler had controlled his kisses in the elevator, but now he unleashed the power of his desire, probing her mouth with his tongue, tasting the warmth of Regan's mouth, bruising her lips with his. She returned his kisses with enthusiasm, her hands running up and down the back of the soft fabric of his shirt until he felt her pull it loose from his pants to press her hands along the bare skin of his back.

His muscles reflexively bunched and released under her caresses as he grew painfully harder and fuller low against her belly. Tyler didn't think it was possible to desire Regan more than he did right now. One of her soft hands skittered across his skin, leaving fire in its wake. The other dug into his scalp, holding his head close as she surrendered everything to Tyler. Regan's lips clung to his and her body clung to him from chin to toes. He savored every inch of his dream woman at long last, molded fast against every inch of him. The idea and the reality crashed in his brain until he wanted to crawl inside Regan and stay there. He craved more, needed to get closer.

Pulling her from the door and toward the bedroom, Tyler stopped to drag at her lips with every few steps. He lowered the short zipper on her dress so the moment they entered the bedroom, with a flick of his fingers over the barely there straps, it slithered to the floor.

Regan stood before him, offering herself to him, naked except a silvery thong, clearly wet with her juices, a pair of too-high heels and a blush that covered her chest and face. She took his breath away.

"Your turn," Regan told him, pulling on one side of his bow tie, jerking it free from under his collar. Tyler took it from her hand as she reached for the studs of his shirtfront. She carefully undid the top two before he yanked hard on the shirt, popping open the rest and causing Regan to laugh her throaty, sexy laugh.

When Tyler reached for the button on his pants, Regan swatted his hand out of the way. "Let me," she suggested, barely above a whisper as her small hands undid the button and zipper, grazing against his hard-on until he wanted to scream.

The tease knew precisely the effect she had on him. It was his turn. Tyler lifted Regan off her feet, high enough to suck on one tantalizing breast while her feet dangled in the air, dropping her gently to the bed and following her down.

Tiny compared to him, Tyler's weight forced Regan deep into the mattress. Her sigh of pleasure was a sufficient signal to keep going. He took her bottom lip between his teeth, nipping at the ripe softness before plundering her mouth with his tongue, tasting the honeyed warmth of her.

Regan was incredibly responsive, little mews of pleasure erupting from her as her hands roamed his back, his shoulders, and the tight muscles of his butt. She left a trail of fiery sensation everywhere she touched.

"I want to discover every inch of you," Tyler told her.

"What's stopping you?"

"With my tongue," he finished, causing her to gasp.

"What's stopping you?" Regan asked again, a wicked smile displaying her even teeth, catching the moonlight in the shadowy room.

Tyler slid down her body, tasting the perfumed skin of her jaw and neck, the hollow of her collarbone and lower, wrapping his mouth around one tight nipple and sucking hard. Regan arched off the mattress, offering herself to him. She was no shy flower, he realized, nipping harder at the tight bud, as his hands roamed lower.

Regan's head was thrashing. Her legs were sliding about the back of his thighs as if she didn't know what to do with everything she was feeling. Tyler moved to her other breast, sucking the mound deep into his mouth, wrapping his fingers around the nipple he had just abandoned as he suckled.

At the same time, he captured her legs between his to still them and shifted his weight to rest his almost painful erection between her thighs. Sinking lower on Regan's body, Tyler worried he wouldn't last much longer.

Regan must have read his mind, clawing at his back. "Please Ty, please," she begged again and again. Did he take what he wanted or deliver on the promise of oral pleasure? Damn. He wanted to please her so much.

Taking a deep, calming breath, Tyler slid lower, until his teeth captured the wisp of fabric barely hiding Regan's center. She lifted her hips, helping Tyler remove the panties without his hands before she kicked them to the floor along with her shoes.

Tyler inhaled the musky smell of arousal, knowing he was the cause, and planted a hard kiss atop the tiny thatch of curls. Dipping lower, he roamed over Regan with his tongue.

"Oh God," she sighed when he wrapped his lips around the hard nub full of nerve endings and sucked. Regan spread her legs wider to allow Tyler freer access. Tyler accepted the invitation, sliding his shoulders between her thighs until she was spread before him like a feast. Then feast he did, as Regan writhed, her legs tightening around his torso, her hips lifting to his face, her juices flowing freely.

Tyler lifted his head. "Do I finish what I started?" he asked her.

"Later." Regan hesitated only seconds before she scrabbled at his shoulders and pulled him up her body. Tyler yanked off the briefs he'd been using to tamp down his need, then positioned himself over her. They both took a deep breath.

Tyler stabbed his tongue into Regan's mouth at the moment he plunged his erection into her. She was hot and tight. So tight, but so slippery at the same time. He glided into her and stopped, fully seated, his body heavy against hers. The feeling was indescribable, leaving Tyler wondering if he would explode too soon.

Control. Tyler willed himself to calm. He focused on her mouth, tasting Regan's sweetness along with the salty flavors of her, on her rapid breathing, on her scent. Tyler felt the urgency of her legs, wrapped securely around his ass, pulling him tight into her. They were gasping like marathon runners as he remained still and deep, savoring the feel of her body wrapped around his in every possible way.

When he thought he could last a few minutes longer, Tyler moved, pulling slowly from the velvet glove that was Regan, tingling with sensation along his shaft, before rocking back into her, thick, hot and hard. Regan rolled her small hips against his movements, straining for release, panting into his mouth.

Reaching under her to grab the globes of her buttocks, Tyler pulled Regan hard against him and plunged into her tight wetness harder and faster.

"Yes, yes," she kept repeating between kisses, her breath soft on his face. Regan's fingers were digging into his muscles, holding him tight, lifting to his withdrawal, sinking with his return. He felt her muscles tighten and cling harder, her breath hitch before she quivered around him, sighing in pleasure, riding him to her climax.

Her orgasm pulsing around him was all Tyler could handle. His body tightened in response, as he thrust deep, retreated and returned to Regan's warm body, striving for his release until his body contracted and exploded. It was too much. He rode the wave of his orgasm, his heart overflowing for the woman clinging to him.

As his body coming down from its high, softening inside Regan's relaxed body, Tyler realized Regan was raining kisses all over his face. They were sweaty and slippery against each other, so much so that he feared he would slip out of her warmth.

"Don't move," he begged her. "I want to stay like this as long as I can. You feel incredible."

"That was incredible," Regan stated, kissing him hard on the mouth. A huge grin split her face as she rained tiny kisses over his cheeks, eyes, and nose.

His smile was an automatic response to her joy and to one of the best orgasms he had ever had.

"I love your dimples," Regan said, gently tracing the dents in his face with her finger. His smile grew wider.

"I love you," he said. Regan stared at him with wide eyes, but said nothing. "I love you, all of you. Everything about you," he repeated. His heart stopped in his chest. She was staring at him. Here he was flaccid, but still inside her, clinging to that closeness, spilling his guts about loving her, and she was silent. He moved to pull out and away.

Regan's arms shot out to hold him to her, not allowing him to pull free of her body. "Don't move," she commanded. "Please. I want this to last forever."

"Forever?"

"This moment, Tyler. Our moment. I finally believe that you love me as completely as I love you. We are going to be together."

Tyler released the breath he didn't know he was holding, felt his heart kick start in his chest and bowed his head to kiss the woman he had loved all his life.

"Hmm, do I feel a certain...resurgence?" she asked, smiling and wiggling against his growing erection.

"Well, if we are going to do this forever, I better be able to keep it up."

"Oh yes, Ty. I plan for you to keep it up again and again."

Tyler stopped Regan's laugh with a searing kiss before beginning to test his stamina for what promised to be a very long night.

Chapter
Twenty-Nine

T yler felt sweat pooling under his arms, and a small shiver of nerves caused his hands to tremble. As long as he kept them out of sight, he was fine. Glancing over at Wyatt, Tyler was astonished to see him looking cool as a cucumber. Sure. He didn't have prison hanging over his head if this went wrong, but still, his family stood to lose millions of dollars and LHRE's best clients.

"Why are you so damn calm?" Tyler finally hissed over to his friend, sitting across the conference room table. "I am sweating like a pig."

"Do I look calm?" Wyatt asked in surprise. "I sure as hell don't feel calm. Where the hell is everyone, anyway?" The two men surveyed the hallways outside the glass-enclosed conference room, seeing nothing out of the ordinary. Assistants sat typing on their computers within their cubicles. People came and went into their offices. To anyone looking from the outside, it was a typical day at Lyons Howe Real Estate.

"I know," Tyler said, looking at the Rolex his friends had gifted him upon graduation from law school for about the twentieth time in an hour. If he ended up with nothing, he would have to sell it. "We have been sitting here for 45 minutes. Where the hell are they?"

"Which they?" Wyatt asked. "I thought by now…"

Both men jerked their heads up like dogs hearing a noise. There was a flurry of activity at the front desk as seven large men dressed in business suits with heavy overcoats ignored the pleas of the receptionist and sailed past her into the conference room.

Tyler rose, surreptitiously wiping his hands along the side of his pants before shaking the hands of his enemies. He offered to take their coats and called for one assistant to bring coffee. They were all playing the game, keeping up the appearances of a typical business meeting. This meeting was anything but typical. It was life and death.

"Andrei, won't you take a seat?" Tyler asked, gesturing to a chair before thinking better of it and shoving his trembling hands in his pockets.

Wyatt sat still, his blue eyes wide, his jaw tight as the men took their places around the table. Tyler knew they would be massive, half were surely bodyguards, but seeing Wyatt's reaction solidified his realization that they were dealing with an entirely different animal.

"He needs to be here?" The apparent ring-leader questioned, nodding his head toward Wyatt.

"He did the software for me," Tyler explained in a voice that sounded calmer than he expected. "He's here in case you have questions."

"The program will speak for itself," a smaller man said in his heavily accented voice. "I will read the software; it will tell me what I need to know."

Recognizing his cue, Wyatt slid a computer printout about one-half inch thick across the table, followed by a laptop, opened to display the same code as printed.

"I guess we have no preliminaries," Wyatt mumbled under his breath, garnering him dirty looks from the ringleader.

"Let it go, Wyatt," Tyler whispered. "Let's just get this over with," he added in a voice loud enough for all to hear.

"We have a different definition of preliminaries, as you say," the ringleader, Andrei, said, gesturing to the two men. The five large, silent men that had entered the room went to work. Two ran their hands carefully over Tyler and Wyatt, looking for weapons, cell phones, wires; Tyler couldn't be sure. The other three were combing their hands along the bottom of the table, the windows, and the light fixtures.

"Clean," one of them announced as all five took seats.

"Good. Preliminaries over. Pyotr, do you have what you need?"

"Where is the client list?" Pyotr looked up from the computer and stared at Wyatt. "We get the code and the list."

"It's there," Wyatt jumped up to come around the table and point it out. Three gigantic men reacted instantly, fast for such large men. Tyler to shake his head furiously and motion Wyatt back to his chair.

"It's there at the back of the printout," Wyatt answered, slowly sinking back into his chair. The three men did the same, and the mounting tension in the room subsided. The only sound was breathing and the rustle of paper as Pyotr sifted through the printout.

"Got it," he said. Andrei relaxed in his chair, shifting his position. Until this moment, Andrei's hand had rested in his breast pocket, likely on a handgun. Tyler took his movement as a positive sign.

"Everything is here, as promised," Tyler assured the men.

"It better be," Andrei said, "or that pretty little blonde won't be running this place anymore."

Wyatt's head shot up, looking first at Tyler, then straight into Andrei's cold brown eyes. "What does Regan have to do with this?"

"Nothing, if you did your job. Your woman is feisty. I would be happy to have her in Russia with me." Andrei licked his lips in a lascivious manner that almost caused Tyler to leap from his chair. Andrei, seeing the reaction, threw his head back and laughed. "Maybe I take her anyway?" he teased Tyler.

"We have a deal," Tyler hissed at the snake sitting across from him. "You don't touch her."

"It's all here," Pyotr announced just as the receptionist wheeled in a coffee cart. Tyler quickly dismissed her. The men ignored the coffee, all eyes on Pyotr. "Everything looks good."

"You're positive?" Andrei challenged.

"No hooks. All the accounts are here. We have the balances and the access information. I even tested two of them randomly while we sat here and they deposited the funds right into our account."

"That fast?" Andrei asked, a wide smile breaking across his sharp features. "How much in all?"

"I can't be positive, but it looks to be in the billions," Pyotr stated, awestruck.

"Billions," Andrei repeated, his face replicating the glee of a kid staring in a candy shop window. "Billions are very good, Tyler. This payment will buy you years and years of freedom."

"This is it, Andrei Milovich. We have a deal. If I hear from you ever again, I go to the police."

"You go to the police," Andrei mocked, "and tell them what? That you embezzled billions with the help of the CEO's brother in order to fund anti-American terrorists? I think you go nowhere. I think you tell no one."

Tyler felt the blood rushing through his veins and feared they would pop with the pressure.

"Tyler," Wyatt called to him softly, "You knew you were taking a chance."

Tyler calmed down and passed three copies of a legal document across the table. "Sign this, all the copies, and we are finished here."

"What am I signing?" Andrei and Pyotr asked in unison.

"A confession," Tyler responded. "I knew you would never leave me alone, no matter what you promised, so I have drafted a legal document admitting all your blackmail, including today. If you ever come near me again, I release it to the authorities."

"Don't sign that, boss," one of the enormous silent men told Andrei.

"No problem," Andrei responded with alacrity. "We will be safely and richly ensconced in Russia, where no one can touch us. No extradition. No trials. I will sign your stupid papers."

Tyler removed a Mont Blanc pen from his interior breast pocket, willing his hands to be steady. He waved the pen in the air to reassure the men it wasn't a gun, then slid it across the mahogany table. He watched as Andrei signed the documents without reading them. Andrei slid the pen across to Pyotr, who did the same before pushing the stack toward Tyler.

Tyler reviewed the signatures with the thoroughness of a lawyer and then returned one copy to Andrei. "For your records," he told the Russian. "One for me and one for the files, in case something should happen to me."

"What could happen to you, Tyler, my friend?" Andrei asked with a menacing smile. "You delivered. We leave you alone. We have a deal."

With that, Andrei rose from his seat, Pyotr stuffed the computer and the papers into a nondescript briefcase and, with goons in front and thugs behind them, the men exited the room.

Wyatt never moved, but Tyler rose from his chair, holding the papers for dear life. Suddenly more confident with the Russians, he spoke up. "What? No kiss goodbye," he teased Andrei. "Farewell, my friend."

Wyatt spoke, but Tyler shushed him, waiting until he saw the men go out the LHRE main doors. When the heavy doors closed behind the last of them, Wyatt reached for his cell, recalled he didn't have it and wandered into the hall, grabbing a cellphone from the first person he saw.

"They are leaving the building now," he said without preamble and hung up.

"What did they sign?" Wyatt asked Tyler. "I wasn't expecting that."

"It could have destroyed everything, but I figured Andrei Milovich would never read it. He is sloppy like that. Pyotr, on the other hand..."

"What did they sign?" Wyatt asked again, his frustration mounting.

"Oh sorry. The idiots signed their extradition papers, of course."

"What?"

"Yeah, Jonathan and I came up with the idea in case they got away," Tyler explained. "They signed an agreement to be extradited from Russia for trial."

"Are you insane? If they read those docs, we are all dead."

"They won't," Tyler reassured his friend. "The legal language is marvelously complicated. They won't understand it even if they read it. I owe Jonathan for that one. Even I had trouble figuring out what it said."

"Okay," Wyatt sighed, sitting back and taking his first deep breath of the day. "Now what?"

"Now we let the FBI do its job. They catch them outside the building with the laptop and printout on them for evidence and the signed docs admitting blackmail and extortion and agreeing to extradition. Sewed up nice and neat."

"Sounds too good to be true," Wyatt admitted.

"Well, it isn't. There is the money already transferred from someone's account, for example. Who knows how much LHRE just lost? We will have a hard time explaining that to our clients, that's for sure."

"Oh no, that won't be a problem. There is a tripwire in the code to boomerang after two hours."

"What does that mean in English, Wyatt?"

"It means the money is automatically transferred back to us after two hours. That was the one piece of code I worried that the Russian guy might spot. The rest was easy to bury."

"The rest?"

"Yeah, we are capturing IP addresses, digital fingerprints, email confirmations, all the data we need to press charges and prosecute successfully and to get to the top of the ring in Russia. I am not sure how successful we will be at the latter, but I will know I tried."

"Who could have ever predicted that I would need my geeky best friend to trap criminals?"

"Who could have ever predicted my lawyer's best friend would risk his entire career to embezzle from my family?"

"Family! Oh, shit, I need to call Regan," Tyler announced, reaching, once again, for his absent phone before remembering he had been barred from bringing it into the conference room.

Reaching into the middle of the table, he hit the speaker button and dialed the outside number for Regan's cell. They had purposely kept her out of the building today, away from the danger. He needed to be careful now, too. The FBI, to avoid suspicion, had left the phones tapped.

Tyler and Wyatt stared into each other's faces as the phone rang and rang. Regan knew to expect their call; she should have picked up by now. Nothing.

"Mr. Winthrop," an assistant poked her head into the room. "You have a call on line three. Shall I transfer it here?"

Tyler nodded yes and smiled over at Wyatt. "There she is," he reassured his friend.

"It's over," he announced into the phone after pressing the talk button a bit too enthusiastically. "They left a few minutes ago. It's over."

"We have them," a male voice agreed. "The FBI nabbed them right outside the elevator."

"Great news, Jonathan," Tyler told the lawyer. "I am so relieved to have this over and done with."

"Who is with you?" Jonathan asked.

"Just me," Wyatt answered.

"Hey, Wyatt. Thanks again for your help. I don't know how you buried all that code, but it was genius."

"Thanks, Jonathan. It was a challenge, but it paid off."

"We don't have to watch what we say?" Tyler asked in confusion.

"The FBI combed the building last night," Jonathan explained. "It's all over."

"So, let's celebrate," Tyler suggested. "We just need to find Regan first."

"I thought she was at the office with you," Jonathan said. "She's not with you? We pulled her security detail when she entered the building this morning." Jonathan sounded alarmed.

"What are you talking about, Jonathan? Regan didn't come to LHRE today. We specifically told her to stay away."

"You may have told her to stay away, but we tailed her to the building."

Tyler looked over at Wyatt, fear clear on his features. He felt the sweat gathering under his shirt all over again.

"She's probably right down the hall," Wyatt reassured, although his face was tight with worry.

Tyler jumped from his chair and ran for the corner office that belonged to Regan. The room was empty; the desk cleared of papers; the shades closed against the bright sun.

Running throughout the building, Tyler randomly asked people if they had seen Regan. No one had. He was returning to the conference room, his hair disheveled, his face ashen when Donna emerged from his office with his cell phone in her hands.

"It's been ringing non-stop, Tyler. Someone must need to reach you."

His walk slowed to a crawl, his heart pounded in his chest, as Tyler stared at Regan's number and her face on the screen of his phone before shaking himself from his fear. If she was calling, she was okay.

"Where the hell are you, hon? I have been worried."

"How sweet of you to worry, Tyler," a deep Russian voice responded. "And to call me hon." Tyler had heard that voice taunt him for his entire adult life. A mid-level lackey, Tyler understood he was challenging the thugs at the top. He was looking for power, and that made him dangerous.

"Taras? Taras, if you touch a hair on her head, I swear I will kill you," Tyler screamed into the phone. Taking a deep breath, he lowered his voice. "Let me speak to Regan."

"She's fine, Ty, I swear," Taras responded. "She is our insurance. As soon as we have our money, we return her to you."

"Let me speak to her now," Tyler demanded, standing taller and puffing out his chest in the middle of the corridor. He was a warrior ready to rescue his lady, and he needed to convey that with his voice. "Now," he shouted.

He heard a rustle at the other end of the phone and then Regan's voice, small and frightened. Tyler melted at the sound, deflating as his shoulders rounded with the weight of his problem.

"I'm fine, Tyler," Regan promised, although it was clear she was not. "They are treating me well, and they swear I can come home when they have what they want. Just give it to them, Tyler. Let's put this behind us."

"Do as she says, Tyler," Taras was back on the line. "Then you see her pretty face again. Otherwise…" Tyler felt his blood go cold, listening to a lascivious cackle through the phone.

The click on the phone set Tyler's brain back in motion. Sprinting for the conference room, he threw open the door, slamming it into the wall behind it.

"Guys," he leaned over the phone, "We have two hours and only two hours to find Regan."

Looking over at Wyatt, desperation filling his face, Tyler shook his head in disbelief. "They boomerang in two hours, right? So the first two transactions will revert in less than two hours."

"Gotta go," Jonathan said before the call disconnected.

"You better pray these guys are too busy to read," Wyatt told his friend. "Or Regan is dead."

"Who are we kidding, Wyatt? We are all dead. If Taras is directly involved and in the States, we are up against a lot more than I expected."

"Oh God, do I tell my family?" Wyatt pondered out loud. "They'll be frantic." Wyatt rose from the chair and moved to the doorway of the conference room. "I'm going to use Regan's office to call home."

Wyatt moved through the doorway and three steps down the hall before turning and standing in the conference door. "Tyler, I love you like a brother," Wyatt shared with his friend, "but if anything happens to Regan, I swear if these assholes don't kill you, I will."

Chapter Thirty

It had been forty-eight hours since Regan had heard anything other than murmurings. She was desperate to catch a word, anything that might help her get out of this predicament. They had locked her in a room the size of her bedroom closet at least two days earlier.

Regan paced from the door, where she pressed her ear to the wood in futility, to the window, covered with a substance that was thick enough to resist both her fingernails and light. She caught a word here and there, but Regan could not understand the language. Russian, she suspected.

For the first two hours, they had been polite and almost kind, treating her more like a guest than a captive. Then everything changed. There were arguments conducted in loud voices, with fists banging on tables, followed by someone grabbing her roughly and shoving her into this room. Since then, every few hours a man passed her sandwiches wrapped in plastic, along with juice boxes. They exchanged no words. No other contact. Two whole days.

Regan knew that spending a long time in captivity was debilitating. Wyatt had shared enough about the software program to explain the boomerang. These thugs had to have felt its effects by now. She suspected they were planning to trade her for a ransom. Someone should have made arrests or paid them off by now. Why was is dragging on?

With no sunlight in the room and the overhead light on around the clock, Regan was unsure about the passage of time. She marked what she believed was an hour with a hash mark on the wall, using the heel from one of her shoes. Based on that, she estimated this was the start of her third day as a hostage. Certainly, she'd been fed, kept in a comfortable room with adequate heat. But a shower would be nice, or a rescue.

Regan was blindfolded to get to and from the bathroom, but using the bathroom fixtures, she determined she was being held in an older apartment building, and there was an 'L' track not far away. That didn't tell her much.

The not knowing, the uncertainty of what was happening in the other room, as well as the uncertainty of what Tyler and Wyatt were doing, wore on her nerves. She was frazzled. She was bored and on edge, unable to sleep more than a few fitful hours.

Was Tyler even alive? Was he looking for her? There were too many risks to their plan. Despite all those assurances from the FBI that this would go down without a hitch, she knew they were all in danger. Had she doubted it before, she doubted no longer.

She should have known that they were oversimplifying the situation when they explained it to her. First, there had been the bodyguards following her night and day, then the tensions between Wyatt and Tyler thick enough to suffocate them all. Tyler's father looked grim all week, and Jonathan Chen uncharacteristically tried to minimize the details to her. He was usually much more of a straight shooter.

She had seen her captors, too. None of them were afraid to show their faces or their arsenal. In the movies, that meant they planned to kill her. She tried to convince herself otherwise, but as the hours ticked by, she feared no one would rescue her.

Regrets swamped Regan. She hugged the pillow to her chest as if it could absorb the pain. She blithely lived as if she had all the time in the world but facing the prospect of life cut short, Regan mourned all the time she wasted, all the friendships she had neglected, how she could have spent more time with her mother instead of only with her father talking LHRE business.

And her work. She pondered all she would never accomplish with CDFI. She considered the plans she would never execute at LHRE—expansion to the west, completing her training and grooming of Ethan, who had such a bright future.

Ethan. She would never see him fall in love or get married. She wondered what kind of girl would appreciate his odd sense of humor and people-pleasing ways? He had turned into quite a player lately, but she hoped he would find a special girl he could love forever.

She would never see her nieces grow up. The list went on and on.

Horrified, Regan realized she had never officially broken her engagement to Brandon. She could imagine him very publicly mourning her passing even as he tried to avoid any taint from a potential embezzlement scandal.

What had she ever seen in him? Was she blinded by his good looks and bright future? Sitting in this room, staring at four walls, she forgave herself. Yes, she remembered Brandon's ambition and grasping ways, but she also recalled how he made her laugh, his whip-smart wit and gentle touch.

Maybe she'd been fooled into believing he wanted only her, the woman, and not Regan Howe, and her considerable legacy, but he had been misleadingly attentive. He must have loved her for herself, at least a little.

Tyler, on the other hand, always had only wanted her. Tyler. Thoughts of him brought tears to Regan's eyes. She tried to remain cool-headed, to hide her gnawing fear, but thinking of Tyler and all the time they had lost, made Regan sob until she had no choice but to mop her red eyes and wipe her runny nose on the pillowcase of the saggy bed provided for her.

She should have known something was wrong way back in high school. His behavior changed so abruptly from loving and devoted to cold and aloof. One summer and a semester of college could not have changed him so much, and his explanations were so feeble. She wished now she'd pushed for answers, seen his pain and stood by him.

Hiccupping away the last of her tears, Regan paced the small space again, stopping at the door to listen for anything she could glean. It was dead silent. There were no noises from the other room, no street noises, nothing. Could they be gone? Regan's thoughts turned to escape.

Thinking better of it, that perhaps it was the middle of the night, Regan took to the bed, flipping the dirty pillowcase over and closing her eyes to rest. Images of Tyler plagued her. All those years he arrived everywhere without a date, hovering near her. He was no milquetoast. If he wanted her—and he apparently did—and failed to act on it. Regan should have known there was a logical impediment keeping him from moving on his feelings for her. She had been a fool.

Tossing on the scratchy wool blanket, Regan gave up trying to sleep after only a few minutes and began to pace again. Stopping once more to place her head hard against the door, she heard men whispering. Did they sound anxious, or was that wishful thinking? She could not understand the words, but she recognized the sound of fear in a man's tone, and she heard just that. She pressed harder to the door.

Regan was sure the activity was increasing. She heard the metal clacking of the men handling their guns, along with their furtive whispers to one another. Was someone approaching from the outside, threatening them?

Before she could listen to more, footsteps reached where she was standing. Regan jumped back unsteadily and fell down on the edge of the bed, watching and listening as she heard the door handle turn.

"So, Ms. Howe," the large man standing in the doorway addressed her in his heavily accented English. "It seems that we must part ways. I had so hoped to enjoy your company," he hesitated as his eyes devoured her body and he licked his lips, "but I fear it is not to be."

"What's happening?" Regan demanded, preparing to argue until she saw another, larger man come to stand behind the first, a long-gun cocked and pointed at her. "Oh god, what is happening?" she asked, her voice barely above a whisper, her knees shaking as she tried to stand.

"Fear not, my dear. No one is coming to shoot you." Someone passed him sandwiches and bottled water and he handed it to Regan, enough for several meals. "But we must say our farewells if we are to escape. Our location is in jeopardy of discovery. You will not be alone long."

With that, all the lights shut off, plunging Regan into total darkness. The door shut and locked. With no sight, her hearing quickly intensified. She heard the scramble in the outer room of men grabbing belongings, footfalls in retreat, and then silence.

Regan counted to 100, breathing in and out, almost meditating to calm down before standing and feeling along the wall for a light switch.

Why did they run? Did that mean rescue was on the way? Did anyone know where she was or would she die here? Regan listened to the quiet until she found the toggle and flicked on the lights. She was sure she was alone in the apartment, so she began banging on the door with her fists, shouting for help.

When her voice was raw, and her hands were sore, she took a break, retreating again to the bed. If possible, she was less confident of her future than when the Russians guarded her. She fought hard against growing despair and accompanying tears.

Tears would not rescue Regan. She swiped her hands across her face to dry them and scoured the room for anything she could use to break the lock on the door or the covering on the window.

Scrabbling at the bolts connecting the legs to the bed, Regan loosened them with bloody fingers. With a hooray no one would hear, she took her metal stick and shoved it through the window. Shit, there were bars on the window. She broke the glass anyway and shouted for help at the top of her lungs. Nothing.

She took a break, listened to the quiet out on the street. When her stomach grumbled, she stopped to wolf down another ham sandwich. It was dark. The trains were quiet. It was late, and no one was out there. The road was tranquil. Regan dozed in and out until she woke with a jolt from a dream of Tyler. They were kissing and laughing together.

Devastated to return to reality and lose her romantic illusion, Regan gave herself a badly needed pep talk. She reminded herself of all the lists she had made earlier and made a vow to see her nieces grow up, to achieve her goals and spend her life with Tyler.

"You have food for another day or two, Ree, so pull yourself together. Someone is going to find you, but you need to help yourself."

Pushing her limp hair from her face, Regan squared her shoulders and, after shouting out the window to silence, grabbed her makeshift tool. She returned to the door, where she began swinging the metal bed-leg with all her might against the door.

After several attempts, the door moved an inch. Frustrated, Regan was about to take a break when she heard voices approaching. Friend or foe? She stood frozen, pipe in mid-air, wondering whether to give away her position.

"Anyone there?"

Regan couldn't believe it. Someone was coming through the building, calling out every few seconds, looking for someone.

"Regan?"

The voice grew louder and closer. Definitely searching for her.

Grabbing the pillowcase and wrapping it around her blistering hands, Regan took up her cudgel and went back to work. The door gave further, boosting Regan with the adrenaline she needed to keep going.

"In here," she shouted.

"Regan? Regan Howe," the voice was growing fainter.

In a panic, Regan pounded on the door with her makeshift tool. The searcher had to hear the noise.

"Hello," she screamed.

"Regan?" The voice was close, a woman's, calling her name.

"In here," Regan shouted.

"Stand back, honey, away from the door," the woman commanded right before shots rang out. The door flew open. Regan stood face to face with a uniformed Chicago policewoman. "You're safe now," she told Regan, wrapping her long arms around Regan and pulling her close.

Regan sobbed, unable to control her emotions now that she was safe.

"You okay, honey? I'm Detective Caldwell. You're Regan Howe?" she asked Regan. Nodding yes, Regan fell completely to pieces and leaned into the woman, sobbing and shaking. "Shhh, it's over now. You're going to be just fine."

After answering dozens of questions about the kidnappers, providing descriptions and learning that she had been missing for almost four days, Regan was allowed to wash her face and use the bathroom before finally leaving the dingy apartment.

A giant movie poster concealed the door to the room where she was confined. Regan was lucky to they found her. She began crying again, pent-up fear catching up with her.

"Let's get you to a paramedic," Detective Caldwell suggested, leading her down two flights of stairs to the small building lobby.

"No, I need to know what happened. I need to let people know I'm alright."

"They sent me to search this building when someone down the block reported shouts and banging sounds. You did a great job, by the way. For answers, you'll have to ask one of those men over there." The policewoman pointed across the dark street full of police cars, fire trucks and paparazzi, to a cluster of men with their heads together.

The group broke apart, and Regan recognized Wyatt's golden hair just before someone rushed across the street and took her into a tight embrace.

"I'm sorry, I'm sorry, I'm sorry," Tyler repeated. "I am never, ever, ever, letting you out of my sight again." Tyler wrapped her in a fierce embrace and held on tight, resting his chin on the top of her head, dropping small kisses on her hair, and hugging her as she cried and cried.

"I can't stop crying now that it is over. It is over, right? Please tell me it's all over."

"It's all over, Ree. Everyone is in custody. The money is safely back in your clients' accounts. There is enough incriminating evidence to put these bozos away for life, and we even got the ringleader."

"What did they want with me?" Regan asked, her arms wrapped around Tyler's muscular body. Someone handed him a warm coat to wrap around Regan, but she continued to hold Tyler close.

"Ransom. Insurance," Missy answered, disentangling her sister from Tyler and wrapping her in a loving embrace. "They expected the double-cross from Tyler. They took you as collateral before anything ever went wrong."

"They were on to us," Wyatt added. "Missy, let Mom have her before she has a coronary."

They passed Regan from family member to family member before paramedics checked her from head to toe. Regan was repeatedly questioned by the FBI and police until her father demanded they take this off the streets. Regan was shivering with cold and belated fear.

"Can I please get some real food?" she asked. "I am starving. Bring me anything but a ham sandwich and orange juice. Anything."

"Come home with me tonight, honey," her mother suggested, "and I will feed you all night long. Anything you want."

"I just want you guys, Mom, and a decent shower."

"Then come home with me, Regan. You can have those, and food for the soul," Tyler told her in a low voice, rough with emotion.

Regan wanted to be with Tyler, but how could she say so in front of her family? Could she choose him over her parents? Regan remembered all the regrets she'd catalogued for the last four days and decided.

Making light of the situation, she did her best, but sorry, imitation of Marlon Brando. "That, sir, sounds like an offer I can't refuse."

"Please, no Godfather references tonight," Tyler told her, kissing her temple, her nose and then her mouth. "We've had enough intrigue to last us all a lifetime."

Chapter
Thirty-One

It was afternoon when Regan finally opened her eyes. She barely stirred in the bed before Tyler was there.

"You're awake?" he asked, despite the obvious answer. "I didn't disturb you, did I? I was trying to be so still."

"What day is it?"

"Usually people start with what time is it," Tyler teased gently. "It's Sunday, just after noon. No more answering questions—for now. You are safe in my bed with nowhere you need to be."

"It all feels like a bad dream right now," Regan admitted, a slightly dazed look about her eyes.

"Let me grab you some coffee, and we will work on easing you back into reality." Tyler jumped from the bed and padded down the hall on bare feet, returning with coffee just the way Regan liked it, together with a blueberry muffin on a plate. "In case you're still hungry," he told her, pointing to the muffin.

"I don't think I will eat again for days," Regan laughed. Tyler had stopped on the way to his place last night and bought her two huge cheeseburgers, fries and a chocolate milkshake from the Shake Shack. She had devoured the food in a most unladylike manner before combing his refrigerator and slicing some Gouda and cheddar, which she ate with a large Gala apple and a half a box of wheat crackers, before finally declaring herself full.

Tyler enjoyed watching her eat, happy to see the fear leave her eyes bit by bit. He ran her a bath, but she insisted he stay with her in the bathroom.

"Stay and explain everything I missed," she begged. Tyler knew she wanted the update but also suspected she was fearful of being alone this soon after her rescue.

Tyler sat on the side edge of the tub, stroking Regan's damp arm as she laid back in the steamy water. She asked questions about the sting that Tyler did his best to answer.

"What went wrong?" she asked first, staring into his dark eyes with her blue ones, searching his face for the truth.

"Nothing initially went wrong. We had the signatures we needed on the extradition and confession papers. Just as I expected, no one bothered to read what they were signing."

"And the software?"

"Worked perfectly." Tyler reached to take the shampoo from Regan and poured a small amount into his hand before massaging it into her scalp with long, slow strokes. Regan sank deeper into the bath with a satisfied groan. "They ran a test just as we knew they would, checked to make sure the money transfer went through, which, of course, it did. The FBI grabbed them, the laptop and the paperwork before they took one step into the lobby and we thought we were home free."

"They didn't spot all those extra security guards?" Regan asked, her eyes closed as Tyler used the hand-held sprayer to rinse her hair free of the suds he had created.

"Half the people were in place the night before. Even I didn't spot anyone out of the ordinary when I came in that morning, but the place was swarming with people. I wish you could have seen it."

A sad, lost look came into Regan's face. "Me too. I would have much rather been there."

Tyler cupped Regan's cheek. "I am so damn sorry, Ree. I would never have willingly risked your safety. I swear."

"I know. I shouldn't have said it like that. I wish I could have seen all the action. Wyatt told the story like he single-handedly captured these guys."

Wyatt had allowed Tyler to take his sister home, probably because he knew Tyler would win that argument, but he stayed by Regan's side through all the questioning and paramedic exams before finally letting Tyler take her for food. The whole time, he entertained Regan with embellished versions of the week's events.

"He did great. Ivy looked cool and calm. I was a wreck," Tyler admitted.

Regan slipped her head out of Tyler's hand, giving him the biggest smile he had seen since her escape. She reached up to wrap her hands around his neck, pulling his face close to hers for a kiss.

"I am sure you played your part perfectly, cowboy. Think of what you have done. You have collapsed a notorious Russian hacking group, blackmailers, and probably killers, and kept them here for trial. That's amazing."

"And rescued the damsel in distress," Tyler added, bending down to kiss Regan once again before moving away to reach for a bath sheet.

"I guess, technically, you rescued yourself. You were unbelievably brave, Regan."

"I wasn't brave. I was desperate. I was getting frantic. And hungry." Regan was trying to laugh it off, but Tyler would have none of it.

"I feel terrible about what you went through, babe. I am just grateful they didn't hurt you." He was baring his soul, gratitude, love and residual fear written on his face.

"You and me both," Regan added with a weak laugh. She stepped out of the tub and Tyler wrapped her in the oversized towel and his arms, lightly patting her damp skin with the towel to dry her gently. She took the sheet from him, turned to kiss him and then moved away to the mirror to comb her wet hair.

"I look like I saw a ghost," she spoke over her shoulder to Tyler, who was mesmerized watching her do these simple tasks.

"Well, I am here to scare all ghosts away from now on."

"No more intrigue, please, Ty. I don't think I can take it."

"Me either," Tyler told her. "I want to be with you, make a quiet little life together, and have a family. Work for you?"

"Oh shit," Regan responded.

"Oh, shit? I ask you to build a life with me, and that's your reply?" Tyler looked crestfallen.

"I need to go back to Washington. I have a fiancé there. I need to get rid of him, and soon.

"Poor Brandon. He's been trying to contact me for four days," she admitted. "Although he didn't look for me when I didn't reply. He doesn't deserve me," she laughed.

"Oh shit," Tyler echoed, "no one ever called Brandon to tell him you were missing. Now he'll hear it on the news."

Tyler almost convinced Regan to allow him to return to DC with her, reminding her that he promised not to let her out of his sight. Regan insisted she needed to do this alone and promised to be quick about it. They laid out a timetable for Regan to recover at home for a few days, then go to DC, sever her ties, pack up and return to Chicago.

She said she needed a week, but Tyler argued her down to four days, by which time she was barely able to stay awake.

Tyler tucked her in his bed like a child, wrapping his arms around her and pulling her back to his chest. He listened as her breathing slowed and she fell into a deep slumber before allowing himself to relax and sleep too.

Now, almost twelve hours later she looked much better, rested and less haunted by the last few days' events. She sat in the bed, wearing one of his old Cornell t-shirts, hair tousled and sticking every which way from sleeping on it wet, and he thought her the most beautiful woman he had ever seen.

"I love you, Ree. I have always loved you," he told her in a voice husky with emotion. "If anything had happened to you, I would never have forgiven myself. I mean it."

"I know, Tyler. I am safe."

"I want to be with you, Ree. I meant what I said last night about settling down and starting a family right away. We have waited long enough."

"Sweetheart," Regan said, snuggling into Tyler's arms. "I think I need to get rid of one fiancé before I take on another, don't you?"

"I have no problem with that, Ree. But I am happy to skip the fiancé part and go straight to husband. Just name the time and place, and I'll be there."

"And deny my mother a big society wedding? Are you nuts? I just escaped with my life here, Ty. Why would I give my mother a reason to murder me?"

"Good point," Tyler conceded before pulling Regan down flat on the bed and kissing her to the point of breathlessness. "But no long engagement, Regan Howe. Promise me."

Chapter Thirty-Two

If Regan was even a bit less empathetic, she might have trouble controlling her laughter. But she put herself in Brandon's shoes as he squirmed his way out of their engagement and maintained a serious demeanor.

Regan had come to dinner prepared to take the lead and break off their plans, but, in typical Brandon fashion, he controlled the evening from the start. She knew by his choice of a quiet, out of the way place instead of his usual high-visibility selection that something was up. He never went anywhere unless he was sure to shake a few hands and get his photo snapped. Publicity and donors, that was Brandon's life. Regan, it was clear, no longer was.

Now that they were seated in a corner under a low light, Brandon was busy tripping over his tongue. Regan sat quietly, twirling the gorgeous engagement ring on her left hand that she knew would vacate her finger in a matter of minutes.

"I was appalled by the scandal," Brandon was saying when Regan returned her attention to him. "And it was unfair for them to drag you into it. After all, you did nothing wrong here, Regan. Nothing." Brandon took a sip of his expensive Cabernet and took a breath.

Regan took advantage of the break in Brandon's lecture to lean forward and confess. "I did allow them to use my company for their sting operation, Brandon. I was fully aware of what they were doing." Each time he reiterated her innocence and became indignant on her behalf, Regan put herself back into the equation.

"But you had no choice, right? You were backed into a corner."

"I am a CEO, Brandon; I always have a choice unless the board overrides me. I don't know when you changed your opinion of me so dramatically. I am not anyone's pawn."

"I wasn't saying you were, Regan. I know how smart and talented you are."

"Do you?" Regan challenged. "I used to believe that you did, Brandon, but lately, I have felt my career was sidelined for yours. You say and do these little things that treat my work as having less importance than yours."

"Regan," Brandon placated, "I helped you get a crucial position at CDFI. Of course, when I am in the White House, when we have a family, things will be different. We both understood that."

"Did we? I think perhaps we have been thinking differently lately. I always wanted to be a wife and mother, but I never said I would be content living in anyone's shadow. And now there is this scandal. Brandon, I understand that my involvement in these arrests creates an uncomfortable problem for you. You have no idea how awful I feel to put you in the spotlight like this." She sat back against the upholstered seat and controlled her smile behind a sip of Cabernet. Regan hoped that her little speech might help Brandon along.

Brandon took the bait. "Exactly, Regan, it puts me in a bad light through no fault of yours or mine. But with elections coming up, I can't afford this type of press coverage. It's very damning." Brandon's upper lip had a sheen of perspiration. Regan wondered if she had ever seen him sweat. Only once, the first time he outright asked Wyatt for money instead of dancing around the topic.

"You understand the way the electorate will think," he continued, running a hand through his short hair. "They will see my fiancé involved with Russian blackmailing and embezzlement and they won't understand the nuances."

"Right, they won't understand that we were cooperating to catch the bad guys. I see how complex that is." Regan looked down at her plate, knowing that if she avoided eye contact, Brandon would entirely miss the sarcasm in her voice. He always underestimated his constituency. They had argued about it more than once.

"Exactly. This scandal will stay with us forever. Years from now when I am talking taxes, this scandal will be all over the internet again. You see the problem, don't you?"

Finally, Brandon stopped talking, having given Regan the setup she required. She pulled the 9-carat diamond from her finger, noting that it slid off quickly as if it had never been part of her. "Well then, I guess I need to give you this back and free you up from the gossip." Regan passed the ring across the table, catching the tablecloth briefly, unsnagging it and sliding it just next to his wine glass. Brandon looked at the ring but didn't pick it up.

"You are breaking our engagement?" Panic contorted his features. "Not so fast, Regan. I didn't say we should split up." A whiny tone entered his voice that Regan found particularly unattractive. It gave her the impetus to end this thing now and stop dragging it out.

"Then just what have you been saying, Brandon?" she asked in a hard voice. "I would argue that you have been breaking up with me for the last ten minutes. I understand your position. We need to go our separate ways." There was no remorse in Regan's voice, no hesitancy, a fact that still hadn't registered with Brandon.

"I need this scandal to go away, Regan, but not you. After all, the Howe family is a powerful force in my campaign. I am counting on our relationship and your family's financial backing. If we break things off now…"

Brandon finally understood that he had boxed himself into a corner and shut his mouth with a snap. He looked somewhat fishlike, odd for such a handsome man. Regan watched as the realization crossed his face, lodging a grim frown in place of the fish face.

"A tough choice is ahead of you, Brandon. Stay engaged for access to my family name and money, or split to avoid being linked to my scandal. You can't have it both ways, Brandon."

Looking up from her plate and straight into Brandon's eyes, Regan squared her shoulders and sat straighter in her chair. "You can't have your cake and eat it too, Brandon. So, let me make this easier for you. My family is not planning to invest heavily in your campaign. I have warned them off of you, now that I am wiser, and see you for the mooch you are. I am not going to be your sugar-mama, so you should disconnect from me and this scandal and spend your time and energy looking for a new rich patsy. Perhaps there is a Rockefeller daughter available. We moneyed women are interchangeable, right?"

Regan felt the weight of the world lift from her shoulders and stood almost as if lifted from the lightness. Finally having accused Brandon, Regan felt free from lying and from wondering. Seeing the truth of it on his face had embarrassed her for only a split second. He may have played her for a fool, but Regan was getting out before it was too late. She squared her shoulders and stood to her full 5'8" plus heels, towering over Brandon, who remained seated.

"Besides, Brandon," Regan said in a voice that carried across the nearby tables causing Brandon to cringe. "I don't love you, and I know you don't love me. So let me wish you luck and say goodbye. Oh, and let me get the check," she ended, reaching for it as she moved to go.

Regan walked away head held high, settled the bill and stepped into the fresh air. She stood there a moment not sure what to do next. She knew that tomorrow's papers would carry the story of the breakup. Reporters would get a quote from someone stating that Regan, not Brandon, had broken it off. He would hate that. Aw, too bad. How had she ever believed she was in love with him?

Love. She knew the real thing now. Taking a deep breath, she reached for her phone to let Tyler know she was finally a free woman. At long last, they would be able to be together, only twenty years later than planned.

He was worth the wait.

Chapter Thirty-Three

Tyler moped around the office. Regan had been away for only three days, but he couldn't calm down with her out of his sight. She sent texts here and there about how much she would miss the CDFI job, causing him to feel guilty.

"I can tell by that long face that you haven't been surfing the net yet today," Charlotte said, entering his office without knocking.

"I am sick of the stories about the Russians. I am sick of the reporters and the lack of privacy. I was no hero, Charlotte. I was the bad boy who got us all into this mess."

"Wyatt is taking all the credit anyway, Ty, so don't worry about hero worship from this corner. I was talking about this." Charlotte walked behind Tyler's desk and placed her laptop front and center where he couldn't miss the story.

A big headline said "Perfect Couple Not So Perfect" with a subheading "What does this mean for DC's Darling?" There were pictures of both Brandon and Regan, but not one of them together, and the brief article quoted people sitting at the restaurant last night who heard Regan break up with Brandon and saw her return her engagement ring.

A huge smile lit Tyler's face like sunshine. He jumped up, hugged Charlotte briefly, and then released her awkwardly. "Thank you, Char, thank you so much." He was dialing Regan immediately.

Tyler was sorry that he had delayed picking up when Regan called last night. He was missing her—and drinking a bit too much with Alex. He had picked up too late and then let her message go unheard. He dialed her now, but Tyler hung up the phone before Regan could answer.

What would he say to her? Congratulations on dumping your loser fiancé?

Tyler was sensitive enough to know it could not have been easy, but he was a man and the winner of this fight. He wanted to crow.

Besides, she still had a killer job in DC that she loved. It was the opportunity of a lifetime. Tyler suddenly decided that he couldn't ask her to give that up for him. He wouldn't ask her.

In the quiet of his bedroom, wrapped in one another's arms, they had made plans for a wedding, for a life together in Chicago. But they had not discussed her forfeiting her job.

LHRE CEO was a plum job, one that Regan had worked a lifetime to achieve, but it was still running a family business. Her father would be looking over her shoulder for years to come. She would be answering to her brothers and sisters. Ethan would be counting the days until she stepped aside and made room for him at the helm. It was important work, but it was not life-changing work.

At CDFI, Regan was making a real difference in people's lives. She felt her impact on a slice of society that few people protected. She put a roof over people's heads and got families with small children out of shelters. Regan's efforts mattered to her, perhaps in ways they never when she was running LHRE.

Tyler's position at LHRE was meant to be temporary, a hold until Regan returned to run her business. Why hadn't they discussed all this before she returned to Washington? He didn't know how Regan felt. Did she expect him to return to his general counsel position at Lyons Software Solutions, or did she expect him to remain at the helm of her family business? He knew that Wyatt was anxious to have him back to lawyering, but what was Regan thinking?

Regan had texted and talked on and on about the projects she was heading up at CDFI, the work she would have to hand off to others. He could sense the pull to her heart, and her head, involved with relinquishing her position. He could hear how much she loved her work and her team. She had barely had time to make a dent in her goals. He wanted her to see them through, as he knew Regan did. He also wanted her home with him. Now.

Tyler paced the office, staring out the window, waiting for answers that would never come. He couldn't call Regan until he knew what to say, but he also couldn't put the call off much longer.

He knew what he wanted. He wanted Regan here, with him, planning a wedding and starting a family. If he asked, she would comply. But, more than anything, he wanted Regan to be happy.

A knock at his office door preceded Ethan, who didn't wait to be invited in before flopping into a chair. "So, my sister's a free woman," he taunted. "Whatcha gonna do about it, Ty?"

"Get off my case, smart ass. Regan only broke up with the guy last night."

"Yeah, and I figured you'd be on a plane to DC by now."

"A plane…" Of course. He needed to go to Washington, talk to Regan face to face so they could decide together what the future held for them. Regan could not fool him if she was looking him in the eye.

He would know if she said she was willing to give up her job when she wasn't.

"Ethan, you are pretty wise for such a dumb fellow."

"I am very wise, Ty. Look how far I have come in such a short time. Go bring home your girl, and leave LHRE with me."

"Not what I had in mind, Ethan. But I think I will."

Tyler strode to the door, not bothering with the intercom, tense with unspent energy and a mission to complete. "Donna," he blurted into the hall. "Get me a ticket to DC. Today. Now."

"With pleasure," Donna replied. "It's about time."

Tyler returned to his office and Ethan, but not before he heard Donna mumble, "If I can't have him, I guess Regan should."

"What's that stupid grin about?" Ethan asked as Tyler stood behind his desk looking like the cat that swallowed the canary.

"Have you ever considered dating, Ethan?"

"Not that I would discuss with you. Why?"

"No reason. I thought that we should find Donna a man."

"Oh no, Ty, not me, and I think you have your hands full enough already."

"Very full indeed."

Chapter Thirty-Four

Regan's nose was entirely out of joint. She could barely concentrate on the meeting she was supposedly leading, her last at CDFI. Why wasn't Tyler picking up her calls? Why wasn't he returning them?

She had been hoping he would pick her up at the airport so they could go out to celebrate. She was a free woman. and she was coming home where she belonged, returning to LHRE, her family and her man.

Her mother had called near tears, watching her big wedding go down the drain. "I am not sorry about Brandon, Regan. Of course, I only want you to marry a man you truly love. But I must admit, I was excited to be planning a big society wedding."

"Thanks, Mom, for being so understanding and giving up your dream."

"I had such high hopes for the wedding of the season, but your wedding should be the event of your dreams, dear, not mine. I know I shouldn't pry, but have you heard anything from the Hockneys?"

"No. I haven't heard a peep, but I didn't expect to. Especially with the news reports all saying that I dumped their son."

"Well, you did, right?"

Regan smiled at the phone. "Yes, Mother, I did. No one dumps a Howe."

"No, they don't," her mother agreed with alacrity. "Still, you would have been a beautiful bride."

"And I will be someday very soon," Regan replied without considering the consequences.

"Soon, Regan dear? Are you trying to tell me something? Is there something I should know? I could hold the venue. You know it takes months of planning…"

"Mother, stop. Please. I am not telling you anything except that I promise not to be an old maid if I can help it."

"You deserve a man who loves you for you, Regan, and I know you will find him if you haven't already." Julia hesitated, hoping Regan would share more. When she didn't, Julia continued. "Your father married my fortune, but I always knew he loved me."

"And he still does," Regan confirmed. "Ooh, I have another call coming in, Mother. Let me talk to you later."

Regan quickly disconnected from her call, anxious to hear from Tyler at last. She was disappointed when she heard her brother's voice.

"Good job, Ree. Brandon was not the man for you," Wyatt told her. "He was too money-grubbing over Thanksgiving. What changed your mind? The kidnapping—scare some smarts into you?"

"I did have time to think then, but no, that wasn't it."

"Tyler? Have you spoken with him?"

"Surprisingly, no, Ivy, I haven't. Listen, I need to get back to a meeting. Let's talk tonight."

Regan was relieved to hang up the phone without answering more questions. Why hadn't she heard from Tyler? All the doubts from high school flooded back, leaving her uncertain and vulnerable. He promised to be there for her, but thoughts of a lifetime flooded Regan.

Was this a Tyler thing? Was he only interested when she wasn't available? He had seemed so sure, promised her the moon. Of course, he had done that years before, then left her hanging. He swore this time would be different, and she believed him. Regan needed to get out of this damn meeting and get on a plane. She

knew her doubts would subside when she was face to face with Tyler.

Regan completed the meeting, handing things off to her successor and accepting good wishes and a cupcake. She was in a limo heading to the airport less than an hour later.

Regan felt an unfamiliar tug in the region of her heart. She would miss the CDFI work more than she had expected, miss making a difference. She started jotting notes about how to incorporate similar work into hLHRE.

Regan hadn't given it a lot of thought when she was laying in Tyler's arms, but she knew he would be on board with her ideas. After all, Tyler knew how much this job had meant to her. It wouldn't hurt that she had completed everything in only three days. He would be so excited that she was home. And surprised. She hoped Tyler wouldn't mind the surprise.

Chapter Thirty-Five

Tyler stood surrounded by photographers who snapped his picture and reporters who unsuccessfully tried to get him to speak into their microphones. He was conspicuous, standing outside Regan's townhouse, not because he lacked either a camera or a mike, but more so for the large armload of flowers.

He expected to find Regan at home when he arrived. He knew she was planning to fly home tomorrow. He wanted to catch her before that happened. He would never have braved this crowd of paparazzi had he known she wouldn't answer the door.

He hadn't called first, wanting to surprise her with his visit, with his offer to help her stay in DC. But now, standing there being ogled, his feet sore from standing on the concrete, he questioned his decision.

Over thirty hours had passed since she left the excited message on his phone saying, "I'm too damn happy. Call me." Nothing more, although her high-pitched voice told him so much more. Would she forgive him for his silence? He hoped the large—ostentatious actually—bouquet would help smooth the way.

Two hours had passed with no sign of Regan. She should have been home. Finally, someone showed up with the key to her door. The large woman dressed in colorful garb turned to the paparazzi with her hands up to silence them.

"Go home, people. Regan Howe isn't here. The movers will be here soon. You need to get out of their way. There's no story here anymore. Pester someone else."

The crowd of reporters dispersed after only a few pictures and shouts asking for the identity of the speaker, who turned out to be Regan's assistant. She had a personal assistant? Tyler had never realized that.

Tyler pushed through the retreating crowd and followed the woman through the door, scaring the life out of her. "I am sorry. I didn't mean to frighten you."

The assistant looked at Tyler, at the flowers and started to laugh. "Tyler Winthrop, I assume?"

"What gave me away?" Tyler laughed, handing her the huge bouquet.

"You're in the wrong city. Regan should be landing in Chicago any minute."

"You're shitting me," Tyler blurted indelicately. "She wasn't supposed to leave for another day."

"She was anxious to see you."

Tyler grabbed his phone, seeing two missed calls. He must not have heard the ring in the din of the reporters. He listened to the messages, frustration growing on his face.

"Hi hon," Regan's cheery voice said. "Just boarding a plane for home. A day early. Aren't you proud of me? I was hoping you could pick me up at O'Hare, but you must be in meetings if you're not answering. I'll try again."

The second message repeated the same information with the addition of the fact that the plane was leaving so her phone would be off. "Oh," Regan added, "I love you, Ty." He couldn't help but smile.

"Everything good?" the assistant, who identified herself as Marilyn, asked.

"It will be," Tyler replied.

He bolted out the door with a hurried goodbye and jumped into a passing taxi. "Reagan Airport," he told the driver, his fingers already on his phone texting.

"Came to DC for you," he wrote. "Be there soon."

Tyler directed the driver to the private jets. One of the perks of his CEO job. Soon he would forfeit the right to the plane or have to ask Regan's permission. He smiled at the idea of needing her approval. He loved her success, her power, everything she had achieved. With a scowl, he remembered that horrible night when she slammed the door of his car after promising him she would succeed and he would never forget her. She was right on both counts, and he was a lucky bastard to win the lady.

Having texted Jetways, Joey, his pilot, was standing at the ready.

"We are cleared for takeoff as soon as you are in your seat, sir," she informed him.

"Let's get moving then. I have a woman waiting for me."

The blonde smiled in spite of herself and schooled her features to be more professional. "Yes, sir," she responded crisply.

Two hours later, he disembarked from his flight, texting Regan immediately.

"Just landed. Where are you?"

"Main terminal, waiting for you," came her response.

"Which one? Stay there. I will come to you."

"Terminal One, sitting at Starbucks."

Starbucks. There must be a thousand of them in the airport, but he would find her. He grabbed a taxi that crawled through airport traffic toward the enormous airport complex. Grabbing his overnight bag, he jogged the last short distance into the terminal. "OK, terminal one, where to now?"

"Near baggage claim" was her response.

Damn. Tyler was upstairs. Regan was downstairs. He went looking for an escalator, anxious to be reunited with Regan. He was almost running when he saw the Starbucks sign overhead, but no sign of his girl.

"I'm here. Where are you?"

"I'm here too," she responded. "Where are you?

"Downstairs," and "Upstairs" came the simultaneous replies. Tyler started to laugh. "Come down to me," he typed.

Watching his phone for her reply, he was surprised when she wrapped her arms around him and peppered his face with kisses.

"That was fast," he told her, holding her still for a real kiss.

"I was anxious," Regan responded, dropping her bag on the floor and pulling her chair close to his. "What were you doing in Washington?" she demanded.

"I went to talk to you."

"I can see this is serious, Ty. You're wearing your lawyer face. Should I be nervous?"

"Of course not," Tyler told her, placing a swift kiss on her lips. "I love you, Ree. I want your happiness more than anything."

"And I want yours," Regan responded, taking Tyler's hand in hers and stroking the back with her fingers. "What is this all about, Tyler?"

"Us."

"Us," Regan repeated. She looked like she was about to cry.

"Oh, honey. Don't make that face. You need to learn to trust me, Regan. I am never leaving you again."

"Okay, then, what about us?"

"Ree, I want to be with you, but I want what's best for you, too. I think that you shouldn't have to give up your job at CDFI." Tyler looked into Regan's face, studying her reaction. She looked confused.

"But Ty, I thought we agreed not to wait too long to be together. I want a family. I am not getting any younger."

"I am not suggesting we wait, Ree. I am suggesting I move to Washington to be with you. I can reach out to my old law firm, or a different firm. I am sure I can land a job quickly enough. You can have your government job and me." Tyler pointed both thumbs at his chest as if he were offering Regan a great gift.

She laughed at the gesture, then sobered. "What about Lyons Howe?"

"Ethan could run it. He's almost ready. We could help. So could Charlotte."

"What about Ivy? He won't be happy."

Tyler rubbed the furrow Regan was developing between her brows until she relaxed her face.

"He'll learn to be happy."

Regan moved her hand from Tyler's hand to stroke his forearm instead. She focused on her fingers running across the strong muscles while she formed her thoughts. "You are talking about giving up a lot for me, Ty. Your home and friends, your job, everything."

"Yes, Regan. I am saying precisely that. What do you say?"

Tyler held his breath and focused on Regan's hand, moving slowly over his arm, up and down, soft as a whisper.

"It's a lot to think about, Ty, but I know what I want. I busted my ass to get to the top of LHRE. I bucked my father's opinion of women, everything. I am not giving that up. And I want to come home, to Chicago, to you."

Chapter Thirty-Six

Tyler was whistling in the shower when Regan entered the bathroom. She didn't remember him whistling before their engagement, but he did it all the time now.

"You're happy," she acknowledged. She stood admiring his hard body, watching it respond to her heated look. "Again?"

"If you keep looking at me like that? You betcha." She handed Tyler the towel and watched his smile fade.

"Sorry, stud, but I have a 9 pm party."

"I thought we just partied..."

"We did," Regan laughed. "We have been partying for hours. But this is with my best girlfriends, in my honor, so let me get out of here."

"I guess when you put it that way..."

Regan swiped a hand over the fogged mirror so she could see herself and began applying makeup. "So, what do you have planned for tonight?" She watched as Tyler approached the sink beside her, swiped clear his slice of the mirror and ran his fingers through his hair, getting it to stand up just so.

"I always wondered how you do that," she observed.

"Magic fingers," he told her, moving into her space and wiggling them up the back of her skirt until they reached and cupped her behind. Regan let out a satisfied sigh, followed by a disgusted huff.

"Now look what you made me do."

Regan was standing facing the mirror with a long line of black mascara painted down her cheek like the scar from hell and a pout that made her bottom lip stick out. Tyler released her butt and took her in his arms, sucking that lip deep into his mouth until Regan pushed him away.

"I'll be late," she explained, "and I have to fix this."

"I think you should leave it, Scarface," Tyler said as he ran from the threat of the towel Regan grabbed to swat at him. Tyler quickly disappeared.

She found him in the kitchen, rummaging in the refrigerator for food. "There's nothing in the house. We never eat here."

"That is obvious," he deadpanned, holding open the refrigerator door to display two containers of takeout, yogurt, two apples, a six-pack of beer, and a bottle of wine. There was a bottle of olives and four different mustards on the door. "Looks like all we do is drink."

"I'll get Donna to order groceries. We should eat at home more."

"Shouldn't your personal assistant do that?"

"I don't have a personal assistant." Regan turned to look at Tyler with a quizzical look. "You know that."

"You did in DC. Don't you want one here?"

"Would you drop that already? I needed one to handle the press stuff, but I don't need an assistant here. I have Donna. And you."

"Me?"

"I seem to recall you telling me you would do anything for me about 30 minutes ago."

"That's not fair. You were teasing me unmercifully then."

"You said it, Tyler Winthrop, and I intend to hold you to it."

"So you want me to go grocery shop?" Tyler asked, confused.

"Oh, no, I have far better uses for your talents."

Tyler and Regan caught each other's eyes in the mirror and laughed.

"Seriously, Ree, I do think you need an assistant. We could share one and see how it works out. Alex has one, and she's fantastic."

"You want one because Alex has one?"

"I want one because it will make your life easier."

"Let me get moving, and we can discuss it tomorrow," she begged until Tyler exited the room after kissing her hard on the mouth, transferring her fresh lipstick to redden his lips.

Less than an hour later, she was laughing with her friends.

"How could I say no when he offered to give up everything and move to Washington for me? That is a man in love," Regan admitted, showing off her ring yet again for the women surrounding her. "Besides, with a rock like this, I'd be an idiot to let the man out of my sight."

The women at the bachelorette party agreed. It wasn't every woman who married the man of her dreams after so many years apart, nor did every woman wear a 7.6-carat perfect diamond on her finger. The stone caught the light and refracted it as Regan moved her fingers this way and that.

"The man's a catch," Charlotte admitted. "I may have been rooting for the other guy—who shall remain nameless—but I am a believer. I didn't have the history."

"All you needed was to see the way Tyler looks at her," Keeli shouted down the table. There were nine women crowded around two tables pushed together in the back corner of Gibson's. In a week, the men would likely have their stag party at this same venue. Then, the next day, Julia Lyons Howe would get her heart's desire, watching her daughter walk down the aisle in one of the biggest weddings of the decade. She had spared no expense, keeping two wedding planners on their toes for six straight months.

"No one could be happier than I am," Missy whispered in Regan's ear. "I have been waiting for this day for too long."

"I think I have been waiting longer," Regan agreed, wrapping her arm around her sister's shoulder and leaning over to kiss her cheek.

"Actually," Missy corrected, "I think I stayed steadfast a few times when you gave up."

"Perhaps, but I learned my lesson."

"Thank God," Sloane interrupted, wrapping her arms around the two sisters and taking over the conversation. "I was so damn sick of watching the two of you moon over each other. It was obvious to the rest of us. Only the two of you would need someone to get kidnapped to realize you were in love."

"Sloane," Charlotte chided, "perhaps you've had enough to drink?"

"What?" Sloane asked the group. "What did I say this time?"

The women laughed and fell into a discussion of whether to stay put or go bar hopping all night. Regan had attempted to remove the cheap tiara and veil on her head as well as the sash proclaiming her the bride to be, but her friends insisted that she wear both. Well-wishers, friends and strangers alike, had been stopping by the table for the last two hours, buying rounds of drinks. The group, in general, was tipsy, but Sloane was drunk.

Keeli, the only one sober as she was expecting, made the decision easy. She pointed across the room at a group of devilishly handsome men approaching the women and proclaimed, "We can't leave now."

Randall got to the table first, signaling a round of drinks for the table. "You might need to carry Sloane home," Keeli warned him.

"It's only fair after everything she put up with in my past." Still, he took the drink in front of Sloane and moved it across the table as he leaned in to kiss her. "Hello, wife. Are you having fun?"

"We're having a blast," Sloane shouted a bit too loudly, making everyone laugh. "But this is a hen party. You aren't supposed to be here."

"We're just passing through," Wyatt assured them as he leaned over the table to kiss Keeli, then moved around to kiss his sisters.

"How's the bachelorette?" he asked, hugging Regan tightly.

"So happy, Ivy. I can't remember being so happy."

"Then I'm happy," he told her, kissing her once more before being shoved out of the way.

"Hey, she's my sister too," Ethan announced, pushing his way closer, only to be pushed aside.

"But she's my fiancé," Tyler announced, wrapping his arms around Regan and kissing her on the cheek. "Doing well?" he whispered in her ear. Regan nodded yes, then spun in her seat to give Tyler a proper kiss. Hoots and howls and calls for another rang around the table. The couple obliged.

"I promised," Alex announced to the rowdy group, "we are not staying. We are not crashing your party. However, you have landed in our usual spot," the men nodded as the women groaned, "so we have no choice but to grab a table across the room."

"No choice?" Joanne challenged.

"No pressure, but remember I hold your job in my hands," Alex teased.

"Not tonight, you don't," Joanne responded, surprisingly cheeky.

"Don't push your luck, dear sister," Clarice told Joanne coolly. "Monday will come sooner than you think."

They all laughed, the drinks arrived, and the men went to move away. "Stay," Regan begged, her hand reaching for Tyler's arm to halt his movement. "Please join us. We have done all our girl stuff already. Right, ladies?"

No one objected, and two more tables were pushed to join the first pair. People moved about the room to accommodate the large group, because of the tiara, because they recognized them, or because Alex bought drinks to bribe them. Whatever the reason, the group swelled to be loud and boisterous.

"Do you realize," Wyatt asked, "how many years we have been coming here?"

"Holy shit, we fought over Sloane here," Randall reminded Wyatt. "And the best man won."

"I let you win," Wyatt shouted down the table, getting a laugh from everyone but Randall.

"It's okay, sweetie," Sloane told her husband. "I let you win too." She reached over to grab his shirtfront and pulled him in for a kiss better completed in privacy. Randall was grinning from ear to ear when they stopped.

"Yeah, whatever," he tossed in Wyatt's direction, raising his glass in salute.

"Look how well things turned out," Keeli piped up, rubbing the small bulge of her tummy. She rested her head on Wyatt's shoulder, the picture of contentment.

"We have come a long way from our bachelor days," Alex stated. "We used to sit here and pick up women on Friday night, not one of whom could hold a candle to this lot." He gestured about the table, acknowledging the force of nature that was this group of women—artists, business executives, CEOs.

"To the women who run the city," he lifted his glass in a toast to them.

"To the women who run our lives," Randall added.

"To the women who have our hearts," Tyler announced, raising his glass to Regan.

Regan lifted her glass. The others around the table followed suit. "Amen to that."

***

Thank You

When I began writing about Wyatt Howe and Keeli Larsen, I had no plans beyond their single romantic story. But, in order for readers to learn what Wyatt was thinking and feeling, I gave him friends—lifelong buddies that he could speak with openly.

When I finished *Bedazzled,* I adored Sloane. She was such a complex, evil, conniving woman. I needed to tell her story. And so the Beguiling Bachelor series was born, four novels and a prequel. But with the completion of *Besotted,* I realized I wasn't actually through with this group.

That's right. Wyatt and his little black book reappear in *Desire & Dessert,* and his brother Ethan is the protagonist in Crazy to Dream, from the *All's Crazy in Love* series. For a taste of the Crazies, continue reading...

Maddy

Introducing the All's Crazy in Love Series

Eight women—seven **single by chance or by choice. One dare—marry in twelve months or less. The stakes are high. Losing is not an option.**

When eight friends from childhood reunite at their twentieth high school reunion, they realize they only see each other at weddings and funerals. This is unacceptable to friends as close as this. The answer—obviously—more weddings. To get the ball rolling, the lone married woman, Gabriella, dares her friends to marry or else. When they laugh off her idea, she doubles down on her challenge and raises the stakes.

Gabriella doesn't care if Avery is so shy she's hardly even spoken to a man, or that Rachel can't choose between the multitude of guys she sleeps with each month. Gabby ignores every argument, instead exacting the worst price for each of them to pay if they lose.

The Dare is on. The women open their hearts to every opportunity that crosses their paths, no matter how unlikely or elusive the man might be. Gabby adds another six months to assure a winner. They'll help each other—as long as it doesn't cost them the win.

Within weeks, Avery finds a fellow cat rescuer, Sofia's heart flutters with new possibilities at work, and Willow spars and sparks with her horrible neighbor. Leah finds a long-distance love. Melinda has to be coached, but not Harper. After twenty years, she's finally flirting with her high school sweetheart.

The *All's Crazy in Love* series offers one dozen steamy romances—from first love to second-chance romance, from unexpected babies to unexpected attraction. Get to know a dozen wonderful women who find each other, themselves, and a chance to snatch the biggest prize of all—love. Read the eight stories of the Crazies and meet their friends and relatives in the *All's Fair in Love* series.

Travel with lifelong friends as they discover love, test friendships, and race to cross the finish line.

Let the games begin...

Crazy to Wed: An All's Crazy in Love Prequel

"What do you mean the wedding's off?" I'm sure the guests heard my mother's shriek. Nearly one hundred of them had gathered for our rehearsal dinner. "You better be joking."

Tears streaked my professionally applied makeup. I know it upset Mom. Hell, I was beside myself, but she didn't make this easier for me. I couldn't keep the annoyance from my voice. "Do I look as if I'm laughing?"

"What the hell." Hell was blasphemy for my mother, but I reduced her to swearing as the truth registered. She became blissfully speechless for once. Sadly, her silence was short-lived. "What did you do, Gabriella?" she asked, pointing an accusing finger at me. Her teeth clenched, and her chin wobbled as tears formed in her eyes.

So typical of my mother, always jumping to the conclusion that made me look my worst.

"Why do you assume it's my fault?" How many times had I said those words to her? At least anger had replaced my misery for a minute.

I flopped into an oversized upholstered chair in the ornate powder room, wondering how long I could hide out and how I would face the remaining rehearsal dinner guests. Thank God it was late, and half had departed earlier.

Do I say the wedding w cancelled or do I let everyone show up tomorrow and find out for themselves?

Less than an hour ago, I looked forward to the happiest day of my life, laughing as Rob and Rachel, the best man and maid-of-honor, toasted our marriage. Now we had no future, and I sat crying my eyes out in a public bathroom, my world in tatters. I watched dispassionately as tears stained the raw silk bodice of my gorgeous Rachel Lowell original dress.

"Was it your fault?" Mom asked, lowering her voice and handing me a box of cheap tissues. My nose chafed. But who cared?

"No, Mother, this time it wasn't. All I did was give him his gift."

Chapter One

"Is six weeks too soon to plan a wedding?"

Strolling the streets of Georgetown with my seven best friends, I should have been sightseeing, window shopping, or choosing where to get lunch. I wasn't doing any of those. Nor was I appreciating this rare time together with the Crazy Eights. No. Not me. I was thinking about Brad. I thought of him morning, noon, and night. Now, I needed to shake him off so that I could stop grinning like a hyena and enjoy my besties. So far, nothing worked.

Images of Brad flashed into my consciousness, moments when he made me laugh so hard, I snorted, or brought me flowers, or sang to me. He wouldn't make it as a front man for a band, but he was pretty good. And he got to me with this head-tilting, eye-locking thing he did, pouring his soul into love songs until I melted.I couldn't ignore Brad's talented hands, either, whether he was strumming the guitar, tinkering under the hood of a car, pounding the keyboard of a computer, or especially caressing my body. Very skilled. I jiggled my head to clear the visions before Rachel caught my dreamy expression and harassed me. Like a sister, we were mind-melded, except she had a dirtier mind.

"Not if you're a professional wedding planner, which you are not. But if you met a guy six weeks ago and think it's time to drag him to the altar, then it's definitely too soon. Besides, Gabriella, has he proposed?" Rachel snapped me back into the moment with her pointed question. "Aren't you getting ahead of yourself here, not to mention breaking your famous four seasons rule?"

Rachel had a point. I was looking at wedding dresses, but I didn't have a groom—at least not yet. Brad and I hardly knew each other. I scowled at the redhead, wanting this conversation to go differently. I was off-the-rails in love and needed my sister-from-another-mother to be on board with me. Instead, she offered a hard dose of reality.

"When I introduced you two, I said you were perfect for each other, and I meant it." Rachel looked away from me, stopping in front of the display window for an upscale boutique to study the merchandise. I watched her scan each mannequin from head to toe, her fingers itching by her sides. Meanwhile, I held my breath, desperate to continue on my favorite subject—Brad.

"I didn't imagine you would start shopping for wedding dresses after six weeks, Gabriella. This may be difficult for you, but you need to relax and let this run its course for a while. Shit, it's not a relationship yet. Before you hire the caterer and florist, someone needs to propose."

Rachel walked away from the window and me without waiting to gauge the impact of her statement. Typical. Not that she didn't care, it was simply that she always assumed she was right. Most of the time, she was.

I expected ridicule for bringing it up, and–not one to mince words–my girl, Rachel, had gone straight for the jugular. Drawing even with her when she stopped at another window, I vibrated with annoyance when she pulled out a tiny sketch pad. My future happiness was hanging in the balance, and she was sketching a chartreuse romper no woman would be caught dead in.

"Rachel." I stepped between her and the display, demanding her attention. She put away the notebook and focused on me with a sigh. Even after twenty years of friendship, her remarkable green eyes distracted me. You couldn't help noticing them, huge in her face, the color of new leaves after a heavy rain.

At that moment, they were staring at me above a mouth twisted with annoyance. "Is it the sex? Because you don't marry a stranger to get laid."

"You should know, I grumbled the words, hopefully quietly enough. Not that Rachel would balk. She knew who she was.

"Of course, you're right," I said. "But it isn't just the sex. I'm obsessed. I understand it's too early to be in love, but Rachel, it feels like the real thing, different from any relationship I've been in before." How could I make her see how Brad tilted my earth to a better axis and how I was a worthier
human being with him? He introduced me to fresh ideas, and I was more optimistic. Especially about love. My cynical friend Rachel would laugh me out
of D.C.

Melanie waved for us to catch up to the rest of the Crazy Eights. These were my friends since third grade when I had created our clique and named it for a card game. The moniker had stuck for twenty years as had the friendships, even if we touched a raw nerve sometimes. We had scattered for college, moved to different cities, married, had children, explored other careers, still the gang held together.

We emailed and talked often, but what helped keep us a unit was our annual long weekend, four days away from home, husbands, obligations. Trips like this one to D.C. assured us we could reconnect on neutral ground—a way to remember why we loved each other. Here we were on a rare vacation, but I remained preoccupied with

Brad instead of engaging with my friends. I was there in body, not spirit. And believe me, my body wanted to be somewhere else, too. The man was like a drug. I was blissfully addicted.

As we rushed to close the gap, I hurried my words, trying to end the discussion before anybody overheard. "I have been looking at wedding dresses and buying those thick *bridal* magazines. I need you to find out Brad's position. See if he feels the same." I yanked on my friend's elbow a little too hard in my enthusiasm. She stopped and looked me in the eye, rubbing her arm. "Sorry," I apologized for the potential bruise, "but you have to help. You know him better than anyone."

Sometimes, I exaggerate a bit. Okay, I might have a habit of hyperbole, if I'm being honest. But in this case, I was right. Rachel and Brad had been thick as thieves for years. She'd dropped his name casually in conversations long before she suggested fixing us up. My curiosity had been worse than any cat's. I was dying to meet him, but Rachel would say the timing was lousy, or he was seeing someone. This had gone on for years until I was ready to rip her red hair out by the roots.

In fact, I hadn't quite forgiven her for taking so long. Had she introduced us six months sooner, I might already have that ostentatious diamond on my hand. Not that I was greedy, or wanted to bankrupt my future fiancé, but it needed to be eye-popping enough to equal Sofia and Melanie's jaw-dropping rings.

When Rachel at-long-last suggested I meet Brad, she confessed why she'd made the match. "You are complete people on your own. I don't see that very often. Neither of you needs a partner, but you would enrich each other's lives."

"What the hell does that mean, anyway?" I was a bundle of nerves and had trouble following everything she said.

"It means he is worth the wait." So worth it, if only she knew. Nah, better if she didn't.

The night in that dark bar when Rachel warned me her friend was going to call, I tried to pick her brain about Brad. But the man-eater was scanning the perimeter of the room. If someone caught her eye, she would be out the door with them in twenty minutes. I needed to work fast if I wanted info before this date. Luckily, that evening the pickings were too young and unappealing, so she returned her focus to our discussion.

"You aren't one of those women desperate for a man," she explained. "You never have been. It'sjust one of the many reasons I love you. Look at your life—you have great friends," she gestured to herself, "a close family, challenging work at which you excel. You travel to cool, exotic locations and even volunteer. You are a complete person, interesting and fun, without some guy on your arm." I rolled my eyes. "It's a compliment," Rachel insisted. "Brad is the same. Lots of sports, tight with his buddies and his siblings, involved in local politics, not looking for a wife."

The pep talk was great, but left me suspicious. "Why is such a paragon interested in meeting me? Is he a dog?"

"No, my dear friend, he's a looker."

Gotta love Rachel. Here I was six weeks later, goo-goo eyed. She'd been right about everything, except being worth the wait. She should have introduced us ages ago.

The moment I saw him, Brad's dark good looks and deep dimples appealed to me—and then some—setting the nerves in my belly fluttering. Finally, they settled, replaced by the welcome hum of sexual tension. He was laid-back, comfortable and when we were together, time flew. Our first drink became dinner, then more drinks, until the wait staff eyed us with longing—longing to see our backs as we left the restaurant. They bounded to lock the doors after us when Brad escorted me to my car.

I remember everything: the velvety purple of the sky, the moon hovering over the trees, and the wind lifting the hem of my dress. And that goodnight kiss—I felt the softness of his lips, the restrained power behind it, a zing to my toes and a shock of electricity everywhere in between.

Brad felt it too, I'm sure, because we sucked face and groped each other like two teenagers until we were on the verge of making love pressed against the trunk of my car. Rachel had nailed it. We were perfect for each other. Reluctantly pulling apart, we scheduled a second date before we left the parking lot.

As for enriching my life, if being a stellar kisser and a stud in bed was what she'd implied, Rachel was spot on. If she'd meant that Brad would make me laugh and cherish me, then she got that right, too. Surprising, really, since Rachel ran through men like a hot knife through butter. One-night stands were her specialty, yet Brad and I were the fourth couple she'd introduced who were talking marriage or already married.

Initially, I was curious. Why hadn't Rachel dated him herself? In fact, I'd been wary. Only natural when you mention Rachel and a man in the same sentence. Settling for her leftovers didn't sit well. Both Brad and Rachel insisted they were just friends. Then I wondered why she wasn't interested. Was something wrong with the man? Eventually, I got past all my suspicions and embraced the relationship.

Once I'd resolved that issue, nothing stood in my way. I clicked with Brad, and knowing he reciprocated, I saw no reason to keep my emotions in check. I was almost thirty So was Brad. Briefly engaged before, "when he was young and foolish," showed me Brad could commit. We discussed vacations and his office Christmas party. He might not be proposing, but he was long-term planning. Wasn't that the same thing?

"Don't tell," I begged Rachel, as we caught up to the rest of the women. The Crazies had halted outside an Ethiopian restaurant. I was out of breath but wheezed out my opinion. "I'll eat anything but Ethiopian."

"That's what you said about Indian," Harper said, crossing her arms and jutting out one hip in defiance. "This town is famous for ethnic food, and you're rejecting everything. You rejected the Thai place, too."

"And that Southwestern restaurant," Avery added.

"You could tell us what it is you want and save us this incessant debate." Harper's scowling face flushed. Her exasperation was palpable. Did I say we got together to remember how we adored each other? Not so much when hungry.

The Crazies were like family. We loved each other, but we didn't always like each other. At that moment, Harper wanted to bitch-slap me. It had been over twenty minutes since she proclaimed herself starving, and I had nixed four potential lunch spots. I wasn't trying to be contrary, in fact I was famous for trying alternative places, but today I needed less fuss.

"We are eating at the next place." Harper gestured her arm to include everyone but me. "Majority rules," she stated with authority. She turned until she was facing me directly. "You can do what you want."

Subject closed as far as she was concerned, Harper spun on her heels and marched down the sidewalk with that enviable athletic stride. I would kill for those long legs, I thought, without resentment. I couldn't be angry with her. After all, the woman was 'hangry.'

I felt a little remorse. Harper was one of my favorite people, and I had brought out the worst in her. These were my peeps, the girls I turned to for advice, for a shoulder, for a laugh. They were the women I most admired and respected.

I'd often wished I could compose one ideal female from the best of each of us. She'd include Avery's logic and compassion, Harper's athleticism and inexhaustible energy, Melanie's faith and sweetness, Willow's sense of adventure. If I could sprinkle in Sofia's poise and unconscious beauty, Sydney's flair for the dramatic, and Rachel's fearlessness, I would be perfect. With Harper's legs, of course. But they would make me taller than Brad. I wasn't sure I would like that.

I halted before a crepe restaurant as sharply as if someone had yanked me by the collar. I vowed to think about food, not my sexy boyfriend, and spoke up. "How about this place?"

Harper scanned the menu posted in the window, calling over her shoulder when something caught her eye. "Ooh, the desserts look amazing. Oh, Willow, they have loads of vegetarian options. Okay, there are tons of choices," she conceded. "This looks great."

"So, we've decided?" Avery asked in her quiet voice.

Before anyone could argue, Harper was through the door, demanding a table. Once seated, Harper reverted to her usual sweet self, commenting on our good fortune. Getting a spot at a Georgetown restaurant between eleven and two was a miracle.

We emptied the breadbasket in less than sixty seconds. With food in her stomach, Harper's face relaxed and her tone softened. "So, Gabs, you've been quiet about your latest conquest." Harper lifted an eyebrow, offering me a sly glance. "Rachel says you've been inseparable."

I threw a look of trepidation in Rachel's direction, but her bland expression assured me she wouldn't share my secrets. Great. I could decide what to share.

"I like him," I admitted in the ultimate understatement. I waited a beat, rearranging my neatly arranged cutlery. "A lot.

"Yeah, we figured." Sydney tossed her head at the dry remark, then pushed a gorgeous mane of curls that fell into her face, securing them with an accessory that resembled a claw. If I envied Harper her legs, it was nothing compared to my longing for Sydney's hair. Total strangers stopped to complement it. "You've been too quiet about him, so Melanie and I guessed you have something to hide."

A pregnant Melanie blushed as she blew a kiss toward Rachel, whose matches stick. She could make a living at it. The pretty blonde would know. Years ago, Rachel introduced her to a serious, somewhat nerdy, speech writer. We attended their perfectly planned wedding last y ear.

I was selfishly concerned that Melanie would be too busy with the new baby to 'do' my party when the time came. She was a high-powered attorney, but her genuine passion was everything on HGTV and Food Network. Her creativity was endless, and I dreamed of an event as beautiful as hers. "We can sit as long as you want," I said, too little too late.

"You've made it through winter," Avery acknowledged to me. I swear I say one hundred sentences for each of Avery's, but I love her—shy, lovely, smart as a whip. She doesn't say much, but when she does, everyone listens. Sadly, I have to keep her at arm's length, or I will sneeze my brains out. A pet-rescuer, Avery is never wholly free of cat dander.

"What does winter have to do with anything?" Willow asked, ordering buckwheat crepes filled with spinach and other disgusting things. How did I end up with such a healthy friend? She was our back to nature girl, no bra, no makeup. She was also a hell of a baker. Someday she would run a very successful bakery, and I would grow fat from patronizing it.

"Remember," Sofia answered, "when Gabriella created that rule. No serious commitments until you've been with a man through four seasons. She's made it through winter, so she has three to go."

Sofia was married to Nico, a handsome devil she'd known her entire life. They were a stunning couple, dark, tall, and fit. Once they got pregnant, and she was trying her best to do so, they would have gorgeous children.

One thing I loved about Sofia? She underestimated her staggering beauty. In fact, she always overdressed to compensate for her insecurities. Sitting beside Willow, she was wearing false eyelashes and make-up more appropriate for a Saturday night. She was an exotic peacock to Willow's brown wren.

Speaking of peacocks, I caught Rachel glaring at me from her seat at the end of the table, but she said nothing. We were so different. I was "the vault." Rachel couldn't keep her mouth shut, but I loved her. Her imagination was endless while I was logical, her behavior wild to my straightlaced. She was even pale skinned to my Mediterranean coloring. Rachel had flamboyant red hair and those eyes. She embraced her freedom and single state while I wanted a husband and a family. The budding designer was the closest thing to a sister I would ever have. She was the first girl to commit to the Crazies and had been in my life ever since.

Rachel couldn't stay silent any longer. "Yeah, Gabriella, what about four seasons?"

"Maybe I wasn't clear." There were seven sets of eyes glaring at me. I had no one to blame but myself for their derision. I was breaking my own rules. "To wed, you should be together a full year, but you can get engaged as soon as you want."

"You're engaged?"

Avery's words acted like a bucket of ice water thrown over the Crazies. Harper stopped chewing bread, Rachel halted doodling on her napkin, Willow nearly choked on the organic juice she had swallowed. Melanie's beautiful blue eyes grew wide as saucers; as did Sofia's gorgeous brown orbs. The clatter of the fork Sydney dropped to the floor brought everyone back to life.

"No, ladies, I'm not engaged."

"But she wants to be," Rachel blurted. I knew I shouldn't have said anything to her. She never could keep a secret, especially not from the Crazies.

The food arrived, offering me a temporary reprieve while the server distributed our orders and took our requests for drink refills and more bread. Everyone settled too soon, and Rachel picked up where she'd left off. "Gabriella is in love, you guys. She wants to marry Brad."

"Waiting four seasons was Gabriella's rule." Melanie used her courtroom voice, getting everyone's attention, including two older women at a nearby table. "She made it, so she gets to break it. Also, you will recall Prom, when Rachel didn't have money for a dress, and we all pitched in to buy fabric?" Heads nodded. "Gabriella stipulated that when one of us wants something, we combine forces to make sure she receives it."

"I said that, didn't I?" my pride was clear in the lift of my chin. If we operated as a team to win Brad, the poor man wouldn't stand a chance.

A cunning smile curved up the corners of my mouth. "Ok, ladies, what's our plan of attack?"

Crazy to Wed is available from your favorite bookseller or at www.madisonmichael.net/books

Books by Madison Michael

The Beguiling Bachelor Series

Bewildered: A Beguiling Bachelor Prequel

Bedazzled

Beholden

Bedeviled

Besottted

All's Crazy in Love Series

Crazy to Wed - Gabriella

Crazy to Believe - Sofia

Way Past Crazy - Avery

Artfully Crazy – Leah

Crazy to Dream – Willow

Crazy Loves Crazy Lies – Veronika

Crazy Lessons in Love – Jules *(coming soon)*

Crazy to Score – Melinda *(coming soon)*

Acting Crazy – Sydney *(coming soon)*

and more...

The B&B Billionaire Series

Desire & Dessert

About Madison Michael

Meet Maddy. She loves romance: reading it, writing it, watching it. So, she made a career of it. Why not reside in an unpredictable, exciting, enticing world where rich, sexy men and smart, sassy women fall in love? Returning to her roots in Chicago after traversing the U.S., Madison embraced old friendships, family, Chicago pizza and hot dogs and began writing, with her trusted feline, Gracie, at her feet.

Maddy creates complex characters who navigate intrigue, suspense, humor and plenty of steamy sex before achieving their happy ending. Setting her stories against the most luxurious and elite Chicago offers, her billionaire heroes—or heroines—quickly learn the value of life-long friendships, and that money can't buy love.

Maddy loves exploring, reading a ton and writing more. She lives on Diet Dr. Pepper and coffee—not imbibed together—and the company of loved ones who provide her inspiration.

Author of more than a dozen romance novels, including the Billionaire series, *The Beguiling Bachelors*, and the humorous *All's Crazy in Love* series, you can sign up to receive exclusive content on her website, www.madisonmichael.net

www.ingramcontent.com/pod-product-compliance
Lightning Source LLC
Chambersburg PA
CBHW030603120726
47904CB00006B/1753